GOING DEEP

WINNING LOVE

SOPHIE ANDREWS

CONTENT NOTE

Going Deep is the stand-alone hate to love sports romance, the first book in the Winning Love series. While you can expect lots of delicious banter and a slow burn, there are plenty of spicy open-door scenes. Also note that the MMC is grieving the loss of his parents throughout the story, and the FMC discusses dubious consent in a past sexual encounter.

CHAPTER 1
CAMDEN

EVERYTHING THEY SAY about Florida is true.

The heat, the bugs, the guy with the beer belly in a cutoff shirt smoking a cigar while wrangling an alligator in the middle of the road…

It's all true.

"Do we really have to do this?" Malcolm, my babysitter for all intents and purposes, groans in disgust.

"*We* are not doing anything, and I have no idea why you're still here."

"Because you're about to make yet another bad decision."

I gesture to the guy trapping the gator as I tell Malcolm, "If you're not going to leave me the fuck alone, why don't you make yourself helpful?"

"That's not in my contract."

"Neither is fucking up my life."

"I'm *keeping* you from fucking up your life." He clicks his tongue and adjusts the collar of his shirt, looking like a real-life Carlton Banks. Minus the dance moves. I might like him more if he did dance. At least then he'd be entertaining, while simultaneously ruining all my fun.

After…everything, Malcolm showed up on my doorstep one

day and has yet to leave. Apparently, my PR team thinks I'm incapable of keeping myself out of trouble. He calls himself my assistant.

I call him a pain in my ass.

"So, let's just pack it in," he suggests. "I'll buy you breakfast tomorrow. Or today, since the sun will be coming up in a few hours."

"Oh boy!" I clap a few times. "Can I get an ice cream too, Daddy?"

He wrenches back, hand on his chest. "Please don't call me daddy. Only Jenson can do that."

I roll my eyes. "So why don't you go home to him. Leave me be."

"Not happening."

I blow out a breath toward the night sky. It's nearly two in the morning on a barren stretch of road outside of Fort Lauderdale. I shouldn't be here, I know that, but lately, none of the *shoulds* have stopped me from doing anything.

Not the partying in Miami when I shouldn't be drinking so much in the off-season.

Not the two blondes in Key West when I've got a girlfriend.

And not that pesky arrest for illegal drag racing.

Malcolm's been at my side for the last two months, hissing in my ear about what I shouldn't be doing and reporting back to Debra Rosenstein, half of Rosenstein & Hill, the public relations firm for the most high-profile athletes in Philadelphia. I'd been hauled into her office after the incident with that motherfucker and his camera, and she chewed my ass out, demanding I clean up my act before it's too late.

But in my defense, it was raining and the sidewalk was slippery. I couldn't help it if I tripped and fell on top of him. He was lucky it was only his camera that broke and not his fucking mouth from running it so much.

Over the past few years, I have earned a bit of a reputation and I'm used to being called names, but living and playing in

Philadelphia is brutal. The "fans" are savage, climbing poles and rioting over *wins*. And they're even worse over losses. Lately, I haven't been able to go anywhere without somebody chirping in my ear or throwing something at me, making my life in Philly hell, probably hoping I'll be traded or quit.

Which is why I got the hell out of dodge, with a pit stop to pick up my car before hightailing it south.

Slim saunters over to me and skims his hand over my 1978 Camaro. "Sweet little ride you got here."

I nod in agreement. I had it customized with a turbo kit that whistles like a banshee and headers that announce my arrival three blocks away. That's what I love most about it, the sound. It quiets the roaring in my head as I'm racing down the drag.

"Yeah, am I finally gonna be able to actually stretch her legs or what?"

Slim's brows arch, and I doubt many people are brave enough to cop an attitude with him. But I think that's why he likes me; I'm just dumb enough to do so. He also can't retaliate like he might want to because I'm in the public eye and he needs to stay out of it. I met Slim a few years ago, and while I'm positive none of his business ventures earn him money legally, I've never had the balls to ask him that outright.

I'm just here to win some cash, and he's here to skim money off one of his rackets.

"I'm tired of waiting around," I tell Slim, earning only a slightly threatening slap to my back.

"Are we all tired of waiting around? You ready to race?" Slim asks, his voice raised so the two dozen or so of us gathered can hear as he holds out his hands, his open button-down fluttering with the movement, a suspicious bulge at his back, something tucked into his pants.

Malcolm notices too and tugs on my elbow. "Seriously, Camden, let's get out of here."

I ignore my paid conscience to whoop it up with the other drivers, joining in on the smack talk that immediately starts. Side bets being placed. I hop on my toes, my adrenaline spiking. I love competing, whether it's on the field or on a street. I want to win, and the familiar buzz in my gut and hands ratchets up.

"*Camden.*" Malcolm's voice is a harsh whisper as he attempts to block my path from slapping the twenty grand of cash into Slim's hand.

"Fuck off," I mumble, tossing the envelope to Slim, over Malcolm's head.

A couple of the guys talk shit about how that's the best play they've ever seen out of me, as if these dumb fucks don't know the difference between a quarterback and a receiver. They all merely want the opportunity to be added to the list of people who beat Camden Long.

But that list is ripped up tonight.

Fuck them. And fuck all the haters. Fuck anyone who thinks they can bring me down.

They can't and won't.

I am unstoppable.

I'm about to open the door on the driver's side when Malcolm slams his hand against it. For being a little guy, he does have some strength behind him, but I brush him away like a gnat. "Go home."

"Camden, don't do this."

I ignore him and slide behind the wheel, starting up my girl, revving her engine. One of Slim's henchmen motions us all to the starting point, and I don't check the rearview mirror to see where Malcolm is. I also don't take out my cell phone to see who has been repeatedly calling me.

I am focused on nothing besides winning this race.

Some chick with huge tits and a tiny bikini sashays out and winks in my direction before waving her hand for all the drivers' attention, one car on my left, three on my right. She says something I can't hear over the gunning of the engines, but then she unties her top, letting it fall off into her hands. But even those perfectly round beauties don't steal my focus as she raises her top into the air, only to wave it back down.

The flag.

I'm off, gunning it down the dark stretch that curves to the right. I shift gears, pulling ahead slightly, only to be overtaken by the red Lambo. I grit my teeth and push it, pedal to the metal. The speedometer ticks up with every second, my heart rate skyrocketing as I clench my left fist around the steering wheel, my right white-knuckled around the shifter. I mentally count down the yards like I'm looking out on the field, and I find my opening to make the turn, pulling ahead on the way back, then hit it with the juice on the straightaway.

I smile as I finish, resting my head back for a moment to enjoy the high before unfolding myself from the car. The flag girl greets me by jumping into my arms, mouth on my jaw, tits against my chest, though she's managed to put her top on. Barely.

Slim congratulates me with a pound, doling out my winnings then proceeding to the second- and third-place finishers, but I don't even have time to enjoy the celebration because Malcolm barrels toward me, pushing the girl out of the way. "Camden."

I roll my eyes. "Just fucking leave already. You—"

He thrusts his cell phone at me. "It's about your parents."

"What?"

He forcibly hands me his cell phone. "They've been trying to get a hold of you. There was an accident with your parents."

Turns out, I'm not unstoppable.

In fact, I'm quite vulnerable.

CHAPTER 2
NADINE

I BARELY MAKE it out of the building and into my car before I lose it. Great heaving sobs that have my makeup running and lungs burning. But somewhere in the back of my mind, I hear Erik's voice, reminding me to settle down and breathe.

All of his usual zen bullshit.

Yet I try to focus on my breathing anyway. After a minute, when my hiccuping finally subsides, I open my eyes to find my cell phone.

Out of my entire family, Erik is my favorite. We're only two years apart, and I know he won't judge me for the decision I'm about to make. He answers my FaceTime call with a smile that quickly drops. "What's wrong?"

"I can't do it anymore," I say, another wave of tears racking my body so hard that I can't speak when he asks me to repeat myself because he can't understand.

"Breathe, Nan. You've got to breathe. I'm gonna count, okay?"

He does his big-brother thing, counting to four, directing me to inhale slowly, hold it at the top, exhale it out until I can speak once again.

"I'm quitting," I say, my throat thick and my voice like sandpaper.

His eyes widen even as his brows narrow. "You're quitting?"

"I can't do it anymore."

He shakes his head, confusion written across his features that are so much like our father. Out of all five of us kids, he looks most like him. "What happened?"

I take a shuddering breath and press my shaking hand to my chest, almost unable to say it out loud. "One of my seniors, Stacey, she's pregnant, and she asked me to be the godmother of her baby. The *godmother*, Erik. Because she said she doesn't have anyone else in her life to ask."

He doesn't speak for a long time, only watches as I find some tissues in my glove compartment to mop up my face. Once I meet his gaze on my phone screen again, he asks, "What did you say?"

"I told her that as much as I love her, it wouldn't be appropriate, and that if she thought about it more, I was sure she could come up with someone else in her life who she could ask. But that's the thing..." My eyes sting with more tears. "She doesn't have anyone else." I stutter out the rest. "Sh-sh-she's in foster care. She doesn't have anyone except m-me. How f-fucked up is that?"

I have to stop because my crying gives way to a distraught moan from the depths of my soul as I think about the rest of my kids, and I smack my hand on the steering wheel as if the physical pain will take away the emotional toll.

With a ragged inhale, I tell my brother, "I gave Orlando money for prom tickets because he couldn't afford them, and he wanted to take his girlfriend. And god, Manny—he and his mom finally received their green cards. He was so happy, but he's worried about his dad because he still doesn't have one. And Christopher has started hanging around with a gang, and..."

I dip my chin, all of my frustration and anger crashing over me so I can't talk anymore, only cry for my students. For me. For all the kids our society continuously allows to fall through the cracks.

Once I feel like I finally have most of it out, I clear my eyes with the back of my hand. "I can't do it anymore. I have to quit. If I don't, I don't think I'll have anything left to offer anyone. I already feel so empty."

"You're burned out," Erik tells me quietly. "It's understandable you feel this way, but don't make any rash decisions. How many days of school do you have left?"

"A few weeks."

"Okay, try to take it easy, but don't quit." When I open my mouth to argue, he holds up his hand. "I know how much you care about your students, which is why I think you shouldn't make any decisions right now. I don't want you to end up regretting anything later on. Then I want you to come stay with me for the summer."

I blot a tissue under my nose. "You don't want me in your house."

"Yes, I do."

"You have your hands full with Kai."

"Who needs to spend time with his aunt."

Sniffling, I give in with a nod because I could use baby snuggles, and Erik offers me a sad smile. "It'll be okay. We'll figure it out. I'll help you."

I do believe Erik thinks that's true. Yet with how barren I feel, utterly useless from constantly giving everything I have to a profession and a school that don't give anything back, I'm not so sure.

But I don't come from a family that quits anything. We don't give up.

We work hard.

We overcome.

We become doctors and PhDs and professional athletes.

We do not settle. *Ever.*

So, I'm sure Erik assumes I'll make it past this momentary

blip and go back to work in the fall after I have some time off to recharge, but I've felt this coming on for a few years. Hell, maybe my whole career.

I made it past the statistic of most teachers quitting in the first five years, but it's this sixth year that has put the nail in the coffin.

Being a teacher is not for the faint of heart. Being a teacher in a Title I school is even harder. Being a learning support teacher in a Title I school? Like building a sandcastle in the middle of a hurricane.

For almost as long as I can remember, I wanted to be a special education teacher. My siblings and I are CODAs, Children of Deaf Adults. With a Deaf mother, I saw firsthand how education needed to be accessible to everyone, and I still believe that. I simply don't know if I'm a person who can do it anymore.

I don't know if I can watch my kids continue to slip through the cracks.

I don't know if I can break up another fight.

I don't know if I can spend another lunch period on cafeteria duty.

As a high school learning support teacher, I assist the general education teachers to adapt their lessons for my students, who read below their grade level, anywhere between third and sixth grade, usually. On top of that, I have a caseload of thirty Individualized Education Plans, which means I spend a lot of time in meetings and writing up reports, making sure my kids receive everything they need during the school day. But of course, they need just as much support outside of school as well.

Because more often than not, these children are the ones who are forgotten about. They come from poor households. Sometimes they have relatives in the prison system. Most of the time, they have only one parent or guardian at home. Some do not speak English. All of them need attention and love, more than I can give them, even as I wish I could.

The school doesn't have enough resources, and the administration is caught between a rock—the government—and a hard place—the local community. The behavior of some of the students is out of control, with no repercussions, and while *I* usually have no problems with my kids, I know they can be disrespectful to other teachers. I'm not sure what even happened, but a few weeks ago, I watched Ronny be put in handcuffs, and I haven't been able to obtain an answer about what happened to him, other than he had a physical altercation with a teacher in the hall, and they were pressing charges. I haven't seen Ronny since I witnessed him chest down on the floor, pleading for me. "Miss, please! Help me! I need you!"

I threw up in the faculty bathroom after that.

I've lost weight, stress stealing my appetite, and every morning, I wake up dreading the day and what it might bring. And I don't know if it's worth it. As much as I love my kids, I don't think I can do it anymore.

But before my thoughts can spiral again, my brother asks, "Where are you right now?"

"Outside of school."

"I'm going to stay on the phone with you until you're home."

"Thanks," I mumble and readjust my position in my car seat, so I can drive home. While I do, he catches me up on his life, which is the same as always, working out and preparing for the upcoming season, except that he has a trip to take.

"I booked a flight out to Iowa for tomorrow."

"Why are you going there?"

"You didn't hear?"

"Hear what?"

"Camden's parents died. It's been all over the news."

I suppose it would be since Camden Long is the leading tight end in the NFL, alongside my brother, who is quarterback for the Philadelphia Founders.

I gasp. "Oh my god."

"Yeah, it was a bad accident with a tractor trailer."

I exhale a low breath. "How is he?"

"I haven't talked to him much, but a lot of the team is attending the funeral. I'm going to spend the weekend out there in Cedar Falls with him."

Although I've met my brother's best friend and teammate on a few occasions, I don't know him that well. Which suits me fine because he's a giant asshole, but I still feel bad for him. To lose both of his parents suddenly is unspeakable.

"Can I do anything? Send anything?"

"No, I'll give him your regards. I think he's in shock right now."

"I'm sure."

"He has a younger sister whom he now has guardianship over. She's in eighth grade."

I wince, imagining being that age and without parents. "How devastating."

"*And*," my brother adds pointedly, "she's Deaf."

"She's in public school?" I ask, my mind immediately spinning with questions and ways to solve problems. "How does she do?"

"I don't know much about her, but I guess he'll be moving her here."

While I'm sure Camden is grieving hard for his parents, the changes his sister will have to go through will make it exponentially worse. I ache for her, knowing how difficult it will be.

"Please let me know if I can do anything."

"I will," he says, then calls out to his wife Molly, explaining to her that I'll be staying with them for the summer, to which she responds happily.

Molly started dating my brother when they were only sixteen, and they've been together nearly fifteen years now. She's more than my sister-in-law; she's one of my best friends. So when she pops on-screen, her voice immediately changes, "Oh Nan, what's wrong?"

I shake my head, unable to talk about it again, so Erik takes over. "She's burned out from school."

Molly makes an understanding sound. "I'm so sorry, but we'll get you feeling better. I can't wait for you to come. You know you can text or call whenever you want."

I blink a few times, clearing my vision before making a right at a red light. "I know, but I don't want to bother you with Kai."

My brother dismisses that idea. "You wouldn't be bothering us. He doesn't do much right now besides sleep and poop. And there is no way you can bother us more than Mom and Dad already do."

Molly agrees. "Your mom won't stop sending us onesies."

Kai is the first grandchild, and when he was first born, Erik had to physically remove my parents from the house so he and Molly could get some peace. I love them dearly, but they are both overbearing in their own ways.

Mom was born in East Germany before the Wall fell, and while we don't know much about her early childhood, she was somehow smuggled out and placed into an orphanage in West Berlin, and she was adopted by my grandparents in the US a few years later. She is quite literally a miracle, born deaf in a time and place where disabled children did not have a high chance of surviving. But she did, and she made it all the way to New York City during college, where she met my father, newly arrived from Puerto Rico to find fame in the boxing ring. But that fateful night in a dance club, they learned they didn't have to speak each other's languages to fall in love.

A few years later, they married and started having half-German, half-Puerto-Rican babies whose first language was ASL and who were raised to be the *best* in our chosen fields. Mom had earned her PhD in psychology after overcoming so much adversity, and there is no excuse for us not to. Not to mention Dad, who won himself a silver medal at the Olympics before opening a string of successful gyms throughout New York and New Jersey.

Felix, my oldest brother, is almost done with his oncology fellowship.

Then there is Erik, one of the best quarterbacks in the league right now.

My younger sister, Emmaline, is about to graduate law school, and the baby, Benedict, is at Harvard on a full sports scholarship for football.

The Riveras do *not* quit.

Except me. The middle child who can't hack being a public school teacher.

Because Molly knows me well enough, she can see it before it happens. "Don't cry, Nan. It may not feel like it, but it will get better."

I glance down to the screen at another red light to find my brother back on it. "Focus on finishing out the year. That's all you need to do. Take it one day at a time, and then you can come here and relax."

Sure. Easier said than done.

CHAPTER 3
CAMDEN

"HEY, MAN." Erik, my best friend and teammate, smiles when I clap hands with him after opening the door to my penthouse in Center City. "How's it going?"

"Terrible." I shake my head and allow him to come in, brushing my fingertips over Kai's head. He's strapped to his dad's chest and seems to be conked out.

"Still?"

Erik spent a few days with me after the funeral, sitting in on meetings with my manager and agent, Malcolm and the PR company. Everyone wanted to decide what the hell I was doing with my life as it crashed around me, but it was my best friend who spoke for me when I didn't feel like I could anymore. For as much as I know how the world sees me, Erik has been there with me from the beginning. We were drafted the same year to Philadelphia with the purpose of rebuilding a dying team, tasked with bringing it back to life. Which we did.

He's the golden boy.

I'm the arrogant asshole. Because I like to have fun on and off the field. What is the point of making millions of dollars a year, doing the thing we dreamed of as kids, if we can't have fun?

But now, I don't know who I am. Or what all of this is for anymore.

Only that the last conversation I had with my parents before they died was how they were disappointed in me, and I'm now in charge of raising my kid sister.

"She barely comes out of her room," I explain to Erik, motioning down the hall. "She hates me."

"She doesn't hate you," he assures me, but she won't talk to me, and she's pretty much cried every single day. Not that I can blame her.

She's lost her parents, home, and friends in one fell swoop.

"I'm not cut out for this. I don't know if I can do it anymore." I grab two bottles of water from the fridge and toss one to him, which he catches with one hand, the other holding Kai's tiny bum.

"You've just started. You can't throw in the towel already."

I heave a sigh. I love the dude. After seven seasons playing together, I know him almost as well as myself. I know what his favorite meals are, how he falls asleep to some English guy on an app telling him to relax his muscles and mind, and that he always has to put his left sock on before his right or his whole game will fall apart. But if he doesn't know by now that I'm not cut out for raising a fourteen-year-old girl, I don't know how else to convince him.

"Everything I do and say is wrong. She won't leave the house, but also, I'm kinda glad because I don't want those vultures outside to say anything to or about her."

The internet had a field day when the news broke. My name and face were plastered everywhere. More than usual. Someone paid for their kids' college with the pictures sold to the tabloids of me in my black suit, bent over two coffins, my hands resting on each, eyes closed.

I can't even fucking bury my parents without the world trying to tear me down.

But I won't let them tear my sister down simply to get a piece of me.

Erik nudges me out of the way to assess the inside of my refrigerator. "You might want to start with buying some groceries."

I don't cook, and I certainly don't grocery shop. I have people for that.

The only items I have in my fridge are water, sports drinks, Greek yogurt, and eggs. I've been ordering in every day since we returned from Iowa, though I have my chef scheduled to drop off some meals tomorrow.

Leaning my elbows on the kitchen island, I focus my attention on the pattern of striations in the white marble. "I don't know what the hell I'm doing. I can't be…a dad. I don't know how to take care of another human. Especially one who's fifteen years younger than I am who cries literally every time she looks at me."

Erik takes a swig of his water and sets it down, eyes scanning my place, pristine from the cleaning service, before pinning me with his dark stare. "Then why don't you try to be her brother instead?"

I huff an aggravated sound. "I don't know how to do that either."

He strokes the back of Kai's little head. "Maybe that's part of the reason she's so upset. You went home, what? Once or twice a year?" I don't need to answer because he knows. "Maybe work on getting to know each other again."

Yeah, sure, that sounds good, but it's easier said than done.

After I was born, my parents had trouble becoming pregnant again, so they figured it would just be me. But then in my sophomore year of high school, after my mom turned forty-one, surprise!

She got pregnant with my sister, but it wasn't easy, and Paisley arrived really early. She was a sickly baby with an infection that caused her to lose most of her hearing. She spent months in the hospital before she could come home, but I recall being attached to my baby sister from day one. As soon as she started walking, she'd come to my high school games, and I doted on her, spending as much time as I could with her. But college came fast—and the draft even faster. She grew up in Cedar Falls, while I spent years away from her in Alabama and then in Pennsylvania. Now, I barely know her.

She certainly doesn't know me, and she doesn't seem like she wants to know me either.

"You talked to the counselor?" Erik asks, drawing my attention up to him, and when I shrug, it's his turn to heave a tired sigh. "You have to. You need to wrap your head around all of this."

Erik is into all that hippie-dippie horseshit of yoga and therapy, but that's not me. That's not what I do. The team is required to have small-and large-group meetings with the psychologist to maintain our mental game on the field and good relationships with teammates off the field, but the Founders also have a counselor on staff for individual sessions. For more personal matters, I guess.

But I don't talk about my feelings, and I especially won't expose any of my weaknesses.

"I'm not gonna give the front office more of a reason to trash my contract."

"They're not going to break your contract." Although his voice isn't as sure as when he calls plays in the huddle. When he knows we're gonna score.

I scrub my hands over my face, thinking about how Coach Roberts wouldn't even acknowledge me after the Bowl game. The phone call from my agent informing me I'd been dropped from all my endorsement deals. And, of course, there was Malcolm.

He'd given me a reprieve for the last few days to "adjust" to my new life, but he's been texting daily to make sure I'm not doing anything stupid.

He doesn't need to. Ever since that phone call weeks ago, I haven't done much of anything besides stare out of windows, remembering my parents' parting words to me.

"We didn't raise you to be this way," my mom said two nights before the accident. "We didn't raise you to throw away everything you've worked so hard for."

"We'll always love you, son," my dad added. "We just wish you'd remember we love you for being *you*, not someone else you think you need to be."

I haven't been sleeping well, haunted by those words.

By the person my parents thought I was, by the persona the world believed was true, by the future I couldn't seem to see.

I can't find a way out of any of it.

"Training camp starts next month..." I meet Erik's eyes. "What am I supposed to do with Paisley?"

He considers this for a while, splitting his attention between the hall that leads to Paisley's room and his three-month-old son. "What does she want to do?"

"Fuck if I know. Go back in time to ask my parents not to go out that night?"

He winces, and I plow my fingers through my hair. "I'm not cut out for this. I can't do it. My aunt offered to take Paisley, and I think—"

"Are you kidding me?" Erik's voice rises enough that it sets me back on my heels. He has a wicked temper, though it very rarely shows. "I know *you* are having a hard time with this new reality, but *she* is your sister. She needs you. She needs to feel loved and supported and not to be shipped off to yet another place she doesn't know. At least here she has her brother. So don't you dare fucking finish that sentence."

As much as I need my best friend in my corner, I'm not about to be lectured by somebody who has two living parents and a bunch of siblings. I cut my hand through the air. "Fuck you and your high horse, assuming it's so easy. I don't have anyone. I'm not like you. I don't have a huge family to rely on. I have no one." I slam my fist on the island, hoping to rid the stinging in my eyes and nose, the sudden pain in my chest. "I don't have anyone to help me. I don't have anyone I can call at the drop of a hat. Fuck, I don't even have…"

My voice wavers, and I lower my gaze to the floor, clearing my throat at the sudden realization that I don't have anywhere to go for holidays anymore. I won't have anyone in the stands cheering me on. Even if they were disappointed in me, my parents still picked up the phone when I called, but I can't do that anymore. I don't have anyone to call.

Erik rounds the island and tows me into a hug, careful of the baby between us. He holds the back of my head, like he does on the field, slapping my helmet. "You have me. You have the team, the coaches, *and* the front office. We will get you the help you need. You just can't give up. Not on yourself, and not on your sister. She needs you most of all."

I nod, blinking away my blurry vision.

Erik pats the back of my head. "I love you, all right?"

I nod again, my throat three times its normal size.

"And I got your back. Always."

I sniff and clear the boulder in my windpipe with a cough. "Yeah, thanks."

"You don't have to say it, but I know you love me too."

That pulls a rough laugh out of me. "Yeah, you fucker."

Really, if I hadn't had Erik with me during that weekend of the funeral, I don't know what I would have done. He stayed when no one else did. Not even Valerie. She came for the service and left almost immediately after. Something about a shoot.

Made me not feel so bad about the Key West girls.

Which only proved my parents' point.

Who the hell had I become?

I blow out a stuttered breath and shuffle toward the living room, with Erik following behind, murmuring a few quiet words to his son. When we sit, he takes the baby out of the carrier and hands him over to me. I wouldn't say I'm comfortable holding him

—this being only the third or fourth time—but in my very limited experience with babies, I think this one's pretty easy. He snuggles up in the crook of my arm as Erik digs through a bag I didn't notice he brought, retrieving a bottle, which he also hands to me.

"What do I do?" I ask, not sure if I'm holding Kai right.

"Keep his head up a little higher. Yeah, like that. You got it."

Kai starts in on the bottle like he's never eaten before, formula dribbling out of his mouth, and Erik finds a soft cloth that he tucks around my forearm, so I can clean him up, and my best friend chuckles.

"You're a total natural. Who says you can't be a dad?"

That's when Kai lets loose a monstrous sound, bubbly and warm against my side, and I nearly throw him back to Erik. "Me. I say I can't be a dad because I am not dealing with *that*."

Erik lays his kid out on my sofa, and when I realize what he's doing, I toss my hands up. "Not on the leather sofa!"

"It's fine." He pays me no mind as he strips Kai's onesie off to get to his diaper. It takes five wet wipes to clean that baby of his mess, and I shake my head.

"Are we sure he's human and not part animal?"

"Nah. Just got those Rivera genes." Erik holds him up, noisily kissing Kai's cheek until he grins, drool making its way down his chin.

"He is cute, though," I admit, and Erik nods.

"Takes after his mother, thank god."

"How's Molly doing?"

"Good. Out with Nadine now. That's why I thought we'd stop by."

"Nadine?" I scratch at my jaw, prickly with a few weeks' worth of a beard.

"She's staying with us for the summer," Erik explains, and I fold my arms over my chest.

"Why?" Not that I care. Only making conversation.

"She's kinda down lately. Her job is…wearing on her."

"Still teaching?"

"Yeah. I thought she could stay with us for the summer to get her out of her funk."

I barely hold back my dubious snort. That girl has always been in a funk. So uptight she could shit diamonds. No sense of humor whatsoever.

"You know," he starts, head tipped to the side like he's studying a new play, "she might be able to help you."

I tug at my ear. "Run that by me again."

"Nadine might be able to help you out." He tucks Kai against his chest. "It's kind of perfect, actually. She's experienced with kids Paisley's age and knows ASL."

Though I can infer what he's implying, I need him to spell it out for me because... No.

Not Nadine Rivera. The first time we met, she called me an asshole. The second time, she told me it was a good thing my head was so big, to make up for the size of my dick.

"What do you think your sister can help me with?"

"You could hire her to help with Paisley. Like a nanny."

"No, that's not... You think... Would she?"

Erik shrugs. "Maybe. You know how she is..."

I stare blankly at him. Because, no, I don't.

"She's always down to help, if needed. When I told her about what happened with your parents, I think she was ready to hop on the plane. Especially when I told her about Paisley."

I sink back against the cushions, cracking my knuckles, thinking of the sharp-tongued woman. For being only a few inches over five feet, she sure carries herself like she's ten feet tall. Looks sweet, but she's poison underneath those blue eyes and soft lips.

"I could talk to her, if you want," Erik goes on. "She understands the demands of your life, and you know you can trust her."

Good points. But still...

After that time I suggested she'd be more relaxed if she got laid, I highly doubt she'd be excited to help me.

But then Paisley skulks around the corner, her long hair down around her face, her T-shirt and shorts way too big for her. She looks miserable and barely spares a glance in the direction of the living room before she opens a few cabinets, searching for food and clearly not finding anything to her liking since I don't keep anything fourteen-year-olds enjoy. Mostly just protein bars and single servings of habanero BBQ almonds. She screeches her annoyance, grabs a Gatorade, and then stomps back to her room.

Erik raises his brows in my direction, and I acquiesce with a dip of my chin. "All right. Talk to your sister."

CHAPTER 4
NADINE

"THIS IS DELICIOUS," I say, shoving a very unladylike bite of homemade pizza into my mouth, this one with prosciutto, peaches, basil, and balsamic vinegar. Since my brother installed a pizza oven outside, he's become an adept chef.

Erik and Molly live on the Main Line, the affluent suburbs outside of Philadelphia, in a house that boasts six bedrooms, eight bathrooms, a pool, sauna, and over an acre of land. It's secluded enough that they live in peace, but Erik can drive to the stadium in thirty minutes, which is perfect for their growing family.

My brother points his thumb over his shoulder to the brick oven.

"I have the fig and goat cheese one in there now."

"You're spoiling me so much, you're gonna have a hard time kicking me out."

Molly grins, aiming her pizza crust my way. "That's the plan."

I've been here for about a week, and I've spent most of that time snuggling with Kai, reading all the books I've been meaning to, and rotting on the sofa. But I woke up this morning, needing to do something.

Like Erik instructed, I did not resign from my position, and while I don't feel all that confident about returning in the fall, I'm also trying to keep my mind off my job and my students. Especially Stacey. She should be due soon.

This morning, when I filled Molly in on all the details—how I'd taken Stacey to her doctor's appointments and purchased her a few things, like baby clothes and gift cards—Molly hugged me close and told me we were going out.

I didn't argue, needing to clear my head and conscience, so we took a Pilates class, went out for a long lunch, and then did a little shopping. By the time we returned home, Erik had started preparing dinner and greeted us each with a smile and a glass of wine, directing us to have a seat on the patio.

Suspiciously.

Not that my brother isn't thoughtful and generous, because he absolutely is, but he's been watching me for the last half hour like he's waiting to drop a bomb.

He does after I've polished off a piece of the delightful fig and goat cheese pizza and replenished my wineglass. "So, I was with Camden today."

"How's he doing?" Molly asks, checking on Kai in his bouncy chair, drooling around his fist.

Erik inhales a big breath. "He's…not great."

Molly winces. "Poor guy."

I don't follow celebrity gossip, but after Erik told me about the situation, I looked it up, curious for more information on his sister. I'm not particularly fond of Camden, but my heart did break for him and Paisley. Especially after I learned someone had sold pictures of the funeral to the tabloids.

The image of Camden with his arm around his sister filters into my mind. The photo had been taken from behind, so her face wasn't made public—small favors—but the infamous athlete was in profile, gazing down at her, the heartache etched so clearly on his features, it was impossible not to feel sympathy for him. Despite all of his faults.

Erik scoots closer to me. "Paisley is having a hard time adjusting, and training camp is going to be starting soon, so he needs to figure out a plan. And I thought you might be able to help."

I wrench back. "Me?"

"He needs someone to take care of Paisley. Like a nanny."

"No." I laugh into a sip of wine. "Absolutely not."

Molly leans over the table to flick my brother's ear. "Erik, did you volunteer her for something?"

"No." He avoids another flick, swatting at her hand. "Only told him I would ask."

"I'm not a nanny," I say more seriously, as my brother shifts his attention to me.

"No, but you sign."

I huff. "So do you. Why don't you do it?"

"You're a teacher," he says, as if I don't know. "You work with kids her age all day long."

"I thought I was supposed to come here to relax and hang out for the summer."

He holds his hands up in innocence. "It was just an idea. It's been really hard on them, their lives being turned upside down. And I know he's got a reputation, but his parents died. That changes a person."

I bite the inside of my cheek. I don't doubt that Camden is grieving hard and struggling with guardianship of his sister, but life is not constant amusement and gratification, as he has always seemed to believe it is. He has to grow up at some point.

And my lingering ire at all the insults he's thrown my way get the better of me. "He's a dick."

Erik shrugs. "Maybe, but he needs help."

I roll my eyes. "I'm not interested in helping assholes."

"What about my best friend?"

I refuse to answer my brother, instead choosing to turn away from him.

He doesn't let it go. "And you know that's not really who he is."

My traitorous sister-in-law agrees. "Underneath all that asshole exterior, he's a nice guy."

My jaw flaps open. "You think this is a good idea?"

She wags her finger. "I didn't say that. But I do think you two got off on the wrong foot all those years ago."

"Yeah? And the arrest is more proof of what a nice guy he is?"

"It was for drag racing, not assault," Erik says defensively. "Other players have done much worse."

It's a pathetic defense of toxic masculinity to say *at least it wasn't assault,* and I count off his other offenses on my fingers. "No? What about the drinking and partying? All the girls? That time he pushed the referee? Or when he trashed your locker room after the championship game that he lost for *you* last year because he couldn't wait one goddamn second to celebrate so he could realize he was on the one-yard line and not in the end zone? No one is more arrogant than he is."

Erik stays silent, only shaking his head.

So I continue. "He's a joke. He takes nothing seriously, and you expect me to swoop in and save his ass because he has to be an adult for once in his life? No. No thank you."

"Don't talk about him like that," Erik snaps, but I'm not done.

"You know all the shit he's said about me? To my face? That I'm uptight and need to get laid, that I'd be prettier if I smiled. He actually said that to me, Erik, and maybe you don't care about that. But I do. I don't work with people like that."

Erik leans away from me, sucking air through his teeth, and I hate that sound. Like nails on a chalkboard. "As if you haven't said shit back to him? This isn't all one-sided."

Molly takes our argument as her cue to leave and swiftly removes Kai from his seat, muttering something about giving him a bath while I silently fume.

Because, of course, I've said things to him. He's a real-life Gaston. Rude, conceited, and I'm positive he's never read a book without pictures in his life. He needs to be brought down a peg or two.

After a staredown, Erik breathes out a noisy exhale. "If you really don't want to, I won't push it, but I'm surprised." He lifts a shoulder as if he doesn't care one way or the other, but then he hits me right where he knows it'll land. "I figured you'd care about Paisley, about getting her the help and support she needs. You're the perfect person to do that."

Then he stands and leaves me to my indignation.

And memories.

Of the first time I ever met Camden Long.

It was at an engagement party for Erik and Molly five years ago in a ballroom in Center City, Philadelphia. Back then, the Founders were still trying to turn their losing record around, but Erik and Camden were the up-and-coming players, making moves for their team, which had previously been called the *Flounders* by anyone who followed professional football. And the story of Erik marrying his high school sweetheart was the kind of made-for-TV stuff producers clamored for, so while the wedding would be small and have no publicity involved, the engagement party was a big affair.

I'd picked out what I thought to be a flattering gown and practiced walking in the sky-high heels for weeks. So it hurt more than I'd like to admit when I'd overheard some of Erik's teammates talking, Camden in particular.

"I can't believe Rivera has such a big family," one of them said.

"Yo, you talk to his dad? I'd love to see that Olympic medal," another one added.

"You meet the sister?" the center asked.

To which another offensive lineman said, "She's in college, bro, barely legal. Stay away."

I'd been about to barge into the conversation to defend

Emmaline when the center said, "Not that one. The other one. The dark-haired one."

That was when Camden cut in. "I think it's best if everybody leaves the Rivera girls alone. Especially the older one."

I hung back, hidden by a potted plant, while the oblivious players had no idea I could hear.

"What's her name?"

"Nadine," Camden answered. "She's a schoolteacher."

One of the other players snickered. "Bet she fucks like one too."

"What's that supposed to mean?" Camden asked as the rest broke up into chuckles while I curled my hands into fists at my sides.

"Haven't you ever had a fantasy about fucking one of your teachers?"

Camden shrugged, his glass, containing some dark drink, appearing minuscule in his giant hand. "Not ones who look like her."

I couldn't stand there anymore, listening to him talk about me or my body. No, I wasn't blond like my sister or super confident like some of the other women strutting about, but I certainly didn't deserve his derisive laughter.

The next time I ran into him that night, I let him know he needed to check himself and maybe switch to water because, "Nobody likes a cocky asshole at their parties."

Now, I grit my teeth, feeling the humiliation all over again. Remembering how every time we met after that party, our barbs went further. Deeper.

I really can't imagine he'd want me working with him. *For* him.

But then I recall that photo of Camden with his arm around Paisley. The way his mouth was tipped down, his usually perfect hair a mess, the glistening streak down his cheek in HD, evidence that the man did indeed have feelings that weren't all about himself.

I think about my students and how I always wish I could do more for them, and even though Camden has the world at his fingertips with his money and fame, sometimes that isn't enough.

It certainly won't be enough for his sister.

With a sigh, I down the rest of my wine and then march inside, where Erik turns to me in the kitchen, expectantly. "I agree to one meeting," I tell him. "But if he makes one snide comment to me, I'm out."

Erik nods slowly, almost as if he's afraid if he makes any quick movement, I'll change my mind.

I point a warning finger at him. "You tell that friend of yours, this isn't for him. It's for Paisley."

CHAPTER 5
CAMDEN

THE FIRST TIME I ever laid my eyes on Nadine Rivera, she was wearing an ice-blue dress, the same color as her eyes, like a frozen river in winter, that flowed down from one shoulder and wrapped around her hips before splitting open to reveal one smooth leg with a mile-high heel on her foot. I'd never before been tempted by the tiny straps of a high heel, but I had suddenly wanted to undo them with my teeth.

It was Erik and Molly's engagement party, and he'd introduced me to his sister by telling me she was one of his best friends. She smiled at that, those plump pink lips spreading wide before taking my proffered outstretched hand, her fingers so dainty in mine. We didn't say much more to each other than the usual small talk, so I couldn't understand why the next time we bumped into each other by the dessert station, and I asked if she was having a good time, she answered by telling me, "The guest list could use a little work." Then she narrowed those river-blue eyes at me, her gaze trailing over me as her nose turned up in obvious disgust. "Nobody likes a cocky asshole at their parties."

"Excuse me?" I said, inclining my head to the tiny menace.

"You heard me." She rolled her eyes. "Other people might

like this bad-boy act, but I do not." Then she stomped away, her dress swishing behind her, and I'd been shocked the floor didn't turn to ice in her wake.

To this day, I have no idea where her complete hatred of me came from, and all our meetings after that didn't fare much better.

Now I'm about to meet her again. While I don't doubt she's perfected her impression of an uptight schoolmarm, I've been warned by Erik to be on my best behavior, and I easily agreed. This isn't for me. This is for Paisley.

As much as I'm not especially looking forward to being in close contact with a porcupine disguised as a woman, I need help, and Nadine is, unfortunately, the best person for the job.

We agreed to meet at my place, and when the doorman alerts me that they're here, I take a few calming breaths before checking my reflection in the mirror. The last two months have taken a toll on me. My hair, which I normally have trimmed every three weeks, is scraggly, and I've grown a beard. From my house and my cars to my personal appearance, I like things to be pristine. Only the best of clothes and barbers.

But lately, I haven't had the will or energy to care, and since I haven't been going out in public at all, it didn't really matter anyway.

I open the door after the few knocks on it and dap up Erik. He pulls me into a one-armed hug, giving me one last warning, "Seriously. Be nice."

"Aren't I always?" I mutter before releasing him then turn to the ice queen herself. "Nadine, how are you?"

She looks exactly as I remember, though her dark brown hair is shorter now, at her shoulders instead of halfway down her back. Her chin is tipped up at that proud angle, and even though she's more than a foot shorter than me, she carries herself like she's a giant.

Especially when she looks me up and down, surprise

coloring her features, probably at my unkempt appearance. "I'm fine. How are you holding up?"

Shrugging, I open the door wider so they can enter. "All right."

She nods, staying silent, and I'm not sure if it's because she pities me or if she received the same warning from her brother. She coasts her gaze around my home, offering no reaction whatsoever, and I almost wish she would. I wish she'd offer some snarky comment, so I could throw one back. At least that would feel normal.

Like my old self.

Nothing about this feels good or right. This new life.

Especially the way Nadine quietly follows me to the living room, all of that addictive venom hidden.

I wave for my sister's attention, and when she turns in her seat, I sign and speak at the same time. "Paisley, my friends are here to hang out with us. You know Erik, and this is his sister Nadine."

She steps up to my side, simultaneously signing, "I'm not his friend."

My little sister's mouth crooks up in a sort of smile, and my heart jumps. For this bit of life and a taste of those abrasive words I've been craving.

"I actually can't stand him," Nadine signs, and my sister laughs.

It's the best sound I've ever heard.

Erik tosses his hands on his hips like he does when the refs won't call a holding penalty.

"Do you mind if I sit with you?" Nadine asks, signing fast.

My ASL is rusty, and I'm having to learn a lot since I'm out of practice. Nadine has no problem with it. Paisley shifts over, making room on the small couch so she and Nadine can face each other while Erik and I take the bigger one. My sister and Nadine easily fall into silent conversation, with Nadine asking questions about Paisley, while Erik and I not so subtly try to eavesdrop, pretending we're not.

I take over the remote and put on ESPN since the girls don't seem to care. Erik catches me up on the workouts he's been doing, keeping his arm in shape for the season. Normally, I spend time with trainers, but I've let everything fall by the wayside since May. I stayed in Cedar Falls after the funeral in my childhood home, so Paisley could finish her eighth-grade year as I packed up my parents' things and sold the home. It wasn't easy, deciding what to do with my parents' entire life, even worse because Paisley did not want to move. She did not want to sell the house. She did not want to give any of their belongings away.

I didn't either, but we couldn't keep all of it, like some mausoleum. But I think that's what she wanted, to keep everything exactly as it was.

I understood that desire to have it like it was before.

But it wasn't possible.

We had to keep going.

At least, that's what I told myself every time I wanted to throw up my hands and give in.

I'm not sure Paisley will ever forgive me for forcing her to move halfway across the country, but I made sure to put multiple boxes into storage, anything I thought she might want from Mom and Dad when she was older. I brought along a couple of old photo albums and some of Dad's button-downs and Mom's T-shirts. Malcolm mentioned I could have them made into pillows or quilts or something, which I suppose is better than what we have now.

Which is nothing.

Watching Paisley chat with Nadine, I blow out a breath, having missed everything Erik said for the last minute. He smacks my side. "You all right?"

I lift my shoulder in answer.

"You wanna watch some tape?" he asks, and when I glance

toward the girls, he waves. "They're fine. Look at them. Two peas in a pod."

So I stand and fetch my wallet to dig out my credit card, handing it over to Paisley. "Order something for dinner," I sign. "Whatever you want. Erik and I are going to the media room. Let us know when the food gets here."

Then we head down the hall to the room with eight recliners and a wall-to-wall screen. The coaching teams had emailed everybody game tape from the previous season, plays that went well or didn't, but I didn't even open mine. Erik, of course, studies a lot more film than me, more than anyone on the team, and he always has a link ready. So he sets it up while I power on the projector before we sink into the chairs, and I lose myself in the only thing I excel at.

The one thing I treated as replaceable.

I have a lot of groveling to do this season, and even though I know it won't be comfortable to face my teammates or coaching staff again, I have to. I need to prove I'm not the careless jackass they think I am. The world can say whatever it wants, but knowing I let down my team is what hurts the most.

So I'll take every minute I can get, earning back their trust, starting with Erik. Because he might be my best friend, but he's also my QB. I let him down most of all. Only days after we—I— lost the championship, Kai was born, and we never talked about what happened. Swept it under the rug instead.

So we spend the next hour discussing plays and strategy until Nadine pops her head around the door, informing us the food has arrived. By the time we make it out to the dining room, she has all the burgers and fries from Shake Shack laid out on the table. She hands a milkshake to Erik, telling him, "It's chocolate."

He nods his thanks and immediately sits down to start eating. Meanwhile, I notice Paisley's got a big vanilla shake in her hand, and Nadine has what appears to be cookies and cream.

"Where's my shake?" I ask verbally, not bothering to sign.

Nadine purses her lips around the straw, sucking some of her milkshake down for five full seconds of torture before saying, "Must've forgotten to order you one."

She offers me a fake smile as her brother chides her softly, but she's not getting off that easy.

Nah.

As she slides into her seat, I intercept her shake, pop the top, and down almost the whole thing before she can argue. It goes down like a brick and I have brain freeze, but watching her jaw hang open is all worth it.

I grin and give her back the little bit that's left. "Delicious."

"You are—"

"Kids," Erik chides, eyes ping-ponging between us. "Let's remember why we're all here."

I slant my gaze to my sister, munching away on her burger and fries, and I deflate. With one last scowl in Nadine's direction, I sit next to Paisley and help myself to grabbing two cheeseburgers, then sign, "I'm glad you're eating."

She huffs. "Because I'm tired of your chicken, broccoli, and rice."

I'm naturally lean, and I have to work to keep on enough muscle for my position so I'm not thrown around like a rag doll by three-hundred-pound defensemen. It's all protein, protein, protein, and I never thought about asking my chef to make me anything different from what he usually does, merely to double it. But I make a mental note to talk to him about making some things Paisley will like.

Erik pretty much carries the conversation since Nadine is completely incapable of having one with me that doesn't involve sarcasm and insults, so he asks Paisley some questions about her hobbies—watching movies—and her favorite subjects in school —art and social studies.

After Nadine breaks into the conversation by assuring my sister that she'd enjoy the art scene in the city, I tell Paisley, "I asked Nadine to come over today because I was hoping she would be your nanny."

Paisley rears back, frowning while she signs, "I don't need a nanny."

Nadine agrees. "She doesn't need a nanny."

"Babysitter," I amend, which makes my sister go absolutely feral, throwing a handful of fries at me.

"She doesn't need a babysitter," Nadine says at the same time Paisley signs it.

I toss my hands up, looking to my best friend for help, but he merely winces.

"What your brother means to say," Nadine starts, though I'm almost positive she signs "idiot." I can only understand about half of the signs as she says, "He's hoping we can be friends, so that when he goes back to work, I can hang out with you. We can explore the city together, learn all the good places to eat, go to museums. I live in New Jersey, so I'm not very familiar with it either. If you don't mind, that is."

Paisley considers Nadine for a few moments then shrugs, not answering one way or the other. Then she shoots her eyes to me, dark like mine, and makes the same sign Nadine did.

And I know it means idiot.

Since I'm the least fluent in ASL, Erik and Nadine are using verbal communication for my benefit. If not for me, and my need to spell out a lot of words, the conversation would be a lot better. Easier.

God. *Fuck.*

I would give anything to make this all easier.

I let out a pained huff as Paisley stalks off in the direction of her room, and Nadine laughs at me, full of disdain. "Nice."

After tossing my paper napkin on the table, I bend to pick up the fries that landed on the floor. "I'm having a hard enough time. You don't need to make it worse."

Guilt flashes across her features before going blank. "I'm sorry. But—"

I scoff. "Of course there's a but."

"She's fourteen. You need to treat her like she's fourteen, not four. Don't talk down to her just because you're uncomfortable."

Her mini lecture hits home, especially when I remember how Valerie interacted with Paisley. In the few minutes they were together, Valerie infantilized my sister, talking slowly and patting her head. At the time, I didn't know what to say. Or, maybe, I just didn't want to say anything. I had the world on my shoulders, and I didn't want to police my girlfriend as well.

But I have to acclimate to the idea that my sister is a teenager, living in my house. She can take care of herself. She simply needs some guidance.

Problem is, I'm a shit person and an even shittier big brother.

"Will you do it?" I ask Nadine, point-blank. "Will you help Paisley and me out for the rest of the summer?"

She gives in with a begrudging tip of her chin. "As long as she's okay with it."

We finish up eating, and after exchanging numbers with the unpleasant little wench, I tell her I'll be in touch.

"I'll be waiting on pins and needles," she deadpans with a roll of her river eyes.

A minute later, I find Paisley in her room, watching something on her phone, so I flicker the lights for her attention then sign, "Can we chat?"

She pushes herself up to sitting. "After you ambushed me with a babysitter?"

"I know you don't need a babysitter. You are old enough to take care of yourself, but I'm not going to be home. I don't want you here by yourself."

She doesn't answer, only stares at the comforter on her bed, white. Same as the walls and furniture, all white. It's a guest room. Or, was. Until a few weeks ago.

Now it belongs to a surly teenage girl.

"What did you think of Nadine?"

"You're asking my opinion?" she signs with a sneer.

I inhale a deep breath and a roll of my shoulders, but my annoyance makes signing even harder, and I go from spelling out words to grabbing my phone to type out a note and then show it to her. While she reads, I say, "I know I haven't been around much the last few years, and I'm sorry about that. I haven't been the brother you need or deserve, and I'm sorry I don't know how to be a parent like Mom and Dad."

Her shoulders sink as she chews on her bottom lip, playing with the ends of her long ponytail, blinking away wetness from her eyes.

I type and talk again. "I need you to understand that my life is really hectic during the season, and there will be days I won't be home at all. I know you're not happy here. I wish I could've kept you in Iowa, but it's not possible. I live here. My job is here."

"You don't have a job. You have a..." She makes a sign I don't understand, so she spells it out. I shake my head in begrudging amusement when I understand she's telling me I have a hobby I'm paid a boatload of money for.

She's not exactly wrong, and she's patient while I give signing another try. "You're right, and the only thing that will make all of this easier is that boatload of money. I can get you whatever you want."

Her brows rise in challenge, and when I nod, she asks, "A dog?"

I slice my hand through the air. "No."

"You said anything."

"Besides a dog. Or any live animal."

She blows a raspberry at me and leans back against her pillows.

"Anything else," I sign. "I know you won't believe it, but I do love you. I want you to be happy."

She turns away from me, facing the big windows, highlighting the glassiness of her eyes again. "Fine," she signs, keeping her focus outside. "I want to hang out with Nadine."

"Good," I say and sign, even though she's not looking at me.

"But I'm not calling her my nanny."

"Agreed," I laugh, and she must see it out of the corner of her eye, because she shoots her foot out, nailing me in the thigh.

"Ouch." I tug on her ponytail, forcing her to turn back to me. "You know how much my body is worth?"

"Eighteen million," she signs, and I grin.

"Nineteen point one, actually."

"I hate you."

I laugh and pull her to me. She doesn't fight when I hug her. In fact, she presses her face into my shoulder and lets me hold her for a little while.

And for this moment, at least, I'm not disappointing anyone.

CHAPTER 6
NADINE

ONLY TWO WEEKS after my school year ended, I'm already thinking of ways to help another child.

Paisley is sweet and funny, in that sarcastic teenage way. In the two hours I spent in the devil's sanctuary, I learned that she loves Y2K rom-coms, because, yes, obviously, they are the best. She enjoys arts and crafts, making online photo collages, and has a TikTok account just to watch cake decorating. She also really misses her best friend from home and thinks Camden is a dick, because, yes, obviously, he is the worst.

Even if he is attractive.

Since I'm alone and no one will be able to tell what I'm looking at besides Russian spies, I enlarge the photo on my cell phone. The one from a few years ago, when he graced the cover of a men's magazine, a football in his right hand and his left holding the knot of a towel that hangs precariously low on his waist, moisture beading all over his golden skin. His mouth is tipped up in that dumbass smirk, his eyebrows raised playfully over his dark eyes.

Like all tight ends, he's tall. Freakishly tall. And muscular. Like, could lift a car, muscular. With those long arms able to catch a pass, strong enough to block a defender.

Each position in football calls for certain traits: offensive linemen are big in height and width, running backs tend to be a bit shorter—which is still taller than the average human—and low to the ground so they can withstand all those tackles when gaining rushing yards, wide receivers are tall and lithe, meant to outmaneuver the defense. The most important physical attribute of a quarterback is their brain. Aside from having an arm, they need to be able to read the entire field and remember hundreds of plays.

I used to help Erik study his playbook, which is how I understand the game and the positions so well. It's also how I know Camden Long is 6'5", 243 pounds, averaged fourteen yards per game last season, scored eight touchdowns, and signed the biggest contract in the league for his position right before the previous season, a four-year extension for a little over $76 million.

But, whatever.

It's not like I keep track.

It's merely difficult to avoid information about him when my brother is his quarterback. I'm proud of all the work Erik has put into his career, and occasionally dealing with his asshole friend is a minor hassle in the grand scheme of watching my brother live out his dream.

But since I officially received the **You're hired** text two hours ago, I figured I might as well do some more research on the minor hassle that has the potential to become a major one when we'll be around each other all the time.

I began with the videos from the championship game in February. When the Founders were down by three with seconds to score, and Erik threw a slant to Camden.

Too bad that fool didn't pay attention to where his toes were —*just* outside of the goal line.

Camden had always been known for dancing on the field, but he got too excited about scoring the winning touchdown, I guess, because he started in on his now-infamous dance, swinging his arms, the ball still in his big hand, only to be tackled, and pushed outside the boundary.

The buzzer went off, and the refs called it.

No touchdown.

The *Flounders* lost.

All because the King of Football, as some other article crowned him two years ago, fucked up. I didn't have any pity for him. He deserved all the scorn he received.

Not to mention, the video of him being arrested for illegal drag racing, grinning at whoever captured it, saying he'd be out in a few hours. Then he turned to the cop and actually asked, "You know who I am?"

I scrolled through old photos of him with some young country star, who had one hit years ago and started dating him shortly after he was drafted. I think they were still together when we met at Erik's engagement party. She wrote a breakup song about him. I don't listen to country, but that line about a strong jaw and weak words really hits.

Then came videos of him sauntering out of bars and clubs, eyes glassy. Celebrity gossip articles about how he was the "right amount" of bad boy. All charm and good looks without the hard drugs or assault charges. Seriously. That's the bar?

Now are the photos of him with his current girlfriend, Valerie Blondeau, a lingerie model turned B-list actress. She's tall with curves in all the right places, and I try not to linger on the picture of his hand on her hip, his fingers curled possessively. Or the one of them on a yacht, her perfectly big and round breasts nearly falling out of her top, him leaning back on his elbows, watching as she danced, holding a bottle of champagne.

"Haven't you ever had a fantasy about fucking one of your teachers?"

"Not ones who look like her."

So what if I don't have big boobs or toned thighs? At least I've never let Camden Long inside me. I growl, angry at myself for being so insecure. Or worse, jealous.

I'm not jealous of her. He's a jackass with a penchant for making bad decisions, and I'm glad I've never had sexual fantasies about him.

There were those couple of dreams, but I can't control what my brain does subconsciously, and I've *never* wanted to have sex with him in real life.

Ever.

Not even when Paisley relayed to me how Camden slept on the floor of her bedroom every day he was home. Said it was to make sure she was all right, even after Paisley told him she was fine.

I didn't find that sweet at all.

And spending the summer helping a grieving girl find her footing again will be fine. As long as her brother keeps his stupid mouth shut.

Three knocks sound on my semi-open door before Molly pops her head inside my bedroom. "Can I come in?"

"Of course." I toss my phone aside and push up to lounge against the pillows.

She smiles, hopping onto the edge of the mattress, pulling a laugh from me. My friend is pure sunshine, from the color of her hair to her persistently optimistic personality. She's in a T-shirt and cotton shorts, her hair wet, and since it's about Kai's bedtime, I ask, "Where's the baby?"

"Your brother's putting him down, so I thought I'd come check in with you. See how it went today."

When we returned home after visiting Camden's pristine penthouse that was more museum than home—cold and devoid of emotion—I grabbed a pack of peanut M&Ms from my brother's "hidden" stash and hightailed it up to the bedroom I've been sleeping in the past few weeks, torn between feeling like I had to learn the meaning of *no* and actually wanting to do this.

I probably should not have agreed, but I had to. I feel compelled to help. As always.

It is not my job as a teacher to talk with my students about their relationship drama or give them sex education—good Lord, do they need it—nor should I feel especially compelled to "lend" them money or give them rides home. I am contracted for 180 days per year, eight hours a day; that is it.

Yet I am unable to draw the line there. I shouldn't want to save every child who crosses my path, but there is something inside me that makes me incapable of saying no.

Not when I know they need help.

It doesn't matter how long or heavy it weighs on my shoulders and heart.

"What's Paisley like?" Molly asks, and I bend my legs up to curl my arms around them.

"She's small…fine-boned. Like she's breakable." She looks a little younger than fourteen, on the shorter side and scrawny. On the drive to Center City, Erik gave me a quick rundown of what he knew about her: that she was a preemie and spent a lot of time in the NICU because of different infections, one of which caused her hearing loss. But she's healthy now. At least, physically.

According to my brother, the Longs had a hard time learning how to communicate with Paisley, but once Camden was signed to Philadelphia out of college, he paid for tutoring for his parents and himself and footed the bill for anything else they needed. ASL is a complicated language, and without anyone for Paisley to communicate with, they ended up traveling to workshops and camps so they could all participate more fully in the Deaf community. Now, she has to start all over.

"She seemed fine when I was with her," I explain, "but it feels like it's just under the surface." I fist my hands by my chest, imagining that elephant on the lungs sensation, the fear of breaking down at any moment.

Molly wrinkles her nose. "Gosh, I feel so bad."

"*Gosh*," I repeat with a laugh. My friend and her good, pure heart.

She smacks me with a decorative pillow before using it to

prop up her head when she lies down next to me. "So you think you'll be all right with Camden for the next few weeks?"

I lift my shoulder. "I don't know. As long as he stays out of my hair, it'll be fine."

Or maybe not.

Molly settles her folded hands on her stomach. "It'll kinda be impossible for him to stay out of your hair when you're the one working for him."

"Can we stop talking about him like he's my boss? He's not my boss. I am not his employee."

"He's paying you."

"Yeah, but this isn't some power-trip situation." I flick my hand in the air, imagining how he'd probably love to hold it over my head. "He is not above me in any way whatsoever."

She huffs a laugh. "You two are so alike. You just hate to admit it."

I jerk back at the insult. "Excuse me?"

She ticks off our so-called similar attributes on her fingers. "You're both stubborn. You can both be quick-tempered *and* quick-witted. But you both have a lot of layers to peel back. I think you misjudged each other. A real *Pride and Prejudice* situation."

"I've never read it," I say as haughtily as possible, still annoyed that she'd lump Camden and me together.

"Me either, but you had to have seen the Keira Knightley version, right?" When I shake my head, she's the one who jerks back. "You've *never* seen it?" She grabs hold of my hand with both of hers. "Nadine no middle name Rivera! How?"

I'm not sure if the question is rhetorical, but I frown. "Not much for historical stuff."

She slides off the bed like I've killed her, though she doesn't let go of my hand when she speaks to me from the floor. "We are watching it. Tonight."

I roll to the edge of the mattress. "How much you wanna bet you fall asleep five minutes into it?"

She shakes her head. "No. No, I won't. It's one of my favorite movies ever. I can't believe you've never seen it. Even Erik loves it."

"Really?" I laugh, though my brother loves anything Molly loves.

"Yeah, come on." She finally lets go of me to push herself up off the floor, only to take my hand again once I'm standing. "But seriously? I think you're going to be great for Paisley. And maybe for Camden too."

I snort. "Doubt it."

She tosses me a mischievous grin before leading the way down the hall. "You might actually start to like him."

"Not happening."

Molly should know me well enough by now; I don't suffer fools.

Like how I knew she'd fall asleep early. Though, she lasted twenty minutes instead of five.

Me? I was too busy scrolling more videos of a fool to pay attention to the movie.

CHAPTER 7
CAMDEN

"CAN you get off my ass for one goddamn second? You just got here."

It's Nadine's first official day as the not-nanny nanny, and already, she's on my last nerve. She arrived with a chip on her shoulder and a small carton of tea bags because she apparently can't live without her Earl Grey in the morning and a chamomile mint in the afternoon.

"Well, who doesn't have a teapot?"

I slap my hand on the counter. "Me. *I* don't have a teapot. Because why the fuck would I have a teapot?"

"To make tea," she overenunciates with a curl to her lip that I'd like to bite.

"I don't drink tea."

"What about coffee? Can I use your coffeepot to heat up water?"

I shake my head. "Don't drink coffee either."

I hate to admit the annoyed, throaty growl of hers really does something to me, and I spin away to show her my state-of-the-art microwave, then proceed to point to the cabinet with mugs. "Help yourself."

She reels back as if she hit her head and ended up in the sixteenth century. "You want me to microwave my tea?"

I shrug and pocket my wallet and keys, informing her, "I'll be home in a couple hours."

"I thought you Midwesterners were supposed to be welcoming."

I paste on a fake smile and offer her a dramatic bow at the waist. "Welcome."

Even though training camp doesn't start for another week, the team has been in meetings, hitting the weight room, and generally remembering what it is to be a professional athlete again. I've been given a wide berth to take personal time, but I need to get back. I need to remind my teammates and the staff that I'm here. I'm ready.

I have an appointment with the speed and agility coach, and I can't stand here arguing all day with this tiny she-devil, who's addicted to fancy teas.

"Paisley is still sleeping," I say, and Nadine ignores me, jamming her index finger at random buttons on the microwave. I don't bother correcting her, but I do send one last parting shot as I leave. "If you want some help removing the stick from your ass, you're *welcome* to use the hot tub to relax. Though I'm not sure the world would be ready to see what a demon looked like after your human skin melted off."

Then I close the door on her grumbles and take the elevator down to the garage, where I start up my brand-new car. I haven't been able to sit behind the wheel of my Camaro since the night of my parents' accident, and I have it covered with a tarp in the corner. Not that I'd use it for city driving anyway, but this Mercedes-Benz will do. It was a spur-of-the-moment purchase when Erik mentioned that I'd now be in charge of my sister's transportation, and my convertible Porsche didn't seem suitable enough, so I went out and bought this GLA SUV. "Perfect for a family," the salesman had said, and I signed the papers on the spot.

Philadelphia appears before me as I pull out of the under-ground garage, a blend of old brick and modern glass that I've come to love. I easily glide through the streets of Center City that once intimidated me when I first moved here, a grid system of one-ways that took me a while to understand, not to mention how to navigate the chaotic traffic. After seven years of living in the City of Brotherly Love, I've found it's become a city of ire.

The familiar landmarks blur past me, a reminder of how the life I used to live is gone.

The bachelor nightlife? Done.

The freedom to chase whatever high I wanted? Crushed.

The old Camden Long? Don't recognize him.

Between becoming the city's number one enemy and the guardian of my sister, nothing is what I remember.

Except the complex that is the Founders' headquarters, including the training and practice facilities, front offices, and a media center. Situated in South Philly, not far from the stadium, it's where I've spent the majority of days in my adult life. It is as familiar to me as my childhood home is.

Or, was. Since it's not mine anymore.

I blink away the sting in my eyes and clear my throat even though no one is around to see. Still, allowing myself even this much emotion is unacceptable. I have too much on the line to break down now.

I have a sister relying on me.

A team depending on me to bring them back from humiliation.

The respect of an entire city to regain.

So with one last deep breath, I step out of my car and into the summer heat. I run my hand through my newly trimmed hair a few times then scrape my knuckles over my clean-shaven jaw, checking my reflection in the driver's side window.

I may look like my old self. But I feel like a shell.

A hollowed-out log on two legs.

Ignoring the few "fans" booing me from across the street, I

jog into the complex, keeping my head down because it's easier to ignore strangers hating on me than it is the people I've worked with for the last seven years. But I can't even retrieve my phone from my pocket to pretend I'm busy before I bump into Coach Roberts.

Tall and well-built, he has a way of making me feel like a kid again, especially when he frowns at me, like he's doing now.

"Long," he says in greeting, crossing his left arm over his torso, rubbing his right hand over his goatee.

"Hey, Coach."

"I saw on the schedule you're here to meet with Monica."

Nodding, I assume he had this little hall meeting planned, and I'm proven correct when he nods. "Let's have a chat in my office."

I follow him down a couple of corridors in silence, the over-head lights reflecting off his bald head. Last year, I would've made a joke about it. He would've laughed. And then we would've had a relaxed conversation among the cluttered space he calls an office.

Now, I'd rather take a hit from Trey Daniels without any pads on than have to sit across from Coach, the whiteboard behind me, trophies and framed photos showing off his famed career, including the one he has front and center of him and President Obama, back when he won a Bowl ring, coaching with his last team.

He could've had another.

If it weren't for me.

"So," he starts once I finally slip into my seat. "How are you doing?"

"Fine," I answer automatically because there is no way I'm volunteering any weakness.

"I'm glad you're back, but if you need more time—"

"I'm fine, Coach. I'm good. I don't need any more time."

"What about your sister?"

Despite how last season ended, a lot of my teammates

showed up at my parents' services. A few dozen men standing like sentries in the back of the room because they couldn't fit in the chairs the funeral home provided. My sister, on the other hand, didn't have that kind of support. As far as I knew, she had her best friend, and that was it. We grew up in a small town, and she was the only deaf student in the entire school. Though she never told me, I assume it must have been a lonely experience for her. Now, even worse.

"Rivera's sister is staying with her when I'm not home," I say, shifting uncomfortably.

"Oh yeah. He's got a whole bunch of sisters, huh?"

"Two," I correct. "Three brothers. Nadine is a teacher and knows ASL, so it's kind of a perfect fit." Why I feel the need to overexplain my decision to hire Nadine, I don't know. Or use the words *perfect fit*.

Coach leans his elbows on his desk, fingers steepled by his chin, his dark brown skin showing almost no sign of his near sixty years. Decades ago, he became one of the youngest head coaches in history when he signed on with Nashville. Since then, he has become known for remaking teams, which is why he was hired for the Founders a season before they signed Erik and me.

Coach Roberts is responsible for my career.

But I have yet to repay him.

"I don't want to continue to rehash last season," he eventually says, and I wipe off my slick palms on my shorts. "We've already had conversations about it, and we can't live in the past."

Conversations is a funny way to say he screamed at me, but...

"I'm glad you're here today. I'm glad you showed up, but I'm gonna need you to continue to show up."

"I understand."

His brows tick up in silent question. *Do you?* "You haven't spoken to Pearce yet."

The team's counselor. It wasn't a question, but I answer anyway. "No."

"You need to."

I start to argue, tell Coach I'm fine, but he stops me.

"I'm not asking. You've been through a lot these last few years, and I'm not putting you on the field without being 110% sure that you are ready."

I swallow down the sick feeling in my throat. He doesn't think I'm ready.

"I can't imagine what you're going through." His tone is the one he uses when we get in our heads after a mistake—missing a block or dropping the pass. I didn't do that.

What I did is much worse.

I let everything outside of the field become bigger than what I did *on* the field.

"I imagine losing both of your parents is hell, and I'm willing to give you all the time you need to sort your head out. But I'm telling you now, if your heart isn't in the right place, none of this —" he sweeps his hand around his office, encompassing all of his success "—is worth it."

I clamp my jaw shut, unable to lift my gaze up from where the organ he's so worried about is splayed out between my Nikes, beat-up and barely working.

"You are one of the most talented athletes I've ever had the pleasure of knowing," he goes on. "But I need you to remember why you love this game. I need you to find the fun in it again. Not what fun you can have because of it, but why you wanted to play in the first place."

I clamp my teeth over my bottom lip and nod.

"Camden."

My attention immediately shoots up because he rarely refers to us by our first names. His dark eyes hold mine, and his chin dips, as if he can imbue his words with extra meaning. "You're not in this alone."

I clear my throat of the sudden dust there, but my voice still sounds like it's been through a wood chipper. "Thanks, Coach."

He stands and offers me his hand, and when I take it, he pulls me into a hug, his other arm banding tightly around me. He doesn't say anything else, but the way his hand lands heavily against my shoulder blade reminds me of the way my father hugged me, and I'm too overwhelmed with familiarity and grief to let myself accept it, so I push away, sniffing a quick, "See you later."

"Make that appointment with Pearce," he calls after me, and I offer a single wave over my head in return.

Having no intention of making that appointment.

But I do let Monica run me ragged for an hour and a half, putting me through the paces before stretching me out while she makes fun of me for whining, busting my balls so much, it makes me feel like maybe things can get back to normal.

By the time I arrive home, I've made plans for Valerie to come over for dinner since she's in town for the night, but I'm not really feeling it. After the short but rough talk with Coach and being reintroduced to shuttle runs and box jumps, I'd rather relax on the couch, but we don't see each other very often, and I owe my girlfriend some time.

Valerie and I met at a party in Vegas. I don't even remember what it was for at this point—I think an anniversary of some tequila company. Or maybe somebody's birthday. All I recall is that she hopped into my limo and had my cock in her mouth before we even stopped at the first red light. Had gotten me off by the time we arrived back at my hotel, so I invited her up.

We've been arranging nights together ever since, but between her shooting schedule and my season, it's rare we spend more than a night or two together, especially because she lives in LA.

When I open the door to the penthouse, I don't immediately see Paisley or Nadine, but there is some god-awful smell coming from the kitchen. Beyond the mess of dishes in the sink and on the counter, the microwave has been left open, and apparently airing out from the burned popcorn, the evidence of which I find in the garbage can.

I peek around, checking the terrace and Paisley's bedroom before heading to the media room, where I find the lights off and Heath Ledger on the big screen, dancing across the stands in *10 Things I Hate About You* with the captioning on the bottom.

Making my way down the steps toward the big recliner they're sharing, I raise my voice above the chatter of the movie. "Hey."

Nadine startles, throwing her bowl of popcorn in the air with a gasped, "Oh my god" while Paisley slowly turns and waves.

"You scared the shit out of me." Nadine slaps hand to her chest, and I hop down the rest of the incline to the floor, where I hit the lighting panel on the wall, illuminating the room. With popcorn strewn all over the love seat and floor.

"You made a mess," I say and sign at the same time.

Nadine answers, signing as well. "Because you decided to sneak in here like a serial killer."

I don't sign what might be considered a threat in a court of law. "While I've had fantasies about wrapping my hands around your neck, I'm not willing to go to prison over you."

She sneers at me as my sister signs, "You want to watch the movie with us? I know it's your favorite."

I shake my head, refuting her. "It's not my favorite."

"Ah, come on. Nothing wrong with a big man like yourself loving a rom-com," Nadine goads with an irritatingly pointed smile, and she really has no idea how often I've thought about my hand around her neck. With a throat that goes red when she's mad and a rose gold chain with a cross on it. As far as I know, Erik isn't religious, more "spiritual," which always earned an eye roll from me whenever he talked about it. But I think I remember him saying their dad was Catholic.

My parents took me to Faith Lutheran every Sunday, and we said grace before every meal, but I easily let that part of me go when I arrived at college and learned I wasn't all that interested in sitting in a hard pew every week if someone wasn't forcing me. Though I assume Nadine is the type to go and sit in the front row. I bet she has Bible verses memorized, believing she's better than everybody else. Certainly believes she's better than me.

"I don't have a problem admitting I enjoy romantic comedies," I say, just to prove her wrong. "I love *10 Things I Hate About You*. That bit when Julia Stiles gets drunk at the party and he rescues her is my favorite."

Again, why I had to go that far, revealing more information than necessary, I don't know, but having Nadine in close quarters has clearly sent my mind reeling. Instead of concentrating on driving off my standing leg during my sprints, I was thinking about the time Nadine and I crossed paths at a Founders' fundraiser for an autism charity. I told her I was surprised to see her in the sunlight since I thought it turned vampires to dust, and she told me I should go back to whatever cornstalks I crawled out of because the crows would eat all the crops. Then I proceeded to tell her my dad was a mechanical engineer and my mom was a dental hygienist, so I didn't come from "cornstalks."

She pursed those lips of hers and lifted a nonchalant shoulder, causing the thin strap of her sundress to droop. "Could have fooled me with all that straw in your head."

I had no reply, my mind scrambled with the way her hips swayed, the hem of the pink dress shorter than I ever might have imagined prissy little Nadine would wear.

Now, she's in my home.

Looking completely comfortable.

As if she has not a care in the world.

Even as she's made a mess of the place.

"Then why did you say your favorite movie was *Any Given Sunday* when your social media people asked for TikTok?" she asks, drawing me back into our sniping.

"You following me on TikTok?"

She rolls her eyes. "The team, you arrogant asshole."

Funny, though, that she would even remember something

like that. The social media managers haven't begun making their content yet this season, so whatever video she's talking about is old.

Then again, if someone asked me what Nadine wore on every occasion I've been in her physical presence, I'd be able to rattle off: ice-blue gown for Erik's engagement party, long and flowy number for the small beach wedding, the tight jeans and black sweater for the surprise birthday party Molly threw Erik, the hot-as-fuck pink sundress for the team's charity fundraiser, this ugly-ass one-piece thing with wide legs and puffy sleeves for Kai's baby shower, and she wore denim shorts and an over-sized T-shirt with *Love Wins* written into a rainbow when she came over the other day to meet Paisley.

But, whatever.

It's not like I ever wrote her a poem about all the reasons I hate her.

Number one being she's a stuck-up shrew with an unfortu-nate ability to get under my skin.

"You need to clean up," I say, motioning to all the popcorn. "Mariam doesn't come until Friday."

Nadine doesn't sign the next bit, too busy shrieking at me as she leaps up from the recliner. "I don't need you ordering me around. Don't mistake my goodwill for submission. I won't tolerate your condescension."

It's my turn to roll my eyes. "Asking a guest in my home to clean up after herself is condescension? I thought it was good fucking manners."

She steps closer to me, having to rise up on her toes, but that only gives her another inch, and she still needs to tilt her head back to hold my gaze, her ice-blue eyes on fire. "Yeah, I do have good fucking manners, unlike you. I always clean up my messes."

I force a laugh. "Little Miss Manners, huh?"

She steps back from me, sneering, "I can't stand you."

That's when Paisley interrupts us, signing that she'll clean up the popcorn. That it's no big deal, but when both Nadine and I start to tell her she doesn't need to, she signs, "Children" with a scoff and then turns to pick up the pieces of popcorn from the floor.

Chastised by a fourteen-year-old, Nadine and I silently trudge out of the media room and back to the kitchen, where we both clean up the mess *she* made. When it's finally done, she glares at me. "Neither one of us knows how to work your stupid robot microwave. We burned the first bag of popcorn."

"Yeah. I got that."

She flicks her hand toward the cabinets. "And you need the good popcorn with butter. Not that plain, calorie-free stuff. It has no flavor."

I comb my fingers through my still sweat-damp hair. "My one mission in life, to fill my house with the groceries you want."

She flings her arm back toward the media room. "Well, it could at least be to make your sister comfortable. You have buckets of money, so you should spend it on her."

I know that. I've already talked to Paisley about it, but Nadine plows on like a miniature bull, stomping around the kitchen.

"You want her to feel at home here, but you're not doing anything to help her. Of course she feels out of sorts—she's in a new city, doesn't know anyone, and you have her sleeping in that hospital room down there."

"Hospital room?" I live in the penthouse of the most expensive building in Center City. It has a twenty-four-seven concierge service, valet parking, a gym with a full-time personal trainer on-site, as well as an outdoor terrace with a pool. When I begin to inform her of all of this, she heaves an exhausted sigh.

"I understand that this—" she circles her finger in the air "—is nice for you, a twenty-nine-year-old bachelor, but not for a teenage girl. There is nothing here that makes her think it's her home. You haven't even tried."

"Yes, I have." The ability this woman has to raise my blood pressure needs to be studied, and I whip my sweat-soaked T-shirt off, tired of having it stick to my body. "I've been trying. I told her I'd buy whatever she wanted."

Nadine's eyes momentarily drift below my chin before zipping right back up to my face. "Your sister doesn't want to live in a museum for the next four years. Start with bedding she likes, toss a couple fluffy blankets around, buy her art supplies. *Try harder*, Camden."

The way she says my name in a plea does something I don't like, making my skin suddenly cold, goose bumps skittering down my arms and up my spine. Like I've been plunged into the ocean.

Blinking away from her defiant stare, I mutter, "Are you always so rude?"

"Only to people who deserve it."

I grunt and push past her right as the doorman calls to inform me Valerie is here. And I haven't even showered yet.

"Guess I better go." Nadine collects her purse and cell phone as Paisley shuffles into the kitchen with the popcorn, which Nadine takes from her to throw away and then loads the bowl in the dishwasher. They hug, signing something I don't pay attention to while I shuck my sneakers off and run my hand through my hair a moment before Valerie arrives at my door.

She greets me with a kiss, her brown eyes trailing over me, mouth quirked up. "We skipping dinner?"

"No, just haven't had time to change," I say, leading her into the house, so she finally sees Nadine next to Paisley.

Valerie stops short, delicate eyebrows winging up. "Oh. You have a visitor."

From the way she drags her gaze over my bare chest once again, she is obviously not pleased that another woman is in my house.

"This is Nadine Rivera, Erik's sister."

Valerie smiles, though it looks like that time she stepped in dog shit in NYC. Cameras were there, so she had to pretend she didn't. "Hi. I'm Valerie Blondeau."

Nadine lifts her hand in greeting. "Nice to meet you. I was just heading out." Then she asks me, "You need me tomorrow?"

"Yeah. Same time. Next week will be every day with training camp starting."

She nods then turns to Paisley, signing, "See you tomorrow."

Valerie twiddles her fingers at Nadine in some weird girl code that I don't understand, not catching what my sister signs out of the corner of my eyes.

Whatever it was, it makes Nadine laugh. A great big chuckle that I don't expect, and I have a hunch it was about Valerie.

I'm not sure how to feel about that, Nadine and my sister teaming up against my girlfriend.

But I have always liked that Nadine refuses to roll over.

CHAPTER 8

NADINE

"SHE'S the Chastity to his Joey Donner," is what Paisley had signed to me on the way out. A very niche joke about her brother and his girlfriend, comparing them to the self-obsessed jock and the self-centered girl who ends up with him in *10 Things I Hate About You*.

Spot-on.

Valerie did exude that mean-girl kind of vibe, and Camden was certainly a Joey Donner. Made me want to draw a penis on his cheek.

But then I walked into his apartment the next day to find a brand-new teakettle on his stove along with a giant box of different teas, all of them in cute, colorful tins.

I'd been so gobsmacked by the gift that I stayed silent when he walked into the room in only a pair of mesh shorts, his mile-long torso and arms on display. He grinned, each of his straight pearly whites glinting like a toothpaste commercial, at my slack-jawed surprise.

"Yeah, I know." He gestured to himself, as if my being in his half-naked presence was the reason for my sudden speechlessness. When, really, it was his thoughtfulness.

But I wasn't about to tell him that and changed the subject. "How was your sleepover?"

He tugged his Under Armor compression shirt on. "You interested in my sex life, River?"

I paused, my hand hovering over the teas, wondering if he'd suddenly lost a few brain cells since yesterday. "Rivera," I corrected, though it came out more like a question. Then I explained, "I'm only interested in so far as I need to know what to tell Paisley when she will inevitably bring it up to me."

He waved away my reasoning. "She's not going to bring anything up. Valerie came over to eat dinner and then left."

I tried very hard to keep my features blank. Because I didn't care about that tidbit of information. Especially when he said, "I wasn't comfortable having her sleep over with Paisley here."

I wasn't glad because I was jealous of Valerie.

I was glad because Camden was being a responsible adult with a young, impressionable girl in his house.

And maybe he wasn't a total Joey Donner. Only, like, 92%.

Because the following day, I arrived at Camden Long's usually spotless lair to find the kitchen littered with reusable shopping bags, an open package of double stuffed Oreos next to a variety pack of snack-sized chip bags. Paisley sat on top of the counter, her legs swinging as she ate her way through a Lunchable.

"Camden took me to the grocery store. Let me get whatever I wanted," she signed, and I opened the refrigerator to find the shelves full of food. Fruits, yogurt, string cheese, milk, and three different kinds of juices. Then I threw open the other hidden door next to it, revealing the freezer full of pizza rolls, Texas Toast, and multiple gallons of ice cream.

And that Joey Donner percentage dropped even more. Especially when he appeared dressed for another workout, hurriedly holding out his fist to his sister for a bump then ruffled her hair, earning a thoroughly happy grin and playful swat. He passed me by with a jut of his chin. "See you, Riv."

Now, the prick left me his credit card and explicit instructions to take Paisley out to buy the essentials. "Whatever she needs to be comfortable."

It's the first day of training camp, so we have hours to test drive his Amex. Being Erik Rivera's sister, I'm used to the luxuries that come with a professional athlete's lifestyle, and it's *nice*.

I have no compunctions about accepting any gifts my brother or Camden wants to offer. They have literal millions to spare, and I live on a teacher's salary. So, like any well-intentioned person with an unlimited budget and a goal to make a teenage girl happy, we start online shopping. We spend the morning next to each other, sharing links and screens, photos of inspiration boards for what will become her bedroom, with a vintage-looking lamp, twinkly lights, and new bedsheets and comforter. We buy a pink and gold rug, bookshelf, and multiple artificial succulents.

After, we head to a salon so she can have her hair and nails done and then enjoy a late lunch, where we chat over fancy mocktails and salads that have no business being twenty dollars. It's while we're eating our caramel cheesecake dessert that I sign, "Is there anything else you want to do today?"

She shrugs. "What else is there?"

"We could walk around and explore." When she wrinkles her nose, I laugh. "It is pretty hot out. We could keep shopping."

She thinks for a few moments, swallowing the last of her dessert, then signs, "I don't really need anything else."

"But there is something you *want*?"

She slants her gaze toward the window, the sunshine streaming in hitting the new purple highlights in her hair. She was worried Camden would be mad, but I told her I'd take care of him. If she wanted purple highlights, she was getting purple highlights.

After all she's been through, there is nothing short of permanent body modification that I wouldn't agree to and defend.

"The penthouse is kind of lonely," she signs after a while, and I wag my head side to side. I could understand that.

It's cold. Not in the physical sense, but in the emotional one. It's like Camden moved in and hasn't touched anything since. Everything in his life is meant to show his status, but nothing of his actual heart.

"I think he's lonely," Paisley goes on. "He would never admit it, but I don't think he ever really enjoyed being away from home all this time." She blows out an audible breath, laughing slightly as she meets my eyes again. "I don't know. Maybe not. Maybe he really is an asshole and likes his weird, sterile house."

"Maybe," I agree with a smile. "Or maybe you're right, and he's covered up all the holes in his life from missing out on important stuff by cultivating this...person he's become. You know him better than I do."

I hate to think she's onto something and her brother isn't actually so bad with all that smarmy charm and inflated confidence, but Paisley seems to agree with me, nodding to herself. She studies her manicured nails, an opalescent mermaid color, then she lifts her focus and her hands to sign. "He didn't always care so much about what people thought about him. He didn't care about clothes and cars and impressing people."

"What did he care about?"

"Making me laugh," she signs, and my heart plummets to the floor. "I remember him making funny faces. He would put me on his shoulders. Give me piggyback rides."

"Sounds like a good brother," I sign, which is just as well because I don't think I'd be able to talk with how my throat feels swollen.

I imagine a teenage Camden, playing with his toddler sister, tossing her in the air, letting her tackle him, carrying her around.

Paisley flips her phone over, scrolling on it for a few seconds before showing me her screen, a photo of Camden in his college football uniform, sweaty and dirty, smiling wide and holding Paisley in one arm, his helmet dangling from his other hand.

"Cute," I sign, and she smiles, admiring it for a while, then clicks on another picture. This one of the whole Long family, sitting on a bench at what appears to be an outdoor picnic or party. In it, Paisley is probably two or three, standing on her brother's thighs, her hands midair like she's about to clap. Camden's attention is on her, smiling. A woman, who I assume is their mother, has her mouth open, laughing, head tilted back, while the man who looks like Camden but older has his head buried in the side of his wife's neck, as if tickling her, the reason for her laughter.

I'd already tried to ease into a conversation about grief and reminding Paisley that she can talk to me about anything, but seeing this picture and the glassiness in her eyes cuts me to ribbons. I don't know what else to do besides slide out of my seat and hug her. "I am so sorry," I say out loud, even though she can't hear me, but I keep saying it. "You are loved," I tell her, squeezing her tight. "You are so loved."

I know nothing will be able to comfort Paisley like having her parents back, though maybe being reminded of their love for her will help. I sit back down again and sign, "How about we print out those pictures and buy some frames? Keep them around where you can see."

She nods and tells me, "I have more pictures. I downloaded them all to my phone from Dad's after…"

"We'll do it today," I say and sign, determined not only to make Paisley as comfortable as possible but happy too. There are times when I find her staring off into space, and I assume she's thinking about her mother and father. I'm sure it'll be a long time before the weight of the loss lessens, but having physical reminders of them might help. "What else? What else will make you feel better?"

"I asked Camden for a dog, but he said no."

I tip my head to the side. "A dog might be difficult to keep in an apartment, no matter how big it is, but… How about something smaller?"

Hours later, I'm lost in a spicy *Jurassic Park* fanfiction, when a monster suddenly appears.

"Nadine!"

"What the hell?" I startle as the sliding door flings open, a deep voice rumbling my name. I rip my sunglasses off my head to find all six feet and five inches of Camden Long looming over me.

"*Me* what the hell? *You* what the hell. Why are there two animals and a shit-ton of hay in my living room?"

I pull myself up from the lounger where I'd been relaxing outside while Paisley got to know her new pets. "Is shit-ton the measurement you used on the farm in Iowa?"

"Nadine," he warns, like a boiling pot of water. "What is in my living room?"

"Your sister said it felt lonely living here, and who am I to disagree with her? So we went over to the animal shelter and spotted those cutie pies."

He props his hands on his hips, glaring. "*What* are they?"

"Guinea pigs. Jelly and Bean."

"Ridiculous fucking names." He heaves a sigh, running his fingers through his hair so it stands on end. "You had to get two?"

I lift my hands because *of course*. "They're a bonded pair."

"A bonded pair?"

"Can't take one without the other, or they'll be sad. Guinea pigs are social creatures."

He rubs the heels of his hands against his eyes. After a beat and a breath, he flops his arms at his sides and narrows his gaze at me. "Do you know how much money you spent today?"

"Probably…" I roll my eyes up to the orange sky, doing the mental math. "A few thousand."

"Five thousand six hundred and eight-three dollars."

I smile. "I was close."

He frowns. "You spent five grand on guinea pigs?"

"Plus a shit-ton of hay."

He closes his eyes, shaking his head. "You're not cute."

Almost like he's convincing himself.

"Paisley picked out all new things for her bedroom, and I took her to a salon for her nails and hair, so make sure to compliment her on it, and then we had a super fancy and overly expensive lunch. It was delicious," I tell him, earning an arched brow. "Don't worry." I pat his stomach. "I'm sure you have suits that cost double what we bought today."

He doesn't argue because he can't.

Only follows me back inside, where I stop to hug Paisley. She thanks me with Jelly in her arm, and I drag my fingertip over his head a few times before I hear a strangled sound behind me. I glance over my shoulder in time to see Camden set down the new frame, filled with a family photo from draft day. Paisley wearing a too-big Founders cap, her arm around Camden's neck with their parents on either side, their mother with happy tears on her cheeks.

I turn, feeling a stab of sympathy under my ribs. "Paisley has a bunch of pictures on her phone, and I thought it would be nice to have them printed. For the both of you."

He nods, pivoting away from me as he clears his throat, and I doubt he'd want me to bring any more attention to his obvious emotional response, so I pass him on my way to the kitchen, where I grab my purse from the corner of the counter, next to the tins of tea. The ones I've been using every day.

By the time I loop it over my shoulder, Camden's next to me, lightly touching my elbow. "Thank you."

I dip my focus to where his long, thick fingers touch my skin and drag my eyes up his muscled forearm, to the bulk of his biceps under his T-shirt. He doesn't have any tattoos. Nothing to take away from the veins and blooming bruise on the inside of his arm.

I skim my index finger along it. He probably wouldn't even know what it's from if I asked. Bruises and injuries all come with the job.

Lifting my focus higher, I trace his Adam's apple with my gaze, the five-o'clock shadow on his jaw to his mouth, parted and wet from a slide of his tongue over his lips. Even higher are his eyes, the color of Earl Grey tea, waking me up like a hot cup usually does in the morning.

He lowers his hand from my elbow at the same time I let my finger slip from the mark on his arm, and we both spin away. As if spending one more second this close would end in violence or fireworks.

He walks me to the door in silence, leaning on the jamb once it's open, but I don't take the two steps into the hall. Instead, I hesitate.

My body won't move.

Not with my heart in my throat and my pulse in my ears.

It's disorienting, letting go of the resentment I've held all these years. Keeping my nails dug into the anger was the only way to shield myself from the hurt.

I'd spent my whole life being unremarkable, the forgettable middle child of the Rivera children, feeling like a disappointment to my overachieving parents. I've become an expert at pretending it doesn't bother me to be *just* a teacher when I am surrounded by professional athletes, doctors, and scholarship recipients.

I know I am important. What I do is, arguably, one of the most important jobs for our society, and yet my list of accomplishments falls short. The constant need to impress people is difficult to shake. I cannot outrun my insecurities, outsmart the voices in the back of my head.

Camden Long is the physical manifestation of everything I am afraid of.

To be judged and found wanting.

Except with the way he stares down at me now, I can't remember much. I don't know anything besides the warm liquid pooling in my belly and seeping into my limbs, the magnetic pull keeping me anchored in place. Anchored to him.

When I try to bring all the memories of my relationship with him forward in my mind, I can't. They're buried in a fog where I can't recall them correctly. And when I finally grasp hold of flashes, those sharp words and even sharper smiles feel dull. The sting of pain replaced by the sting of pleasure and the need for more.

I can't understand it, and the longer I stay here, the more confused I become. With a stiff shake of my head, I finally step into the hall, leaving him with a last piece of advice. "She only wants you to see her. That's all. *See* her and love her."

CHAPTER 9
CAMDEN

NADINE ANSWERS my phone call with a wary voice. "Camden? Are you okay?"

"No. I am absolutely not okay."

"What's going on?"

"Paisley got her period."

A beat passes before the cruel little witch laughs at me.

"This isn't funny."

"Kinda. Why are you calling me about it?"

"Because!" I fling my hand out to the rainbow of products in front of me, even though she can't see it. "My sister got her first period, and I'm at the store and I have no idea what the fuck I'm supposed to buy."

The last thing I want to or should be doing is buying menstrual products for my fourteen-year-old sister, especially after another grueling day at camp, but when Paisley shuffled into my bedroom in near tears, I was ready to bring the apartment complex down to rubble.

She'd apparently learned about the birds and bees and everything that goes along with it, but without Mom here to guide her through this, she doesn't know what to do.

I don't either.

So I'd kissed the top of her head, told her to hang tight, and then I sprinted out to the closest CVS, where I very quickly realized I was out of my depth. Which is when I reached for my cell phone. And the contact for the not-nanny nanny.

Nadine hums. "What does she want to use? Pads or tampons?"

If anyone on my team heard the sound that escapes my throat, they'd never let me touch a football again. "I have no idea."

She breathes a laugh, amused at my discomfort. But it's not that I'm disgusted at the biological function; it's that I don't know what to do. I don't know how to help.

I've been staring at the wings and no wings, light or super, cardboard or plastic, organic and non-organic options for what feels like an hour.

"Why don't you buy her one package of pads and one box of regular tampons? Can you do that?" Nadine suggests, as if she's speaking to a toddler.

"Yeah. I think so."

"Okay, you do that, and I'll be over as soon as I can."

I blow out a relieved breath. "You sure?"

"Yeah. I'm getting my keys now. See you in half an hour. Just stay calm."

Stay calm?

Yeah, sure, okay. I'll stay fucking calm.

I pluck one box of everything off the shelf, every type of pad, tampon, and panty liner available, and then head directly to the candy aisle, throwing in a few bags of chocolates and gummy candy. Then because I hate feeling useless, I add a pair of socks, a few face masks, and a *Get Well Soon* card.

By the time I make it home, Nadine is pulling into the parking garage at the same time. Once again, she laughs when she spies me and the five bags.

Only she would laugh at a time like this.

"What did you buy?" she asks, casually walking toward me

in an oversized T-shirt that reads *First of all, I'm a delight* with a snarling raccoon on it—appropriate—and itty-bitty shorts, some of her hair wrapped up into a bun on the top of her head, flip-flops on. I wonder if she was in the middle of getting ready for bed and darted out of her brother's house.

I don't know why I like that possibility.

I hold up the loot. "Is it enough?"

"Yeah." She smothers a grin, closing the distance between us. "It's enough."

She follows me into the elevator up to the top floor, silence stretched thin between us, and I know I should thank her, tell her that I know she didn't have to show up, but I'm so glad she did. Except when she angles her head my way, lips pursed, as if waiting for me to speak, I can't. I don't want to say the wrong thing.

I don't want to go back to what we were before, snipping and sniping. It's only been a few days since we crossed an unseen ceasefire line. Everything is too delicate and new for me to go and fuck it up, so I keep quiet and jut my chin in the direction for her to exit first when the elevator stops.

I gave her the key code for my place before training camp, so she hits the numbers now—2280, my birthday backward—then holds the door open for me. Inside, I set all the bags on the kitchen counter, while Nadine snorts beside me, taking in exactly how much I bought.

"You didn't stay calm, did you?"

I find a pen and scrawl my name inside the card, but before I can place it in the envelope, she intercepts it from me, eyes wide as she takes in the cartoon chocolate chip cookie with the words *You're one tough cookie* around it.

"Camden," she says in a voice low with barely constrained amusement that sends a shiver down my spine. "She's not sick."

I snatch it back from her. "I know that, but there's no *Happy first period* card, so I got this one instead."

She covers her mouth with her hand, blue eyes tipped up in

the corners, head shaking at me like I'm the dumbest man on the face of the planet. Possibly in the universe.

I feel like it.

But there is no training for this.

No class or pamphlet and certainly no warning about this when I talked to the lawyers and doctors about taking guardianship of Paisley. Feed her, keep her safe, make her happy, of course.

Walk her through her period?

Fuck no. I'm not equipped for this.

Nadine plucks the card from my hand, along with the bags, before patting my shoulder. "I'll take it from here. You did good."

"Yeah?"

"Yeah." She nods, eyes clear like she means it.

After she disappears down the hall, I inhale a ragged breath and snag a sparkling water from the fridge before returning to my room to remove my contacts and put on my glasses. Before Paisley had told me about…everything, I'd been in the process of winding down, but there will be no winding until I know she is all right, so I head out to the terrace. It wraps around much of the apartment, and I pace the length of it, taking in the glittering Philly skyline as I finish off the La Croix. My teammates have always made fun of me for drinking it, but during the season, I'm strict about my diet and alcohol consumption. It's the off-season when I indulge.

Too much.

It's been good to be back to work, doing what I do best, though it's been a rocky start. Not that I expected much different.

My teammates are still pissed.

A lot of them did come to Iowa for the funeral, but when it comes time to play, they hold a lot of resentment.

No matter what anyone says about team sports, it's still too easy to take the blame for a loss on yourself, especially when it's true.

When I'm on the field, I have tunnel vision. Like a lot of players, I only see what's in front of me. And I know I've earned a reputation for being a dick; I've been arrogant and played up my showmanship on and off the field for some fun, enjoyed it all a little too much—the money and women and fame. But when I caught that pass from Erik with zero seconds to go, I legitimately thought I was in the end zone. Maybe I'd imagined it too many times, scoring the winning touchdown so that I saw myself already there instead of taking that extra step, but in the two seconds I spent dancing to when I was tackled, the entire stadium went silent.

Then it all came roaring back, and instead of cheers, it was boos. They loved me for being an asshole, and now they hate me for being an asshole.

To lead off the team meeting last week, I asked Coach Roberts if I could address the elephant in the room. I thanked my teammates for showing up when I needed them and apologized for letting them down, promising I would make it up to them.

I know they don't all believe me, but there isn't much I can do besides show up.

So I have been.

I've been working as hard or maybe harder than I did my rookie year to prove myself. And it's exhausting.

It feels a lot different at almost thirty than it did coming out of college.

Having the boulder of guilt on my back feels even worse.

Carrying the new responsibility at home? It's made me reevaluate everything.

Reflecting back on the last few years of my life, the last one in particular, it's like watching a horror movie with the guy running to the barn where the murderer is hiding with the machete.

To know he's making all the wrong choices.

And sprinting straight to his end.

That's what it felt like standing at the graveyard, the double tombstone bearing the names of my parents, Lorraine and Kenneth Long.

The epitaph of *Forever in our hearts* inscribed underneath their first and last days.

I rub at the pressure in my chest, grief hitting me all over again, and it's too hard to remain upright, so I lean against the railing, allowing my head to drop, the tears falling down toward the sidewalk, twenty-two stories below.

I know I was already disappointing them, but I don't want to continue to. I promised them I'd change. That I'd be different. Take care of Paisley. But there are moments when I think it's too late.

That I've fucked up too much, and they'll never forgive me.

Not my team, the city of Philadelphia, or my parents.

I'll never be able to speak to them again to know.

"Hey, there you are."

I quickly wipe my face with the collar of my T-shirt, readjusting my glasses before turning around to Nadine. Under the glow of the outdoor lights, she looks angelic, all soft lines and even softer eyes when she tilts her chin up to study my face. "You okay?"

I nod, sniffing away the emotion, though I doubt she believes me. Still, she doesn't push, only meets me at the railing, close enough that her elbow brushes my forearm. A dozen heartbeats pass before she speaks again. "I didn't know you wear glasses."

"Since I was a kid," I tell her, thankful she doesn't ask about the reason I have yet to look her in the eyes. "Started wearing contacts in middle school."

"You should wear the glasses more. Makes you look smart," she says, back to her regular waspish attitude, like a shot of adrenaline in my veins.

"I am smart. Have a college degree in math, graduated magna cum laude and everything."

That has her whipping her head toward me. "You're shitting me."

"Nope." I finally meet her surprised gaze, eyebrows up to her hairline. "Can't use any more dumb jock jokes."

"I'll still use them. Because you do dumb shit."

I pointedly lower my focus to her shirt. "You are always *such* a delight."

The way she smiles is more feral animal than human, and I love it.

We fall into a companionable silence for a little while, until I think about the link I sent her yesterday. "Did you look at the school?"

"Yeah." She sets her hands on the railing behind her, forcing her back to arch ever so slightly, her breasts to push out. I don't think she's wearing a bra underneath the T-shirt that's way too big on her.

Nadine is petite, curvy with wide hips and thick thighs, and even though I've always gravitated toward women with big tits, I can't seem to stop staring at her bare legs, her shorts barely more than underwear.

"It seems like a good fit, but you need to talk to Paisley about it."

With the academic year around the corner, I need to register Paisley in a school, and I had heard about a school for the Deaf, one of the oldest in the entire country.

"But in your professional opinion..." I start, inclining my head to the special education teacher, hoping she has more to say.

"In my professional opinion, she'll be more comfortable there than in a mainstream school. Even though Philadelphia is so much more diverse than the cornfields of Iowa, she would get so much more support in a Deaf school."

"What is your deal with cornfields?"

She shoots me a withering glare. "Don't you know anything about your own state? It's the number one producer of corn. Or did they confer that degree on you simply because you can carry a ball good?"

"*Well*," I correct with a smirk. "I can carry a ball well."

"So, anyway." She heaves an exasperated sigh. "Paisley might have had trouble with her peers in her other school because there weren't many she could communicate with, but in that school, she'll have all the support she needs, and everyone will know ASL."

I scratch at the back of my neck, asking Nadine the question I've been afraid of. "Do you get the impression she was bullied or anything?"

"Not bullied, but definitely left out." She obviously had this conversation with Paisley, and it makes me feel like shit for not having it myself.

Almost as if Nadine can read my mind, she explains, "She didn't outright express that, but I am assuming from everything she's told me about her old school. About the difficulty your parents had with the administration pushing back on some accommodations, having the interpreter in class. Some bad experiences with teachers."

"Like what?"

Nadine puffs up her cheeks and blows out a breath, her eyes staring into the house through the glass doors. "Common microaggressions deaf and hard of hearing students may face, talking down to her or outright ignoring her. The closest Deaf school in Iowa was three hours away."

I knew that. I remember my parents considering moving to send her there, but that meant them giving up their jobs, unsure if they would be able to find new ones. That's when I stepped in and offered to pay for anything they needed, even a new house, if that's what they wanted. They refused a new house, but they did accept my paying for her to join clubs and go on trips to meet up with other children in the Deaf community. It was good for my parents too, learning how to navigate that world. Still, it wasn't enough. As Nadine tells me, "It's lonely to live in a hearing world when you're deaf. It's exhausting and sometimes very depressing without friends to build a support system."

"I had no idea she was struggling so much." Because once again, I'm the fucking worst. I spin around, gripping the railing tight, a punch of self-loathing hitting me worse than that tackle. "I should've known. I should've asked. Been there."

Nadine doesn't disagree, but she also doesn't blame me. "You are her brother, not her parent. It wasn't your job to know."

"It is now."

"And you can help her now." She sets her small hand on my back, rubbing a small circle, soothing the tension gathered along my spine. "She'll be okay."

I'm not so sure of it.

"She will," Nadine promises quietly as her hand slides off my back, settling on the railing next to mine, our pinkies separated by only an inch of space. "You see her," she says, repeating the piece of advice she gave me the other night. All I need to do is see Paisley and love her. See the person she is and love her, no matter what. "She'll be okay."

I tip my head back, face up to the night sky. It must be almost eleven now. And Nadine is still here. Going above and beyond for her job. For my sister.

Maybe for me too.

"I'm not sure I'd be able to do any of this without you," I confess, and when she doesn't respond, I turn my focus on her. She's staring out ahead of us, her profile is in shadow because I'm so much taller than her and blocking the light. Though I notice the way her chest rises and falls with each of her breaths, the tip of her tongue when it pokes out to wet her lips.

It's an eternity before she finally replies, tilting her ice-river eyes up to mine, a familiar challenge in them. "I'm positive you'd have figured it out eventually since you're so *smart*. But if you need some emotional support, Jelly and Bean are waiting for you."

"Those are dumb fucking names."

She huffs, pivoting away from me to step back inside the apartment, and I follow as if she's got me on an invisible leash. "I like them. I think they're cute." She bends, sticking her finger into their oversized cage to pet the black one with a white stripe on its nose, cooing, "Yes, you're cute. Yes, you are, aren't you?"

I'd like to make a joke about me being cute, but her ass is too distracting, and it isn't until she struts away from me that my brain comes back online. I once again escort her to the front door, a pattern we've developed lately. I stop at the door, and she turns to me, one hand curled around the strap of her purse, the other pointing in the direction of my sister's bedroom. "Nice work staying so calm."

When I roll my lips into a flat line, she laughs at my expense. "You might just be all right."

"Yeah." I watch as she saunters away in her short shorts, oversized raccoon T-shirt billowing around her. "You too."

CHAPTER 10
CAMDEN

"WHICH TEAMMATE WOULD you not want to date your sister?"

One of the social media managers stands at the fence as we exit the practice field, a tiny microphone held out in front of Erik and me. Momentarily caught off guard by the question because I'm suddenly thinking of Paisley dating, I'm stunned into silence. My best friend is not.

He punches me in the chest with his helmet. "Easy... Long."

"What?" I guffaw. "You don't want me dating your sister?"

"I don't want you dating *any* sisters, but *especially* mine."

Laughing, I push him. "Fuck you. I'm a gentleman with women, especially sisters." I wink at the camera. "What teammate would I not want to date my sister? JD," I say, naming our cornerback, then shoot another smile at the social media manager. "Sorry about the cursing."

"It's fine. We'll bleep it out. All part of the Camden Long persona, right?"

"Right," I say with a forced laugh. That same persona I've been trying to drop.

Erik and I head into the locker room to shower and change. We have our first preseason game coming up, a chance to see what the rookies can do and for the veterans to stretch our legs. While the team has been jiving well at training camp, I can't seem to shake the extra emotional weight I'm carrying. It's like running with chains on my ankles. I'm moving but in slow motion.

Coach reminded me twice about seeing the counselor, and Erik even offered to go to the appointment with me, but I can't.

Because if I ever let it all out, I might never recover.

Fearing the yawning hole I'm desperate to crawl out of would only grow wider if I admitted everything out loud.

So, thanks, but no thanks.

After dressing and looping my duffel bag over my shoulder, I round the corner of the locker room door, only to run right into Malcolm. "How the hell did you get back here?"

"Nice to see you too. I'm doing well, thank you for asking."

I stare blandly at him, waiting for his answer.

He shrugs. "You shouldn't be surprised the front desk is happy to give me the necessary credentials so I can rein in their favorite troublemaker."

I start walking out to the private parking lot, knowing he'll tag along at my side. "I haven't been making any trouble lately."

"Yes, and I'd like to keep it that way, which is why I'm here to check in. We're lifting the media embargo on you, so you'll be doing press, and you *will* be on your best behavior."

I offer him a salute as I hit the key fob to unlock my car. "Anything else?"

"Yes." He blocks me from opening my door. He studies me with a tilted head, his off-white suit a contrast to his brown skin, and I'm not sure how he can stand it in this heat. I motion for him to get on with it, and as always, he takes his time, careful with his words. "How is Paisley?"

"She's good." I chuck my bag into the trunk. "Really good."

"And you?"

"Good."

I don't think he believes me, but he nods anyway. "As much

as I enjoyed our time together this year, I don't want to have to go back to babysitting duty."

"I thought you were my *assistant*," I say, repeating his oft-told lie.

Even though he'd been hired to follow me around and keep me out of trouble, he did really help me out in my hour of need. The guy knows how to deal with tough situations and communicate with people from all walks of life. It takes a special talent to keep a level head when emotions are high. I would know because I'm not all that good at it. But he has the ability to take in the storm around him and settle the waves.

"I've been meaning to thank you," I say, swallowing my pride. "For everything you did for me. It's... I'm not sure I'll ever be able to pay you back."

A genuine smile unfurls across his features. "I was happy to help you, and the way you can pay me back is to keep your head down. Prove to the media that you are the person I know and not the arrogant prick they think you are."

I huff. Before, his words would have bounced off my armor. The *persona*. Now, they stick to me like the cotton of my shirt. I wish I could peel them off, but I can't. I am still an arrogant prick.

Hell, part of me wants to tell Malcolm to piss off and *I'll do what I want*, but there is another part, a bigger one, that knows I can't. I can't fuck up again.

I can't keep letting my worst instincts take over, when I have my sister waiting for me at home. A reputation that will now affect her.

As much as it would be so easy to pretend nothing bothers me and hide behind parties and lavish trips, for once, I like doing the hard thing—I love being with my sister.

"We've already been contacted about a special sit-down interview. It's totally up to you, but I wanted to run that by you and let you think about it. We don't need the answer right away." Malcolm scrolls over his cell phone. "Also, I have a list of questions you can expect to be asked at your press calls. I wrote up some answers that I'm sending to you right now, so if you don't like them, rewrite them with your thoughts and send it back to me. I just don't want you going off the cuff."

I suspected all of this was coming, that the press would eventually circle like sharks. Drama sells, and I've created a lot of drama on my own. Add in this sad story? I'm sure they've already written up the pieces. They're merely waiting to hit publish.

"I'll do what you think is best," I say, earning a surprised sound out of Malcolm.

"Okay, then. Think about the interview. I've already talked to the front office about it, and everyone is in agreement that it would be your choice. There is absolutely no pressure, one way or the other."

"I'll think about it, but I do not want Paisley involved at all. I don't even want her name mentioned—at no press calls, no interviews, nothing, and if she is brought up, I'll leave."

"Okay, I'll—"

"I'm serious, Malcolm. My sister is completely off-limits."

He actually appears proud of me when he says, "Of course. I'll make sure of it."

Then he pats my shoulder and finally shifts, allowing me to reach the driver's side of my car. I slip into the seat as he offers me a wave with one hand, busy lifting his cell phone to his ear with the other, already relaying this conversation to the PR firm. I guess no matter how much he may act like my friend, he's still on the payroll, my babysitter.

I crank the air and blast some Kendrick as I make the twenty-five-minute drive back to Center City, parking as a text from Valerie arrives. She's in Manhattan for a few days and wants to know if I can visit for a night or two.

Even if I wanted to, I can't leave my sister.

She's more than shown me she can take care of herself, but I'm not comfortable leaving her overnight on her own. I'll need to figure something out for games since Nadine will be going back to Jersey soon, but I'm hoping she might be willing to help me find a replacement before then.

I shoot a text back to Valerie that I won't be able to make it then head upstairs, where I spy my sister on the terrace through the glass doors. I stop to pet Jelly and Bean, though I've been referring to them as Rocky and Balboa, before stepping outside. Only to stop short.

Laid out on a beach towel, Nadine has her top off, and I can't see anything because she's on her stomach reading something on an iPad. But, still.

Shouldn't she be, like, covered up?

"Shouldn't you be covered up?" I ask, waving my hand around at her.

She angles her head back, scrunching up her face. "What?"

"You're…" I trail off, my attention catching on her dewy tan and the line on her left ass cheek, delineating where her bikini bottom has ridden up, revealing the difference of where the sun has touched and not touched.

She carefully moves, clasping the ends of her bathing suit top and tying it at her neck before rolling over to face me. "Didn't realize you were such a prude. Sorry."

"I'm not a prude." Far from it, actually. "But you're supposed to be watching my sister."

Said sister is fast asleep, mouth hanging open, head lolled to the side, where she's laid out on a lounge chair, rolled-up towel behind her head.

"Took your Amex out for another walk today," Nadine explains as she stands, smelling of coconut and looking like a goddess with her wavy hair and sun-kissed skin. Her bikini isn't all that revealing, but it highlights the curve of her waist and roundness of her hips. Does great things for her breasts.

I'd be able to hold them in my hands, cover them completely, and I'm suddenly aching to know what color her nipples are, if she'd like me biting them.

"Got her a new bathing suit." She points to Paisley in a one-piece, then to herself. "And I didn't want to be left out, so... Thanks for the bonus."

"Yeah," I grunt because it was worth it. Whatever it cost. She could spend it. All my money. "Did you, uh..." I scratch at my jaw, forcing my gaze past her to the skyline. "Check out the pool?"

"We did. For a bit."

"Good. That's good."

She starts to clean up, bending over right in front of me, and I wonder if she's doing it on purpose. Tormenting me like this.

Proving that I've been wrong my entire life, thinking the best part of a woman is her breasts.

Because, no.

It's her ass.

And thighs.

That jiggle when she walks. Have dimples I can trace with my fingertips. Or tongue. The soft place I suddenly want to dive between.

I clear my throat, rubbing at the back of my neck, attempting to look anywhere but at the heart shape of her ass.

Because, seriously.

How long does it take to pick up a cup, iPad, and fold a goddamn towel?

"Gimme that," I snap when she's finally upright again, snatching the blue towel from her. "Cover up already. You'll get sunburned."

She removes her sunglasses, frowning at me. "What the hell is your problem?"

I take the empty cup too. "Your shoulders are red."

"You don't have to have such an attitude about it."

"And you could put on a shirt."

She rears back, and I know it was the wrong thing to say, yet I like this back-and-forth. I like her feisty, hands on her generous hips, eyes narrowed at me. "And you could go back to 1800 when you think a woman would listen to a fucking thing you told her to do."

"Maybe I will. Find me a woman less mouthy."

She scoffs. "Go ahead, Magna Cum Laude. Put that degree of yours to good use and build a time machine. Since you have yet to prove you're not the most overpaid tight end in the league. I caught some of the practice footage, and you're slow off the line."

I should probably be embarrassed, but I'm more pleased than anything. "You watched my practice footage."

"Of the *team*." Irritation sounds so good on her tongue. "And if I were you, I wouldn't be grinning so hard for somebody who got their shit rocked by a twenty-two-year-old rookie linebacker."

I don't think I've ever been more turned on in my life.

By my best friend's sister and her snarky attitude.

I was wrong before. She's not uptight.

She's simply been waiting to be unleashed. All the pent-up frustration needing a target.

I don't mind taking a few arrows.

I like the pain.

CHAPTER 11
NADINE

IT'S WELL after nine o'clock, and my tea has long gone cold by the time the door opens, and I attempt to fix my features into a semblance of calm. But with the way Camden's shoulders sag as he drops his bag by the entryway, I don't think he'll notice or care about why I have a heap of tissues in front of me where I sit at the eat-in counter.

He scrubs his hands over his hair a few times then finally lifts his head, doing a double take when he spots me. "Hey."

I set my chin in my hand. "Game didn't go well?"

He shakes his head. It was the first preseason game on their home field, and I can only imagine how he was crucified by the press and fans if he didn't play well. Probably all up in his head.

Like I am.

"Where's Paise?" he asks, crossing to the fridge for a sports drink.

"In her room, talking to her best friend, I think." I turn my cell phone over so I don't have to see the email anymore. "We watched a double feature of Kate Hudson rom-coms tonight."

He nods a few times but makes no comment about it. No teasing or sarcasm.

That's okay. I don't much feel like trading barbs anyway.

He coasts his gaze around the penthouse as if searching for something out of place. It does feel different, being here in relative quiet with him. Neither of us reaching for the closest verbal weapon. But I'm too exhausted from running mental circles. And he seems exhausted, period.

"You all right?" he asks eventually, tipping his chin to the pile of tissues I push into the garbage can. "Are you sick?"

I shake my head, dumping my tea down the drain. "I'm fine."

He halts my steps after I load my mug into the dishwasher, his big hands landing on the counter, on either side of my hips. "You look like you were crying."

I don't answer, rolling my lips over my teeth, and he bends slightly, waiting for me to meet his gaze. "What's wrong?"

I lift my shoulder. "Just work stuff." When he rubs his hand over his mouth and jaw, I turn the question back on him. "What's wrong with you?"

"Work stuff."

I bite back the growing curl of amusement on my lips and move to push past him, but he stops me once again, this time with his hand on my arm. His fingers are so wide and long—almost twice the size of mine—they easily wrap all the way around my biceps. "I can tell you're upset. Don't go driving yet. Stay for a little while."

Stay?

With him?

To calm down?

That's not a thing that has ever happened in our past. Historically, he has only ever made me upset.

But maybe he needs me to stay for him, what with how he looks like a kicked puppy, so I agree with a beleaguered, "Fine."

His mouth tips up in a half smile as he repeats, "Fine."

If I'm going to stay here, I'm going to drown my sorrows with one of the tubs of ice cream. I dig out the chocolate peanut butter but don't bother with a bowl, then take my seat once again and help myself to a spoonful.

On the other side of the counter, Camden watches intently, arms folded over his chest. When I raise my brows in question, he shakes his head at me. "Barbarian."

"I just watched you down an entire Gatorade in three seconds flat. Me eating ice cream out of the carton is no worse or better."

"Germs." He motions to the spoon I stab back into the frozen dessert after having it in my mouth, and I cough a laugh.

"I'm sure you've picked up far worse germs in far grosser places than my mouth."

I realize only after his attention locks on my mouth what I said, how it's basically an open invitation to talk about what I've put in my mouth, where it's been. Where *his* mouth has been.

And suddenly, his 3,000-square-foot apartment feels like three feet. A yard.

Sunk down to mere inches when he leans his elbows on the counter, snagging the spoon out of my hand to scoop some ice cream. His square jaw is covered in a day's worth of growth, dark hair that I know would feel like tiny pinpricks against my skin, abrading the softest part of me when he pressed his mouth there. The idea of him dragging his tongue over me, making sure he tastes *all* of me, has liquid heat pooling in my belly, and not even the spoonful of ice cream Camden offers can cool it down.

Not with the way his dark eyes are practically black, following my every movement, from the way I part my mouth around the spoon to the lift of my throat when I swallow. His voice is broken glass when he speaks. "I should eat this more often."

I crawl over the shards to hear more. "It's not against your diet?"

He holds up the spoon between us. "You should know by now, I like to break the rules."

Yes, I know.

The whole country knows.

But I've never wanted to break rules more than I do with him, which is ridiculous.

The man is reckless and inconsiderate. Arrogant and impulsive. A selfish prick.

At least, he was.

I *thought* he was.

Now, he's become…a friend?

Or, at the very least, an acquaintance I no longer wish would drive off the Walt Whitman Bridge.

"What happened today?" I ask, accepting the spoon back from him to scrape up a big chunk of frozen peanut butter.

"I only played a few series," he explains, eyes cast down on his hands on top of the marble countertop, a bruise forming on one of his knuckles. It's not unusual for veteran players not to play much in the preseason since the rookies need to battle it out for their positions.

"The fans were brutal." He saws his teeth across his bottom lip. "I couldn't…can't block them out."

I offer him another bite of ice cream, which he accepts by wrapping his fingers around my wrist to keep it steady as he guides the spoon to his mouth. "Have you talked to the team counselor?"

"Not you, too," he says around the ice cream.

I shrug. "That's what they're there for. Might as well use them."

He rubs the heels of his hands against his eyes, mumbling, "I've got to take my contacts out. Be right back."

He disappears for two minutes and returns with his thin-framed glasses on like the Clark Kent version of Superman. He places his hands on the counter again, fingers spread out and pointing toward me. "Why are you upset tonight?"

I shove a huge spoonful of ice cream into my mouth, but to keep me from avoiding the question anymore, he steals the tub and the spoon from me. "What's up, River?"

I press my thumb to the roof of my mouth to relieve myself of brain freeze before asking, "Is it one too many concussions that makes you call me River instead of Rivera?"

He puts the ice cream away, places the spoon in the dishwasher, then faces me again. "No concussions recently to speak of. Why are you upset?"

I tuck my arms around my torso. "Got an email from admin about in-service days before the school year, and I..." Shrugging, I exhale a long breath. "I'm a little nauseous about it."

"Nauseous about your job?" He studies me for a long time. "That seems like a bad omen."

"You believe in luck?"

"Not really. But I do always listen to the same song on game days and have to tape my laces down, right foot first."

"That's not luck?"

He grins at me. "It's betting the odds."

"What's the song?"

"'Mama' by Cam Cole."

He lifts his cell phone from his pocket and plays it, setting the device on the counter, both of us leaning in close, heads bent together as the guitar riff fills the space between us.

"I like it," I say once it's over, and he nods.

"Yeah, so I do what I can to make sure I feel comfortable playing. What do you do to make yourself comfortable?"

I allow my gaze to drift around his apartment. What used to be as white and pristine as a church now has color and life, random magnets on the fridge, a pair of high-tops in the hall that clearly don't belong to him, photos I helped Paisley frame, and of course, Jelly and Bean in the corner of the living room.

"I don't think there is anything to make me comfortable."

"Why not?" His voice is low, curious, but as if he doesn't want to admit it. "I thought you loved teaching."

"I do." I curl my hands into fists, letting my nails pinch into my skin, keeping my emotions tethered to earth. I so easily fall into the storm, and I don't want to break down in front of him. I clear my throat. "I love teaching and I love my kids, but I don't love having no support from the administration or the parents." I press my hand to my chest, feeling myself losing it. "I'm the last line of defense for these *children*, and I'm..." I close my eyes to the burn in them. "I do everything I can. I give and give and give, and it's still not enough."

When I flutter my eyelids open, Camden is next to me, so close I can smell chocolate and peanut butter on his breath. He wipes my cheek with his knuckle, and I lean into the touch, telling him, "I had a kid who graduated this past year. He shouldn't have. Aside from never completing any work, he was rude and disrespectful, in fights all the time, but he also needed a lot of support and was clearly crying out for help."

I huff, thinking of Christian. This kid who told me he trained his pit bull for fights and was proud of it. I couldn't stand him, but he was my student. A child who needed help. "Everyone was tired of him," I say, "and I got a call from the head of the department, asking me to change his grade because they weren't going to keep him another year. They weren't going to, quote, 'waste any more resources on him.' And..." I exhale a rough breath. "We sent him out into the world unprepared. I passed him on so society can deal with him. But you know how it deals with kids like that?"

Camden shakes his head, sinking his hand into my hair, holding the back of my neck, though it feels as if he's holding me together. Keeping me from another torrent of tears.

"He'll end up in prison. Or worse." I bite my cheek, trying in vain to stop my chin from wobbling. My throat is clogged, and I can barely force the rest out. "I don't think I can do another year, and I feel so guilty, but I..."

Camden hauls me into him, face pressed against his chest as I give in, letting out the emotion I'd tried to hide from him. Instead of making fun of me or being awkward about it, he tucks me in close to him, one hand on the back of my head, the other smoothing up and down my back. He murmurs things I can't hear but that soothe me, nonetheless. His heartbeat strong under my ear, his steady hold an anchor until I'm able to sit upright again, wiping my face with the back of my hand.

He combs my hair behind my ears, tracing the shell of each one, his fingers surprisingly gentle for their size. "No job should make you anxious like this. Nothing is worth you getting sick over it. Because even though you love your kids, you'll be no use to them if you send yourself into a depression."

Erik and Molly have said the same thing, but the idea of actually quitting sends me further down the spiral.

"Maybe you should talk to a therapist or something," Camden suggests, and I snort.

"Like you?"

"I'll go if you go."

I don't believe him. "No, you won't."

"Sounds like a challenge."

I lift my shoulder. "More like a dare."

He holds out his right hand between us. "I'll take it. We both go to therapy. Get our fucked-up brains to work for our work."

I clasp his hand with mine. "I suppose I can sacrifice some of my own time for the greater Philadelphia area. Maybe Pennsylvania in general. It'll owe me when your team starts winning again."

The way he licks his lips, as if he'd like to kiss his reflection, sends a chill down my spine. Because I'm the one he's staring at. There is no mirror in sight.

"Would it make you feel better if you didn't go back to school?" he asks, and I shake my head.

"I couldn't leave them in the lurch. I don't know if I could leave my students either."

"What if you exchanged a bunch of students for one?"

"What are you asking?"

"Don't go back to Jersey. Stay here with Paisley. Whatever you were making at the school, I'll double it."

I blink once. Then twice. "You'll *double* it?"

"Triple it?" he asks, as if it's a negotiation and not my brain stalling out.

"You want me to keep nannying Paisley?"

"You're not a nanny, but yes. You know what the season is like. It'll save me from having to find someone else to be with Paisley. All those nights I'll be away from home, you can stay here. Move in if you want. Whatever you want, however much you want. Just stay. Paisley needs you." His focus dips to my mouth for a moment before drifting back to my eyes. "*I* need you."

The idea is so wild that I don't know what to say. All I've ever wanted to do is teach, but my gut reaction is to stay. To take the money. It'll be the easiest paycheck I've ever earned.

And yet... I can't my quit my job.

What would my parents say?

What would the school say? My co-teachers? My students who are expecting me to return?

There are only a few weeks until the start of the year, and leaving now would screw them over, needing to hire someone immediately.

"You're serious?" I ask, and he nods, turning my stool—literally picking it up and rotating it—so I'm facing him, and he steps close enough for our knees to touch. "I don't like seeing you anxious over something you're supposed to love."

I could say the same, but I don't. I stay quiet as he places one hand on the counter next to us and the other on the back of the stool, effectively boxing me in. "You could continue working with Paisley, and I will pay you whatever you want. Enough for therapy and shopping sprees and time to figure out what you want to do. If it's going back to teaching or doing something else —but just don't say no right this second. Think about it, okay?"

Even if I could answer, I don't because his doorbell rings, and both of us whip our heads to the front door as if we can see who's there. The number of people who are on Camden's list to be permitted up without calling first is short.

Only me, Erik, and—

"Surprise!" Valerie throws herself at Camden when he opens the door. "Since you couldn't come to me, I decided to come to you."

She climbs him like a tree, arms around his neck, legs around his waist, and it's only when he walks a few steps into the house that the barnacle notices me.

"Oh. You're here."

Camden pats her thigh, a sign for her to get down, which she does, but she keeps her arms around his middle, and I think that's my cue to exit.

"I was just leaving," I tell her and gather my things, keeping a few feet of distance between myself and the happy couple as I head to the door.

"Think about it," Camden reminds me, and I lift my hand in a silent goodbye.

I feel his gaze on me as I head to the door, but it's her voice that follows me out. "Oh my god! Are they rats?"

CHAPTER 12
CAMDEN

AFTER VALERIE surprised me by showing up at my apartment, we spent the night in stilted conversation. Aside from the fact that she never asked about Paisley or tried to spend time with her, I felt ambivalent about Val. I couldn't even scrounge up enough energy to argue when she said she didn't like that I "changed so much all of a sudden," including but not limited to bringing "rodents" into my home. Which had me getting defensive about Rocky and Balboa. Then she asked how much longer Nadine was going to work for me, and when I informed her that I asked her to stay full time, Valerie went completely quiet, dropped to her knees and offered to suck my dick.

I'm not sure if it was because I'd been so physically wrung out or the sudden aversion to my girlfriend, but my dick wasn't having it. And she promptly huffed, ordered me to "get my shit together," and to make sure I kept my bye week open for her.

We haven't really spoken since.

But I have seen Nadine every day, both of us dancing around the topic of her job. She needs time to think, and I need not to get my hopes up. Especially when I have so much of my own stress to deal with.

Malcolm catches my eye in the back of the media room, offers a subtle nod, a silent direction to stay on the script and keep my temper. I plop into the chair in front of the microphone with the maroon backdrop behind me, the team's logo and sponsor on it. After a sip of water, I settle my elbows on the table and wait for the first question.

It's an easy one.

"First of all, happy birthday. How does it feel to be thirty, and do you have anything special planned?"

I smile, knowing there are multiple cameras on me, and accept the inquiry with a thanks. "Feels the same as twenty-nine. I don't have any special plans beyond a team meeting later." And some cannoli from my favorite Italian bakery on 8th Street. "I'm focused on the game against Washington."

The reporters were already informed I would not be answering any questions about my family, but the second question alludes to them. "How does it feel to be back? After everything you've been through, how are you doing?"

Rubbing my thumb over the ridge of my plastic water bottle, I manage to lift my gaze out to the sea of faces staring at me. "It's good to be back. It's good to be on the field. I'm doing well."

"Where's your head at?" someone asks from the corner. "After the catastrophe of last season, what's the locker room like? Any problems? How's your relationship with the team?"

I scoot the water bottle between my hands, giving me something to squeeze. "I'm focused on winning this season. The past is the past, and this is a new season. So I'm concentrating on my future, on the team's future. As for the locker room, there are no problems." That isn't completely true; there's still some lingering tension, but I'm not about to tell these fuckers that. "We all have one goal in mind—to win the championship."

Another reporter. "How do you feel physically? I'm assuming your off-season wasn't as productive as you would have liked it to be, so do you feel like you've lost your edge?"

I stare down at the bottle top. "I've been working with the

position coaches, working hard in the weight room, with the agility trainer to make sure I'm quicker off the line, so, no, I don't feel like I lost my edge. If anything, I have more to prove." I shrug and meet the reporter's gaze, making sure they know I'm still Camden Long. "I'm still the top tight end in the league."

A few murmurs ring out before another question from the back. "Your reputation in Philadelphia has tanked. What do you have to say to the fans?"

"They want a win, and we're going to do that for them. I owe them that, and I'm going to do everything in my power to bring the trophy to Philly."

Someone in the front row. "Yesterday, Lionel Barry from ESPN said about you, quote, 'I feel for the guy, losing his parents and all, but he has proven to be a clown. He cares more about showing off than showing out for his team. The Founders flushed nineteen million down the toilet with him.' What is your response?"

I pinch my eyes shut for a moment, hearing Malcolm on my shoulder, reminding me to keep my head, but Lionel fucking Barry is a washed-up has-been, known for talking a lot of shit because he wishes he could still play. "My parents have nothing to do with any of this, and I'd politely ask Mr. Barry to avoid mentioning them any further. If he wants to come after me, fine, but don't use their deaths as an excuse to try to take me down."

"What about addressing his saying you care more about showing off than showing out for your team?"

I flick my gaze to Malcolm, who pleads with wide eyes for me to stay on track, but I can't help it. My mouth is moving before I've fully formed the answer. "If I didn't care about my team, I wouldn't have returned. I would challenge Lionel fucking Barry or anyone else to do what I had to do, to bury both of my parents and endure the chatter in the media and online about what a shitty person I am and how I deserved it." I dig my finger into the table. "You think I want to come back to a city that hates me after saying goodbye to what feels like the only two people who loved me? You think it's easy to sit here with all of you looking at me, knowing you want the nitty-gritty details of the worst moments of my life? Yes, I fucked up. Yes, I am taking responsibility, but there is no greater challenge than coming back here and fighting for my team. I am rising to it, so you can take whatever sound bite you want back to prove to the world I am every bit the asshole you think I am, but I'm here, and I'm not going anywhere. Even when most anyone else would have quit, I haven't. I'm still here."

With that, I stand and exit the stage, marching right out the doors with the patter of feet behind me, probably Malcolm or any one of the team's media people, pissed about what I said and leaving early, but fuck that.

"Hey." Erik intercepts me in the hall, probably having been watching it on one of the televisions mounted there. He gestures to whoever is behind me, clearly ordering them to leave me alone then directs me away from the fray. "That was great. Good for you."

"You think it was great?"

"Yeah. You needed to get it off your chest."

I nod and step away from his grasp to turn down another hall, feeling much lighter now than I did when I walked into that room. He follows, keeping step with me. "Where are you going?"

Since this isn't the way to the locker room, the team meeting room, or the cafeteria. "To see Pearce."

Erik pats my back twice in solidarity. I suppose it is time to see the therapist. I made a promise with Nadine. I won't break it, especially after that presser. I'm sure every single reporter, paper, sports program, and idiot on social media will have a field day with it, but no one has any idea what it's like to be in my shoes. They have no idea what it feels like to be dragged to hell and back and still sit in front of a firing squad after to answer questions as if they haven't already killed me.

"What's the name of the school your sister taught at?" I ask, and I can feel my best friend's attention on the side of my face, but I keep my focus in front of me.

"East Central. Why?"

"I want to buy everything on the teachers' supply lists there, but I don't want her to know it's me." I pause, finally meeting Erik's surprised stare. "Or maybe I should do the whole district. How much ya think that'll cost?" I wave it off, reaching for my cell phone. "I'm doing it."

I take off again, but Erik keeps up. "I'm proud of you, man." When I try to swat his words away, he stops me with his hand on my forearm. "I'm serious. What you told the reporters? How almost everyone else would have given up? It's true. You're still here fighting, and I'm proud of you." He hugs me. "Be proud of yourself."

I'm trying. I am, but it's hard to do when it feels like everyone is rooting for me to fail or, at the very least, "get what I deserve," which is to say, utter humiliation. They want me humbled.

I have been. More than they could ever imagine, but they'll never see me on my knees. I will never show them how much pain it causes me to know the last conversation I ever had with my parents was about how I had disappointed them. They will never have to face an inconsolable fourteen-year-old girl and tell her it'll be all right, when nothing is all right.

Knowing I've experienced the worst thing that could ever happen to me and come out on the other side, I feel invincible. They want me humbled, okay. They want to see me battered and bruised, I am. But I cannot be broken.

I *will not* be broken.

The list of people who I allow in, who I'm happy to lay down my shields for, is very small.

"You're doing it for your sister," Erik reminds me, releasing me from his embrace. "For your parents."

And a woman I shouldn't be thinking about while her brother stands in front of me, comforting me. A woman who gave me a birthday card this morning that read *Happy birthday! You're still an asshole.*

"Hey." I hold out my fist for a bump from Erik. "I'm gonna take it from here. Thanks, though."

He slaps my shoulder and pivots around as I continue down the hall, finding my text thread with Nadine to type out a new message.

> On my way to see the counselor.

> Look at you! Next, you'll be using manners and everything. Like a real human boy.

> Have you made your appointment yet?

> I did. This afternoon actually. After I talked to my parents.

> Is that supposed to be a scary cliffhanger?

> That's when you ask me

> "What did you talk to your parents about, Nadine?"

> What did you talk to your parents about, Nadine?

> Told them I was resigning.

Despite being happy she's staying, I know she was worried about what her parents would think. Yesterday, Nadine told me she decided she wouldn't be returning to school after having a long discussion with one of her coworkers, who told her burnout is real, and she'd rather see Nadine leave and be healthy than stay at the school and be miserable, because not only would she hurt herself, but she'd hurt her students too. "Burnout leads to bad teaching" is what Nadine said resolutely, and I hugged her after, lifting her up off the floor. Completely forgetting that I shouldn't be touching her like that when I have a girlfriend, but I am just so relieved.

Nadine is staying with me—I mean, my sister.

I text Nadine back.

How did it go?

Not terrible but not great either. They think I'm having some sort of mental breakdown. They suggested I move back in with them.

They also don't fully trust you.

They can take a number to join the club.

Like in the media room, my fingers are typing before I've fully fleshed out my thoughts.

I only care that you trust me.

Do you trust me?

I want to.

Hope you weren't lying about tripling my salary.

I couldn't contain the shit-eating grin on my face if I tried as I email my accountant to make a wire transfer.

Hours later, after I talk a bit with Pearce and arrange weekly meetings with him and speak with Coach Roberts, who tells me not to lose my cool with the press again but that Lionel Barry is a "fucking weasel," I pull my cell phone back out to find a litany of texts from Nadine.

This isn't a joke, is it? You sending me this money.

$200,000 is more than triple my salary.

But I'm not giving it back. You better not be expecting this back.

I've never had this much money in my life.

This many zeros!

Do you know what I can buy with this?

A small house.

Or at least a trailer.

Who knows in this economy!

I think I might take all of it out of my account in single dollar bills and put it on my bed to make a money angel. Swim around in it. Do my best impression of Donald Duck counting money.

You've created a monster.

An awfully cute monster.

Who surprises me with a round of birthday mocktails when I arrive home. Nadine, Paisley, and I ignore the shadow of grief lingering just beyond the corners of the room while we eat cannoli, and I realize thirty feels wholly different from twenty-nine.

CHAPTER 13
CAMDEN

AUGUST'S HEAT rolled right on into September. After multiple conversations and a visit to meet the faculty, I enrolled Paisley at the School for the Deaf, and so far, she has been loving it. She said she hasn't had to worry about fitting in, which has made learning a lot easier. Nadine shows up early every morning to drive Paisley to school because I don't have time to take her before I need to be at the complex. I'm not sure what Nadine does during the day, spending some of her $200K, I guess, but she picks up my sister in the afternoon and hangs out with her until I return home.

Although, this is the first weekend I'll be away. With the regular season kicking off, I'll be out of state basically two weekends every month, and Nadine will be sleeping at my place while I'm gone. Including the nights before home games, when the team all stays in a local hotel to make sure we're in peak form for the game. And I try desperately not to picture what she sleeps in. I'm hoping it's a full-on onesie so she's covered from neck to toes. It's the only option that doesn't give me a semi when I think of it.

After the team's walk-through today, we had a short meeting to go over some last-minute details for our trip, then Coach

Roberts sent us home with instructions to get a good night's sleep and that he'd see us tomorrow to board the bus, which would take us to the airport to fly us to Kansas City. We lost our first game to Dallas last weekend, and while I played well, I was still basically treated like the enemy even though we were on our home turf. One guy even threw his beer on me as I walked into the tunnel after the game.

I've been working on visualizations with Pearce to help keep me grounded, so I visualized ripping that fucking guy's head off. Not doing so earned a couple of backslaps from teammates, and the ones who still held on to some anger from last season seemed to let it go after that incident. Because, I suppose, it's one thing for me to be booed, but it's another to take a can to the head without a helmet.

I open up the door to my apartment to blaring music, "Don't Go Breaking My Heart" coming from a speaker in the kitchen, where Paisley and Nadine dance in front of the stove, something cooking that smells delicious. I quietly set my bag down and kick off my sneakers so my socked feet don't make a sound as I cross the hardwood floor, sneaking onto a stool at the counter, their backs to me.

Nadine signs something to Paisley that I don't catch, but it's clearly a direction to grate some fresh Parmesan cheese over the pot, and when she struggles to, Nadine helps, showing my sister how before going back to bopping around, hips swaying, using a big spoon as a microphone to sing terribly off-key to Paisley, who laughs at her antics.

"Voilà!" Nadine says and signs. "Nice work. See how easy it was to make this? Once you make it enough, you'll remember all the ingredients and how much." She slides her arm around Pais-ley, gives her a quick squeeze, and then signs, "You get the plates, and I'll get the drinks." That's when she swings around and notices me, jumping in place. "Oh my god!"

She lowers the music as I wave my hand. "No, please, continue. I was enjoying the show."

It's the first time I've ever witnessed Nadine blush, and it's cute. Even if she tries to cover it up. "You're a creep. How long have you been here?"

Paisley pivots around too, smiling in my direction, signing, "I made dinner."

"Smells great," I say and sign then look to Nadine. "I've been here long enough to know you are a genuinely terrible singer."

"Your sister doesn't think so."

When I shoot Nadine a bland look, she asks my sister, "Should we allow him to eat with us?"

Paisley plays it up, tilting her head side to side, but eventually gives in, signing, "I guess."

"So nice of you both."

I help them scoop out servings of the butternut squash and rigatoni as Paisley explains how Nadine loves to cook, and that she promised they'd make a new meal together every week. "It's a life skill everyone should have." Nadine sits opposite me at the dining room table that I've never used. Until now. "This one is so easy, even you can make it."

I ignore the jibe and dig into the meal. It's delicious. "I have a chef so I don't have to cook."

"But do you really enjoy all those reheated meals? Putting everything in the microwave?"

I shrug. "It's easy, and it's not like I have a lot of time on my hands to make something like this."

"I can make this for you again," Paisley volunteers, though she reconsiders with a wince, her hands dropping so low, I almost can't see her signing behind the edge of the table. "If you like it, I mean."

"I love it," I tell her, and she grins proudly.

And I am so proud.

Only a few weeks ago, she was miserable, would barely come out of her room or meet my eyes, and now she's talking and having fun. She's happy.

We chat for a while about Paisley's classes and the friends

she's made. Nadine chimes in that she thinks she's going to sign up to volunteer at the school, which has Paisley wiggling like a puppy. Then after the girls have ice cream for dessert, and I swallow down a protein shake, we all clean up together.

Like some quaint little family.

I used to get itchy thinking about kids. Didn't like the idea of settling down. Couldn't imagine wanting to come home instead of going out. Except I look forward to opening my door now. I enjoy being here with my sister. With Nadine.

Paisley heads to the living room, letting the guinea pigs out to make a mess of the cream rug with all of the hay and blueberries she sets in a line, hoping they'll follow it. They don't.

Nadine watches, leaning in close to me, murmuring, "She's been trying to train them, but..."

My sister lies on her stomach, clicking her tongue, holding out a blueberry in her hand, but neither one of the little guys comes to her. Instead, they share a piece of hay, munching on it like the spaghetti scene in *Lady and the Tramp*.

An elbow digs into my side. "Admit it. You think they're cute."

I refuse to give in to the twitch of my lips. "They're pointless. They can't do tricks. You can't take them for a walk."

"Technically, that's not true. They have itty-bitty leashes you can buy. There's nothing stopping you from taking Jelly and Bean down Broad Street."

"Rocky and Balboa," I correct, and she gasps quietly, moving to stand in front of me, head tilted up, amusement shining in her eyes.

"You gave them new names. You *love* them."

"I like them," I grumble, and Nadine whacks at my chest.

"You big softy."

"Don't tell anyone."

She winks theatrically, and my heart thumps behind my rib cage. I find myself back in a ballroom five years ago, a beautiful woman in an ice-blue dress that matches her eyes floating toward me. Shaking my hand. Smiling shyly.

And then turning right around to call me a prick.

"What happened?" I ask, hands shoved into my pockets so she doesn't see how tightly they're curled into fists. "That night of Erik and Molly's engagement party. What happened?"

She doesn't need any more explanation. Her face slowly falls, the playful smile I've become so familiar with slipping, along with her shoulders. Those eyes—the ones that have haunted me since that night—cloud as her chin dips. Still, she doesn't answer.

"Tell me what happened. Tell me what I did. Aside from… everything."

She stays quiet, brushing by me, but I catch her wrist. "I need to know. Because when I first saw you… We were… We had…" I shake my head, trying to make sense of my jumbled thoughts. "What did I do to make you hate me?"

She lifts a shoulder, tugging her hand out of my hold, and it feels like all the goodwill we built up between us over the summer is gone.

"Nadine," I say, bending to close the distance between us, my voice completely unfamiliar when I plead, "Please, talk to me."

She inhales audibly, angling her gaze away from me. "Why do you care all of a sudden?"

I don't know.

I don't know why I'm suddenly unable to be in my home and not see her in every corner. I can't help the innate sense of right-ness when I'm around her. Like a light has turned on after I've been sitting in the dark for my whole life.

"Because I'd like to know how we got so…lost."

And why it's taken so long for me to find my way back to her.

"I heard you talking," she murmurs. "You were with your teammates."

"Talking about you?" I guess, and she nods, but I can't

remember anything much about that night besides her. Besides the deep-seated fire that came roaring to life and then was immediately snuffed out. I think that's why I've been so willing to spar with her all these years, hoping it would spark another fire.

"One of them said something about me."

"What? What did they say?" The hairs on the back of my neck stand up. Did they insult her? I will kill them. Whoever it is.

"Nothing much. Alluded to…possibly being attracted to me."

I slowly lean back, doing my best to remember. None of this rings a bell. "Okay?"

"You…" She trails off, scuffing her heel against the floor.

"What? What did I do?"

She takes a breath and spits it out all at once. "You kind of warned him—all of them—away from me and Emmaline. Said it would be better if everyone left us alone because we were Erik's sisters."

I nod. Yes, that makes sense. Plus, I wanted Nadine for myself. None of those other douchebags.

"You told them I was a teacher, and when one of them made a joke about me fucking like one—"

"Oh." It hits me like a ton of bricks. It was Donaldson. He had a problem keeping his dick in his pants and ended up retiring early after some sexual assault allegations popped up. I believed them, and he deserved to be in a jail cell, instead of enjoying a quiet life somewhere in Michigan.

"He asked if you'd ever had a fantasy about fucking one of your teachers," Nadine starts.

"And I said not ones who look like her," I finish, and she nods, eyes cast down. But it still doesn't make sense. "Why didn't you say anything?"

That makes her lift her gaze, an angry divot between her brows. "Why would I? You humiliated me."

"Humiliated you? How?"

She tosses her hands out. "By making fun of me. By even

participating in that conversation, basically talking about me like I was a piece of meat."

"No." I slice my hand through the air. "I shut that conversation down. I wasn't going to let anyone talk about you like that."

She scoffs. "You didn't shut anything down. You played into it."

I tunnel my fingers into my hair, not knowing what to do. It's like we heard two different conversations that night. "I didn't. I didn't want anyone talking about you or to you because I wanted you."

"I didn't—what?" She cants her head back, whatever argument she had dying on her tongue. "*What?*"

"I said I never had a fantasy about fucking one of my teachers because I never had one who looked like you."

Her eyes dart back and forth between mine, as if working to translate my words, make some sense of them. "You... That's not..."

"Is that all you heard? Because after that, I told them you were completely off-limits." Looking back now, I don't know what I was going to do, play some kind of long game? Telling everyone to back off because eventually I'd make a move? I don't know, but it was all overturned anyway.

"I was trying to stick up for you, in my own stupid way, I guess. But I swear I wasn't aiming to put you down. When I saw you that night, I thought you were stunning. Took my breath away."

Her jaw works, but nothing comes out for a long time. And when she finally does speak, it's not what I expect. "Your sister started making bracelets. She made one for her best friend and me." She holds up her left hand, where a colorful woven bracelet winds around her wrist. "She made one for you too. You better wear it, okay?"

"Okay," I agree, my voice barely audible.

Nadine licks her lips, takes a deep breath, and then spins

away from me, saying, "I've got to get home. Pack a bag. I'll see you tomorrow."

She practically sprints out, and I'm left staring at the spot she stood moments before, a myriad of emotions crossing her features: hurt, shock, denial, and most interesting of all, something that looked a lot like satisfaction.

Since I can't dissect the female brain—especially one like Nadine's—I make my way over to Paisley. She has Rocky in her arms, and I stroke my index finger over his head.

"Where's Nadine?" she signs.

"Had to run out. She said you made me a bracelet."

My sister hands me the guinea pig to scurry away, and I ask the—truthfully—cute thing, "You like the name Rocky better, don't you? Yeah, I'm sure you do."

His tiny nose scrunches, and I bring him to my chest as my sister rounds the couch again. "Here," she signs, then holds out the bracelet, maroon and gray thread braided together. "For good luck."

I hold up my hand so she can tie it around my wrist.

We win against Kansas City.

CHAPTER 14
NADINE

WITH SO MUCH time on my hands, I've been doing a lot of introspection. I started journaling and have explored a variety of graduate programs, which would allow me to look into different careers in the education field. With so much extra spending money from Daddy Warbucks, I can easily pay for another degree. Especially because I paid off my student loans in one big chunk.

I never realized how stressed my money situation made me. Sure, I was single and had a full-time job, but not having any savings was like being followed by the Grim Reaper, his scythe ready to drop at any moment. Money really does make life so much easier.

Like staying in this penthouse every day, I feel like I'm auditioning for a reality show. After dropping Paisley off at school, I might run an errand or two, but for the most part, I enjoy my morning cup of tea on the terrace, which is really more like an outdoor living room, and then I might watch said reality shows on the wall-to-wall screen in the media room. Take a dip in the heated pool on the third floor. Or glide across the penthouse bamboo flooring in socks and an oversized shirt just for funsies.

I've done it all, but today is the first day I'm daring to enter the gym. It is everything you'd expect from a gym in a luxury apartment building with a near 360 view, sauna, and personal trainer at your beck and call.

"Hey," he says, strolling around a small desk toward me to extend his hand out to me. "I'm Brendan. Are you new to the building?"

"No, but I've never been to the gym before, so I thought I'd come and check it out." I'm hesitant to tell him who I work for, although I know the employees know Camden lives in the building.

"Great. Well, it's nice to meet you…?"

"Nadine."

He grins. "Nice to meet you, Nadine. There is always a person on staff here to help with whatever you need." He gestures around us. "For now, I'd be happy to give you a tour. Make sure you're comfortable with everything."

An older man is working out in the corner with some kind of machine, and a woman who appears to be in her 30s or 40s is getting in a good sweat on the elliptical. When I shrug in agreement, I earn another friendly smile. "How often do you exercise now? What do you like to do?"

"I'm not much into weights." I glance around again, mostly interested in seeing if there is some new magic machine that can shave the cellulite off my thighs without my having to do much work. "But I've done group classes. I like them."

He nods, rubbing his hands together as if he's about to rock my world. With a bit of a farmer's tan and a gap between his front teeth, he has a Woody Harrelson quality about him that puts me at ease. "Okay. Well, for starters, let me walk you through all the equipment, and you can let me know if you have any questions."

I agree with a nod, and he spends the next ten minutes showing me the free weights, an array of cardio and weight machines, how to use the sauna, and the small area in the back for personal training sessions. He says all I have to do is make an appointment in the online system, and he'd be able to design a program for me.

Since I have some time, and he seems nice enough, I let him show me a few exercises now, and he makes me feel proud of myself for lifting even the tiniest weight. I never would have been able to walk into a public gym, too embarrassed by my lack of knowledge and intimidated by everyone who actually does know what they're doing, but Brendan is so relaxed, it's impossible not to enjoy it. He has an easy smile, a gentle spirit, and a body carved from the side of a mountain, so of course when he asks if I'll be back, I agree and make an appointment with him right then and there.

Afterward, I head back up to the penthouse to shower and change so I can pick up Paisley from school. While I'm waiting in the car line, my mind drifts to my former students and how my old colleagues are doing. I text Lindsey—another special education teacher there—to check in, and it's the usual stuff of kids being annoying, a fight over a boy, stress over reevaluations. Until she informs me of a huge anonymous donation that bought all of the supplies every single teacher needed. For the entire district.

Teachers spend hundreds of dollars of their own money for classroom necessities like tissues, hand sanitizer, folders, pens, and decorations. It doesn't seem like much, but it adds up, and for every single teacher to receive what they need, it had to be at least half a million dollars. I'm not sure who would have done that, but it's an incredibly generous gift to the students and teachers.

And something about the coincidence makes me start to sweat, even though the temperature has cooled off enough that I'm wearing a long-sleeved T-shirt today. I yank the cotton up to my elbows, exhaling a big breath because it wouldn't have been...

Camden wouldn't have done it.

He would have no reason to.

Except me.

And...

When I saw you that night, I thought you were stunning. Took my breath away.

I've been replaying those words in my head for the last week and a half, wondering if he meant it. If he still thinks that way. If it's possible that we've been fighting with each other this whole time because my feelings were hurt over a misunderstanding, and I've refused to see how judgmental I can be.

I open the text thread with him, to the latest message he wrote, informing me that he wouldn't be home until the early morning hours. He doesn't have a lot of Thursday night games, but this one is against Tampa Bay. And when he left yesterday, he once again reminded me to use his credit card to purchase whatever I wanted for the guest bedroom I've been using while he's away. To buy anything I might need.

But ever since our conversation about that night, I haven't been able to take him up on the offer. Spite purchases? Absolutely yes. Buying something when I know it's coming from a genuine place? Makes me feel like a shrew.

I don't want to believe that I was the asshole in that situation, but I very well might have been. It's even made me view all of his well-reported bad behavior through a new lens. All the stupid stuff he's done, it's never involved anyone else. He's never hurt anyone. At least, not that I know of, and certainly not on purpose.

If I am to believe what he said is true, he never insulted me and only ever wanted to protect me.

Could I have gotten it so wrong?

It's the question that has been troubling me every day as I enter his apartment and find my tea and the kettle he bought, the guinea pigs he's become attached to and can never leave the house without saying goodbye to, the bracelet he wears from his sister, the smiles and hugs he offers her, the way his gaze coasts over me from head to toe every time I enter a room he's in, as if he's making sure I'm all right before ever uttering a single word to me.

I never thought of myself as a particularly prideful person, but it has been a struggle to accept that I was the one who fucked up. I was the one who jumped to conclusions. I was the one to kick off this sparring relationship. *Me.* I'm the problem.

And I don't know how to begin to apologize.

But there is also another part of me that doesn't want to because he may not have deliberately hurt my feelings that first time, yet he continued to every other time. I am not the only one who acted out of anger.

We were like bickering children, poking each other until the other one flinched.

Well, he's got me flinching.

So much so that I've been keeping as much distance as possible from him.

Physically and emotionally.

Except that's hard to do when Paisley and I turn on his game later. Paisley is mostly uninterested, texting her best friend, only lifting her attention to it every few minutes. I have the volume up and the captions on, and as the camera zooms in on Camden, he tunnels his fingers through his sweat-slicked hair, his woven bracelet still on his wrist. I notice Paisley smile to herself until the commentators start dissecting his private life.

"Long's comeback after an embarrassing display, which cost the Founders their national championship, and a terrible tragedy in the off-season has had a surprising upward trajectory."

"Yeah, I didn't expect him to come back so well, or at all. With a personal loss like that, you never know how it's going to affect a player."

At that moment, they cut away to a prepackaged video, a montage of Camden's highest and lowest moments. Next to me, Paisley shifts as the commentators go on. "Long's a smart player, a natural-born talent. We saw that in his rookie year. Coming out of college, the kid threw up statistics that matched veteran players."

"But you said the keyword there—*kid*. For as mature a player as he is on the field, he doesn't have that same maturity off the field."

"It's still early in the season, but it seems he did a lot of growing up."

"He had to. You don't lose both of your parents at the same time without it changing you as a person."

The camera pans back to Camden as he stalks to the fifty-yard line with Erik and the other two captains for the coin toss. The Founders win and choose to defer, but Paisley doesn't stay. She tells me that she's going to her bedroom, leaving me alone to watch the game.

I don't have to, and yet I don't turn it off. Instead, I curl up under a blanket with a mug of hot tea and watch as Camden Long once again displays his maturity on the field. If only they knew what his life has been like off the field these last few months.

He plays well, and though he doesn't score any points, he has a couple of catches and a great block in the third quarter so my brother can score on a rushing touchdown. I try to stay awake to watch the postgame wrap-up and interviews, but it's almost midnight and I pass out right there on the couch in the living room.

I don't know what time it is when I come to with a gentle hand on my shoulder and a quietly rumbled, "River, honey, wake up."

I feel like I'm moving in mud, and it takes my brain a moment to process that I'm still on the couch in Camden's penthouse. He's in front of me, sitting back on his haunches, his face mere inches from mine. All the lights in the main areas of the condo turn off automatically at midnight, so only the glow of the television remains to illuminate the room, casting his face mostly in shadow.

But he's wearing his glasses, and I find myself smiling in my exhausted delirium. "I like when you wear them," I murmur, forcing myself to sit up. "I like the Clark Kent version of you."

"Yeah?" I can hear more than see the arrogant tilt to his lips. "You don't want Superman?"

I shake my head. "Too many people know him. But I know the real version. Only I know Clark."

He doesn't reply, merely makes a soft sound, one I can't interpret, but then his hand is under the blanket, wrapping around my calf, his thumb stroking the back of my knee. And I reflexively extend my leg farther out, giving his fingers more room.

"You feel okay?" he asks. "These couches can't be too comfortable to sleep on."

I yawn. "It's okay. The blanket makes up for it."

The plush fleece in the color Cappuccino, the one I bought with his credit card.

He brushes his other hand along the edge. "You should order a few more of these if you like them."

"A few more items to ruin your bachelor aesthetic," I tease, and he mutters an assent before tugging the blanket off me to find my hands.

"Let's get you to bed."

"Yes, just give me a few minutes, and I'll head out."

He pauses. "Head out?"

My brain is still fuzzy with sleep, and I don't understand. "Yes...?"

"It's almost four in the morning. You're not going anywhere."

I nearly trip into him when he tows me up to standing, my hands landing on his chest. His palms come around my waist, holding me steady, and I blink a few times. "I figured now that you're home..."

"I'm not sending you out driving now. You're going to sleep here."

"But I—"

"You're sleeping here." He slides his hands to my shoulders, and with him towering over me, I can't see anything but the reflection off his glasses. "Now, can you walk, or do I need to carry you?"

It's a tempting offer. To give in to the heaviness of my limbs and let him take me in his arms, but even in my sleep-addled brain, I know it's not a good idea. Not for my heart or our fragile truce.

"I can walk."

He lets me step away from him but keeps his hand on my lower back, guiding me through the living room and kitchen to the hall, where I suddenly remember an idea I had. I don't want to forget in the morning.

Spinning around, I grab his biceps, my fingers barely spanning the round muscles. "I was thinking about Paisley's birthday. She really misses Ava, and I was hoping we could plan something. Maybe fly her out here."

"Ava is the best friend, right?" When I nod, he inclines his head a few inches, his fingertips tracing over my hips, slipping under the hem of my T-shirt and over my shorts. "Yeah, that's a good idea. That'll make her happy."

"Happier," I correct, and I can smell mint on his breath when he exhales harshly.

"I hope so."

"I know so."

"Mostly because of you."

But I won't let him escape the credit on this. "No. It's because you're taking care of her. She adores you."

He digs his fingertips into my hips, and with my heart jackrabbiting so loud in my chest, I can't be sure if I heard it or if I imagined it.

I adore you.

"Come on." He urges me to the guest room. "You need sleep, and so do I."

"I'll be up to take Paisley to school tomorrow."

"I'm going to. It's our rest day, and you need time off."

"It's okay."

"River," he warns, opening the door for me, flicking on the light, which makes me wince. Although being able to finally see him makes it better.

He smiles down at me, runs his hand over my sleep-mussed hair that probably looks like a rat's nest. "Sleep well."

Then he nudges me inside, closing the door after me.

I adore you too.

CHAPTER 15
CAMDEN

IT HAS BEEN A WEIRD WEEK. Between trying to sneak around behind Paisley's back, planning the big surprise for her birthday, I also contended with constant reminders of Nadine and that night I came home from Tampa to find her asleep on the couch.

Unfortunately, she does not sleep in a giant onesie. But thankfully, it is also not an itty-bitty top and thong like the picture my imagination had conjured up. She fell asleep in a billowing charity 5K T-shirt and cotton shorts that rode up high when she walked. Torturously, though, I do know how soft they are from when I had my fingertips buried in the material, both of us cloaked in shadows with only our breaths between us.

She was so warm and sleepy and smelled so good. She doesn't wear perfume, but whatever it is—a mixture of her soap, tea, cotton, and mornings in bed—her scent is addictive. It haunts me. Lingers in my senses and mind. Slowly making me lose it.

Especially when my sister informs me of where Nadine has been spending so much time.

"An hour every day," she signs in between bites of breakfast. "She said this guy has been helping her."

"What do you mean a guy has been helping her for an hour at the gym every day?"

She pauses with the spoon of her Fruity Pebbles halfway to her mouth and stares at me like I have two heads.

"What did she say about him?" I sign, and my sister pops the cereal into her mouth, shrugging.

"Not much." And then a moment later, she gasps and signs, "Oh my god! You like her! You like Nadine."

"I do not." I huff.

"Then why are you being weird?"

"Because I don't want anyone harassing her."

"He's not harassing her," Paisley signs. "It seems like she likes him."

"Likes him?" *Like* likes him?

At the realization that I've turned into a middle-schooler, I push my breakfast potatoes and slice of quiche away. It's my favorite, packed with turkey sausage, cheese, and veggies, but I've lost my appetite for the chef-made breakfast.

"What about Valerie?" Paisley asks, and I sink back against my chair.

"What about her?"

"Are you still with her?"

I scroll idly through my cell phone, finding the last text messages exchanged with her. **Nice game** with an attached photo of her tits. She loves when we win. She loves being on the arm of a winner.

I didn't use to mind.

Never really cared about having a relationship with much more substance beyond the image. It's not above me to admit I liked the status of dating a model. I think any twelve-year-old boy who has wet dreams of his favorite model or actress would take advantage of the position I'm currently in. She was in the right place and right time for me.

And I highly doubt Valerie thinks of me any different.

She likes going to games, when the camera pans to her for the jumbotron. She enjoys posting photos of us on her social media. My notoriety brings her more fame and paychecks with every job booked. She went from being a voluptuous runway model before we were dating to a voluptuous actress in cheap thrillers who runs around in white tops with no bra, tits bouncing all over the screen. If *Baywatch* were still a thing, she would have been great in it.

But I'm not really interested in the facade anymore and didn't respond to her messages, aside from **Thanks**.

Because I have a not-nanny nanny falling asleep on my couch and making friends with some guy in the gym.

"Are you almost done?" I sign to Paisley. "We're going to be late."

"You're grouchy in the morning," she signs back then slurps down the milk from her bowl.

I don't have many days that I'm able to take her to school, but our Fridays before home games start late, so Nadine has the mornings off.

My sister finishes up her breakfast and grabs her things before we head to the parking garage. It's not until we're walking to the car that I sign, "What time does she usually go to the gym?"

Paisley rolls her eyes with a snicker. "The afternoons, I think."

Great. Might make sure to be home in time to check it out.

After a focus on special teams and a quick team meeting, I skip out on the late lunch most of the players are taking in the cafeteria and practically sprint out of the complex.

By the time I storm into the condo's gym, my pulse is hammering and my gaze immediately homes in on where some blond asshole has one hand on Nadine's back and the other on her hip as she does reverse flys. He smiles as if it's no big deal. As if there is nothing wrong with touching her like that. As if it's totally appropriate to be "training" her alone, so no one could intervene if his hands continued to find other places on her body.

But I'm glad there will be no witnesses when I rip this motherfucker's spine straight out of his body.

"Hey," I say a lot louder than I need to. "What's up?"

Nadine freezes, eyes shooting to where I stand by the leg press as the soon-to-be dead man flattens his palm between her shoulder blades, sliding the other down her right arm to help her set the weight on the floor, then he grins at me. It's unnerving how he's so comfortable touching her.

"Camden Long, nice to meet you." He strolls over to me, leaving Nadine by herself. I don't take my eyes off her as she holds my gaze in the reflection of the mirror in front of her.

"What are you doing here?"

"I got out early." I ignore the sack of shit's hand when he extends it to me. "What are *you* doing?"

"Working out." She gestures to herself as if it should be obvious. In bike shorts and a loose tank top that shows off her sports bra, she has half of her hair up in a little ponytail on the top of her head that makes me want to smile, along with bright-white New Balances.

She's so fucking cute.

And this guy has had his hands all over her.

"Hey," he says at my side. "I'm Brendan."

Finally, I turn to this human who looks like a penis. I can't say exactly why, if it's the odd bowl cut or the shape of his head, but he looks like a penis, and I want to break his fingers.

"You working out with my girl here?"

His eyes widen. "Oh, uh… I didn't…"

"Camden," Nadine hisses. "What are you doing?"

"Nadine works with my sister," I explain to this so-called personal trainer. "Did you know that?" It's a rhetorical question, but he opens his mouth as if to answer, eyes flicking toward the woman digging her claws into my forearm. I don't let him speak, holding up my hand. "I need to make sure no one is going to take advantage of her."

He lifts his hands in innocence. "Hey, no, I—"

"There's no one else here right now," I point out as Nadine attempts to physically push me out of the way.

"What is your problem?"

I let her ram my side and fold my arms across my chest, staring down Brendan. If that's even his real name. "Do you normally work one-on-one in an empty gym?"

"Usually—"

"Because isn't there some policy against that?"

He shakes his head, shoulders up by his ears, obviously thrown off by my presence. Good. "There are cameras everywhere. There is no need—"

"To be putting your hands on a client," I finish for him, and he goes scarlet.

He stutters out a few syllables before finally stepping away, mumbling an excuse. "I'm gonna go use the restroom. You got her?" he asks me, barely glancing at Nadine. "Okay, great. I'll, uh, yeah..."

He scampers off, leaving me with a tiny raging bull.

"You have some fucking nerve, coming in here like that." She pushes at my chest, and when I don't move, she growls. "You are the worst!"

"No, you're lucky I came in here when I did. One more minute and his hand would have been on your ass."

"Don't be ridiculous. He has never treated me inappropriately."

I swat her hands away when she shoves at me again. "He doesn't need to be touching you like that."

"He's training me."

"He's pawing at you."

"I'll give you pawing." She grits her teeth, yet again trying to take me down, but I've got over a foot and probably one hundred pounds on her. I catch her hands, holding them tightly between mine and tow her into me. She seethes, cheeks flushed, with tiny baby hairs sticking to her temples. "You had no right to come in here swinging your dick around."

I can't help it. I let a smile loose. Feisty thing. "If I really came in here swinging my dick around, then maybe your smart mouth would be quiet for once." She has no quick-witted response, so I take the opportunity to tell her, "If you want to work out with someone, I'll hire them. Somebody much better than that prick."

"You're the prick." The fight has mostly drained out of her, though I still don't release her hands. Instead, I press them against my pecs, her fingers butting up against my collarbone. Her fingernails are painted a dark orange. She and Paisley have standing weekly nail appointments, on my dime.

Makes me think I should ask her to get my favorite color— the same blue as her eyes—or maybe Founders colors.

But with her still huffing and puffing, I figure I'll stick with one request at a time. "It would make me feel better if you worked with a professional."

"Brendan is a professional."

"*Brendan* was staring at your ass when I walked in."

"Was not."

"He's not here to actually help you."

She eventually breaks and straight up laughs in my face. "You are..." She loses her smile. "You're serious."

I nod, letting her go when she tugs, and I can't make out the series of emotions that crosses her features. A mixture of confusion and acquiescence, maybe.

That she can tell how serious I am. How knowing another man had his hands on her made me want to tear down the whole building. How having her in my life, in my home every day, sleeping down the hall every weekend, has made me no better than an animal.

Over these past few months, I have felt different, more focused and less concerned with finding my latest fix of adrenaline. Because this, right here, having Nadine in front of me, her lips parted, chest rising with each breath, nipples pebbled beneath her top, is my adrenaline.

No race or car, drink or drug, paycheck or ring could make me feel as alive as she does.

And I don't want to give her up to anything or anyone.

She licks her lips and brushes her hand over her hair, her throat lifting on a swallow as her gaze coasts around the empty gym. "I don't know what you're doing here."

She knows. From the way she can't hold my gaze, she knows.

I try to play it cool and shrug. "Since I'm home, I can pick up Paisley from school. Do you want to come with me?"

"No." The venom is back in her voice. "Not after how you embarrassed me."

"Better than having him assault you," I say to her back when she stomps past me.

"He's a nice guy."

I follow her to the elevator and use my key card to call it, pressing the button for the penthouse when we step inside. "You know how many nice guys take it too far after earning your trust?"

She fumes at me over her shoulder. "You don't need to mansplain the female experience to me. I know what it's like for the nice guy to go too far."

"You *what*?"

I reach for her hand, but she brushes me away. "Nothing."

She clearly didn't mean to blurt that out, though I'm not going to drop this subject. "It's not nothing. Did someone hurt you?"

The elevator opens to the entryway of my apartment, and she marches off, trying to get away from me and this conversation. Not happening.

"Who was it? When?" I place my hand on her shoulder, forcing her to stop right inside the door. "Nadine, please."

I don't beg, but I will. I will beg her to explain this to me. Because I won't rest until I know.

Stepping in front of her, I gently tilt her chin up, finding that stubborn look in her eyes. "River." I stroke the pad of my thumb over her jaw. "What happened?"

She leans away from my touch, shifting her attention away from mine. "Every woman has a story. I'm not special."

She is. She is so fucking special, and I force myself to keep my hands at my sides. I'm consumed with the need to break something because *this* is something every woman experiences. *This* is something I need to worry about with my sister. *This* is something Nadine has been forced to suffer through.

"You shouldn't have a story. No one should have a story."

Her snort of laughter is part condescension, part exhaustion. "I don't really want to make it a thing, okay? It happened, it's over, and there isn't anything you can do to change it, so I'd really like you to stop the nostril-flaring and fist-clenching."

I take a deep breath and cross my arms so she can't see my fisted hands anymore. "What happened?"

"I was friends with this guy in college. We flirted and kissed a few times, whatever." She waves a flippant hand. "We were at a party at his off-campus house one night. Both of us had been drinking, and I had been making out with him—"

"Please don't make excuses," I grit out, my voice so low even I'm surprised at what it sounds like.

"I'm not. I'm just explaining to you what happened, and why I felt..." She slips past me to the kitchen, stuffing her keys and cell phone into her purse. "We were hooking up, but I was still a virgin and I wanted to stop." She presses both of her hands into the counter, closing her eyes. "I just wasn't comfortable enough to tell him to stop. He was my friend, so I didn't want to disappoint him, I guess. And he kept going, kept taking his clothes off, kept taking mine off, and I..."

She lifts her head, glancing over her shoulder at me as if I could fill in the rest. I can, and it makes me furious. "You never actually consented?"

"I kept quiet. I don't know why. He wasn't violent or disrespectful, but he kept telling me how long he'd been waiting, how he was so happy to finally be doing it, and that he'd make sure it felt good."

My jaw aches with how hard I'm clenching, barely grunting out the words. "But it didn't?"

"No."

I think my jaw cracks from the pressure of grinding my teeth. She lifts a shoulder, and I'm getting tired of her shrugs. Then again, womankind is probably tired of my existence. Of men, in general.

"I didn't say no, but I also didn't want it to happen. I didn't fight back, I didn't leave, I just…let him do what he wanted. I didn't want to hurt his feelings, and I was too embarrassed to admit I didn't like it."

It feels like a physical blow, and I hunch over, holding back a shout of frustration. "Consent, enthusiastic consent is the fucking bar. The lowest bar. And he didn't wait. He didn't ask. It was as—"

"Don't." She throws her bag over her arm, car keys in hand. "Please don't say it out loud because it makes it worse. It's a thing that happened, a bad experience I've dealt with and learned from, okay? I've never let it happen again. I stand up for myself now."

Yeah. I know that firsthand, and when I step toward her, she shakes her head. She doesn't want me in her space. So I stay right where I am, helpless.

She pushes a loose piece of hair behind her ear. "I told you because I don't need you bulldozing into my life, talking about what nice guys do. I *know* what they are capable of."

"Have you told anyone else about this?"

"Some girlfriends." She smiles the saddest smile I've ever seen. "These are stories we share in whispers over wine. Battle scars we show off to each other."

I don't have words for how utterly useless I feel. "I'm sorry."

"I'll see you tomorrow." She ignores the apology and brushes past me. I don't bother chasing her, understanding that she needs time alone. *I* need time alone. But I do stop her with one more question.

I stand in my open door as she waits for the elevator. "What happened to him?"

"Don't know. He never talked to me again after that night."

Motherfucker.

"And just so we're clear," she says, the spark I love so much back in her eyes. "I am fully aware of who is a nice guy and who is not."

With the way she scowls at me, I assume she means I am *not* a nice guy. Well, if the shoe fits…

A day later, as I'm on my way to the team dinner in the hotel, I receive a text.

Did you get a second trainer hired?

Don't know what you're talking about.

There is a second trainer in the gym now. A woman named Mina.

Good.

This is an overreaction.

No. An overreaction would be getting him fired.

OMG

You wouldn't.

If he crossed a line? Absolutely.

You can't get him fired.

I'm just saying, if it doesn't work out there for him, it'll be for a good reason.

Meaning you got them to hire a second person just in case?

No comment.

Like you don't know anything about the donation made to every teacher in my former school district for their entire supply lists?

Doesn't ring a bell.

And none of that has to do with me?

It has everything to do with you, I want to say, but instead, I send a different text.

I didn't realize you thought the world revolved around you.

I learn from the best.

You.

Now that, I'll own up to. Being the best.

But just so we're clear, I'm not a nice guy. I won't hesitate. I'm not afraid to hurt anyone's feelings.

Except yours.

CHAPTER 16

NADINE

IT TOOK a few phone calls and emails to put all the plans in place, but it came together perfectly. Camden arranged for Ava, her parents, and younger brother to be picked up from the airport and transported to a hotel, so they would be able to meet Paisley and me for brunch at our favorite restaurant. The same one I took her to the first day we went shopping with twenty-dollar salads.

Brunch is my favorite because of the mimosa flights. She likes it for the stuffed French toast, so she doesn't think anything of it at first when we walk into a private room. It is her birthday after all.

"Your brother wanted to do something special," I sign and gesture to the flowers, card, and presents all set up in the middle of the table. I'm not sure what he bought for her since he didn't run it past me, but I'm learning Camden can be quite thoughtful, if a little over the top.

I'd taken her to get her hair trimmed and highlighted again yesterday, this time with pink. Our glittery nails match, and I'm wearing the woven bracelet she made me in pink, purple, and blue.

This morning was really difficult. She woke up crying, her

first birthday without her parents. I suspect every first will be difficult, and I pray that I'll always be in her life to help her through it, if I can.

But seeing her tear open her birthday card from Camden, smiling as she reads it, lets me know she'll be all right. They both will be.

I hold out my hand so I can take a look at the card. It's simple with *Love you, Sis!* on the front in rainbow colors, while the inside contains a few lines of his chicken scratch.

Happy birthday, Paisley. I'm sorry I can't be there with you right now, but I hope you have fun at your party. I'm so proud of you, and I can't wait to see what you do this year. Love you, Cam.

I'm not sure what it feels like for ovaries to weep, but I think mine do, and I stuff the card back into the envelope as Paisley opens her gifts. The first is a new laptop, which has her excitedly hopping on her toes, telling me how she'll be able to video chat with Ava on it instead of using an iPad, and I have to bite my cheek so I don't give away the big gift. Next, she opens a box with the latest trendy sneakers, and then a third with a belt bag that she loves. She immediately transfers her cell phone, lip gloss, and hair ties to it but promptly forgets about it when the door opens.

When she recognizes who it is, Paisley throws herself across the room at her best friend, hugging and crying and shrieking. Behind them, Ava's parents, Hank and Kate, step inside with their eight-year-old son, Bryson. I wave to them, careful to step around the girls to shake their hands, and formally introduce myself.

"This is amazing," Kate signs, moving to my side. "I really can't thank you enough for doing this."

"It wasn't me. It was all Camden."

"I don't think Ava's slept the last two days, she's been so excited to come." Her eyes turn glassy as she watches her daughter and Paisley talk, hands moving at the same time, both of them repeating over and over how they can't believe it and how much they've missed the other and that they love each other. Makes me tear up a little too.

"I'm just happy it all worked out. Why don't we sit?"

Kate nods and motions for Hank and Bryson to sit at the large circular table. The girls follow, but they're too busy catching up to really pay attention to anything else.

We take our time over our food, since Ava and Paisley do more chatting than eating, both of them only taking a break when the server brings in the cake, and we all sign and sing "Happy Birthday." We dig into the four layers of chocolate with chocolate mousse in between and cascading flowers on the outside. I clean my plate of it as Kate explains how Ava and Paisley have been friends since they met at a Deaf camp, and while they're from Des Moines and the Longs lived in Cedar Falls, they made sure to get the girls together as often as possible. Kate was born deaf and understands how important it is to build a community for her Deaf daughter.

"We were all so devastated about the accident," Kate signs, after sipping on her second mimosa. "I think of Paisley as one of my own, and I've been sick to my stomach ever since. How has she been doing?"

"Good." I wipe my mouth with the linen napkin before continuing to sign. "Or as good as can be expected, I suppose. She's doing well in school, and I try to keep her as busy as possible with different things around the city. She started taking an art class on Saturday mornings. We've seen a show at the Kimmel Center. We cook together and watch movies with popcorn every Friday."

Kate smiles as Ava shows Paisley something on her cell phone that makes both of them crack up. "And you said you're a teacher?"

I recross my legs under the table. Aside from the weekly check-in with my parents, no one has asked me about my career. "I was. I taught learning support at a high school in Jersey."

"You live close?"

I shrug. "About an hour away. I'm living with my brother right now while I help Camden and Paisley out."

"It's incredible that you stepped up the way you have." When I try to wave off the compliment, she taps my wrist for my attention before she signs. "Not everyone would give up their life the way you have."

I stare at my nearly empty mimosa glass, an orange slice barely clinging to the edge. I didn't give up much. Besides oncoming depression and my students. Other than that, I didn't have much else in my one-bedroom apartment. No boyfriend, no pets, not even a plant.

Here, though, I've gained so much. I'm happy, and I feel like I can finally see a path for myself in the future, something in special education administration. Making sure every child has their needs met from the top.

"I appreciate you and what you're doing," Kate continues. "And I know Lori and Ken would feel the same way."

I clear my throat of the sudden thickness there, surreptitiously dabbing at the corners of my eyes. "Thank you."

After a moment, she points to her empty glass and signs, "Do you think it would be okay if I had another mimosa?"

I break out in a big laugh. "Definitely."

Later, we pile into a limo to take us to the stadium, where we're met by a woman in a suit, who leads us to a suite only for us, filled with more food, drinks, and a few pieces of signed memorabilia. Bryson freaks out about the football with the signatures of what looks like the entire Founders team on it.

Hank snaps videos and pictures of everything, including a selfie of him in his Detroit jersey, and when I notice, I volunteer to take it for him, making sure to include as much of the stadium as possible in the background.

"So you're not a Founders fan, huh?" I tease verbally, handing his phone back.

"Never was, but this might change my mind." Then he turns to watch the pregame stuff happening on the field, the cheerleaders dancing while the small fife and drum corps plays. The eagle mascot wearing a colonial military uniform runs around, pumping up the crowd. On the jumbotron, fans wave and cheer, beer is spilled, and a stomach flashes with Erik's name painted on it.

Beside me, Hank makes a curious sound. "I didn't know what to expect with all this. I always thought Camden was…"

"A jerk?" I guess, and he winces.

"I hate to admit it, but yes. I feel bad about that. He's paying for all of us, being so generous. He didn't have to fly us all out here. He didn't have to put us up in a room at the Four Seasons." He huffs. "I mean… I think my wife likes that hotel room more than she likes our house."

"I think that has more to do with the housekeeping services than your actual house."

He puffs up his cheeks, blowing out a breath that turns into a good-humored chuckle. "I don't know how I can compete with this. Every birthday and anniversary, she'll think *This isn't as nice as the time Camden Long paid for a weekend away in a four-star hotel.*"

"I doubt that, but I'm glad you're all having a good time."

"Hey, Dad, catch!"

Hank spins around to catch the football Bryson tosses him, effectively ending our conversation, so I move closer to the window as the team runs out of the tunnel, through a cloud of fog.

Camden really did go above and beyond, and I find him immediately, toward the back of the pack. He always used to lead in the front, flapping his hands up and down, riling up the crowd, but now he's more subdued. Still jumping around, though clearly focused on himself as opposed to the people in the stands.

He does a few lunges, shakes out his arms, then pulls off his helmet, pivoting with one hand on his hip, head up, as if skating his gaze around the stadium. I'm not sure if he knows where we are, but he seems to be looking in this direction, and I lift my hand. Just in case he can see me.

He does, pointing his index finger at me. I grin back before swinging around to Paisley. "Hey, look. Do you see your brother?"

She joins me by the window, waving wildly, and Camden holds up the sign for *I love you*, which Paisley returns. Out of the corner of my eye, I notice the camera catches it, and we're on the jumbotron, Paisley and I. My smile immediately slips, and I motion for her to sit back down, hoping the attention of the entire stadium is no longer on us. The camera focuses on Camden then, but he either doesn't notice or care, his attention on the field. *My* attention is on the maroon and gray woven bracelet around his wrist that he idly toys with.

They beat Detroit 42-35.

After the game, Paisley and Ava beg us to let them have a sleepover, which we expected. I'd already planned to stay at the penthouse, so Ava and Paisley can sleep in her room while I'm right down the hall, and we all hop back in the limo to drop Kate, Hank, and Bryson off at the Four Seasons then head home, where Paisley asks if we can order pizza. As if they haven't eaten their faces off all day. But what Paisley wants, Paisley gets with Camden's Amex that I've now memorized the numbers of.

They settle in the media room with their large pepperoni, garlic knots, two liters of soda, and *She's The Man*. By then, Camden arrives, all smiles. "Where is she?"

"Watching a movie with Ava."

He nods and turns that way while I clean up the mess of gifts, flowers, and bags in the kitchen. A few minutes later, he reappears, hair still wet from a shower, wearing joggers and a hoodie.

"You played well," I say, trying to find a home for the left-over birthday cake.

But he doesn't let me stick it in the fridge and plucks the box right out of my hands. "Thanks, and thank you for taking care of everything today."

I sidle up next to him as he cuts himself a big slice. "It was fun."

He grabs a fork and scoops a hefty portion of the cake onto it. "You're wearing your brother's jersey."

I pinch at it with a laugh. "Yeah."

He grunts and then stuffs cake into his mouth.

"Is it a problem to support my brother? Your quarterback?"

He shakes his head, scoops up another piece of cake and then holds it out to me, his hand underneath in case it drops. "Open."

I mindlessly follow his direction, opening my mouth so he can feed me the cake. It's as delicious as it was this afternoon, and I lick my lips of the frosting. "This is really good. Where'd you get it from?"

"Same place as the cannoli." He forks himself a piece of cake. And then one for me.

That's how we finish the whole slice. One bite for him. One for me. His eyes on my lips, his hands serving me. His voice quiet as he asks what we did, interested if Ava's family enjoyed themselves, wanting to know every detail. He smiles satisfactorily when I tell him that everyone had fun. That Bryson said it was the best day ever. "And I think you've won over your sister for the rest of her life."

"Yeah?" He wipes his thumb over the corner of my mouth, a smear of pink that he licks off, and my knees go wobbly. "What about you?"

"Have you won me over?" When he nods, I feel myself sinking into him, leaning so far into his space that my hip brushes the knuckles of the hand he has wrapped around the edge of the counter. His index finger scratches at my maroon jersey with the number 12. Camden's number is 88, and I wonder what he would think if I wore it. If it would make him feel like an electrical current is running through his chest, like it does mine at the mere idea.

If I ever actually put on a jersey with his name and number, I might never want to take it off.

This man I used to hate.

And now can't seem to stop falling for.

"You won me over today. This *one* day."

He saws his teeth over his bottom lip, pressing hard enough that it briefly turns white, and heat pools in my belly, between my legs.

"Take it day by day then, hm? See if I can't win you over tomorrow?"

He inclines his head, setting down the fork to place his hand on my waist, smoothing it to my back, curling around the hem of the jersey, almost like he wants to rip it off.

I think I would let him if not for the buzzing.

Camden's eyes close, an audible exhale rushing from his mouth at the interruption that might as well be a bus crashing through here.

I step away, realizing it's his cell phone when he slides it from his pocket. "It's Valerie."

I catch my breath, pressing my hand to my temple, reining in my racing imagination.

He has a girlfriend. One who is currently on the other end of his FaceTime call.

The one I'm obviously on-screen for because instead of a greeting, Valerie snaps, "Why is *she* there with you again?"

CHAPTER 17
CAMDEN

I FLICK my eyes to Nadine to find her face flushed. I don't know if it's because of the kiss we almost shared or Valerie. Either way, I'd much rather find more ways to make Nadine blush than be on the phone with a woman I don't care very much about.

She's been on my ass lately, calling and texting every day, but I've been avoiding her, knowing we'd have to have this conversation. Because I'm not *that* much of an asshole to call it quits over a text, I wanted to do it in person. After more than two years together in this semblance of a relationship, I owe her that.

But I can't keep pushing it off.

Clearly.

"I'm sorry," I mouth to Nadine then turn away from her, taking this call outside on the terrace. It's cool, and I pull the hood of my sweatshirt up over my head before lounging on one of the chairs. When I'm finally settled, I ask, "What's up, Val?"

"What's up?" she parrots, scowling at me. "I've been trying to plan this trip, and you won't even give me an answer."

"Because I don't want to go."

She screeches. "What?"

She's been asking to go to the Caribbean for a while, and in a moment of delirium and grief after having just brought Paisley back here, I agreed when Valerie said we should get away. I told her we would go during my bye week. But now it's bye week, and I don't want to go.

"You promised," she whines, and I rub my hand over the back of my head.

"I know, but I want to stay here. I want to be with Paisley."

"You want to be with Paisley or with Nancy?"

I sniff out a derisive laugh. I didn't date Valerie for her personality, but this is so childish. "You know that's not her name."

"Like I give a shit."

"Clearly, you do. You're jealous. Is that why you've been up my ass lately?"

"I'm up your ass because you won't answer me. Because you're too busy with her!"

I lift my gaze up from Valerie's frown on the screen to peek in through the windows of my home. I don't see Nadine, so I assume she went to bed. I'm glad of it. I don't want her to hear any of this.

"You know she's been helping me out. Nothing is going on between us," I say, although it rings false. *Something* is going on, but nothing I can name.

"She's around all the time," Valerie snaps, refocusing my attention back on my phone. On her.

Valerie is objectively hot. She has some mix of ancestry that left her with hazel eyes, creamy light brown skin, thick black hair that is halfway down her back, and an hourglass figure. But she's too wrapped up in being famous, in documenting every second of her life for social media, selling every part of herself that she can.

And I'm not into it anymore.

"Nadine is around all the time because I can't be. I don't know why you're so surprised. You were at my parents' funeral. You were there," I say, finally getting to the crux of the problem.

When I needed her, she wasn't there.

In body, sure, but not in any real way.

She took no interest in my sister, didn't help while I packed up my childhood home, and hasn't bothered to even talk about any of it with me. She hasn't once asked how I'm doing or feeling.

If she did, she'd know that I often cry in the shower and sometimes wake up in the middle of the night breathing hard with my heart beating in my ears, reliving the night of the accident. I dream of winning the race and Malcolm holding his cell phone out to me. That's when I sit up straight in bed, my skin damp with sweat.

"I can't take care of Paisley on my own," I tell Valerie, and she huffs.

"She seems to be taking care of a lot more than Paisley."

I rub my knuckle against my eye, thinking I'd like to take my contacts out. Valerie always hated when I wore my glasses. "I'm not going to argue about Nadine with you. This isn't about her. It's about us."

"This is absolutely about her."

"No. It's you."

On-screen, Valerie wrenches her head back. "Me? What did I do?"

I heave a sigh up to the night sky. "I'm in a different place in my life. I thought we might be able to stay together, but it's not working for me anymore."

"You're kidding," she says flatly.

"No."

"This isn't working for *you* anymore? It's not like you put all that much effort into it to begin with."

That's fair, but she hasn't either. "I need more than you can give me right now."

"You need more from me or from *her*?"

When I don't answer, Valerie shakes her head, lips pursed in an angry pout. "You're going to regret this. When you realize what you're missing, you're going to come crawling back."

I don't know what else to say besides, "Okay, Val. I've got to go."

She hangs up before I can, and I spend a few minutes in the night air, letting it cleanse me with every breath. Valerie was the last piece of my past I needed to rid myself of. The former Camden Long was an arrogant prick. The new Camden Long is probably still an arrogant prick, but at least now he thinks about how his actions affect other people. Only, like, 75% arrogant prick.

Back inside, I check on the girls one more time, but I doubt they'll be going to sleep anytime soon since they're still wide awake in the media room, on to movie number two. But I don't care. They can stay up all night if they want. It's the most I've seen my sister smile since she moved here, and as long as she's happy, they can do whatever they want.

I pass by Nadine's closed bedroom door, half tempted to knock on it, but I've already asked so much of her today—hell, every day for the past few months—that I don't want to disturb her peace.

Even though I know her feelings about me have changed, I don't want to fuck up the good thing we have going by barging in there and doing what I want to do.

Fucking her up against the wall. Coming so deep inside her that my DNA will be dripping out of her for weeks.

I tug off my sweatshirt as soon as I step into my bedroom, on the opposite side of the penthouse. My skin is a little too hot, a familiar tingle building in my spine when I think about Nadine's thighs smeared with my come. Marking her with it. Claiming her as mine.

I've never been one to care much for making a mess. Physically or with feelings. It was easier to hook up with women who only cared about being with me because of who I was. Didn't take much for them to get on their knees or hike up their skirt.

Relationships went as far as I let them, only until I was tired of what they could give me.

I didn't care about making them happy or reciprocating orgasms. I didn't have to.

Yeah, I'm a dick, but no woman ever made me face it before.

Nadine is different.

What I feel for her is different.

I care about her. I care about her happiness and safety. I don't want to disappoint her, and I especially don't want to ruin the good thing we have going.

So all my fantasies about fucking her without a condom and making a mess of her stay inside my brain, let out only when I'm alone with my hand.

The knowledge that she's asleep in my home makes my blood pump even faster, and I reach for the lube in my bedside table. I barely have my pants and underwear pushed down before my erection is in my hand.

I hiss at the first touch of the cool gel then unconsciously thrust into my fist, envisioning her naked and laid out for me. Pushing those thighs of hers apart. Knees up toward her chest.

Or maybe sliding into her from behind. Her ass up. Jiggling with every push. My fingers digging into her soft hips.

I'd make sure she liked it. Make sure she was begging for it. For me. For my cock.

Hear my name from her lips. Those winter eyes heavy with lust.

Yeah, she'd love it.

I grunt, closing my eyes, leaning over my bed, hand on the mattress, thinking of what it would be like to sink between her legs. Going down on a woman has never been on my list of needs in bed and none of them has ever complained about my not doing it, but it is *necessary* to put my mouth on Nadine.

Learn what she tastes like. If her pussy is as delicious as the biting words that fall from her lips. I know once I have it, I'll never want to give it up. I think I might like to live down there with her thighs permanently attached to either side of my head.

I'd make her so wet from my mouth that I would slide right in.

Squeezing my fist tighter, I fuck harder, gritting my teeth, imagining the sweet clench of her. It would be so good I'd have to focus on not finishing too fast.

Because the tensing of her muscles as she wraps her legs around me would be heaven. Her skin flushed and damp. Hair a mess from my fingers. Nipples tight little beads that I nibble on until she's bucking up into me.

"You like that?" I mumble to an empty room, though my mind is nothing but Nadine. Her familiar scent and the quirk of her mouth, the arch of her brow when she throws attitude my way.

That's when I come, giving in to that perfect mix of sweet and sour, because I don't want one without the other. I need her giving heart and her sharp tongue. I want her kindness and her ferocity. She is both tender and strong, yet unwilling to concede when she knows she's right.

Which is almost all the time.

Because she is right about me. I am a jealous, demanding, conceited asshole.

And when I finally come, spilling inside her, I will stay there until it seeps out between us. Only then would I slip out of her, except I won't clean her up. No, I'll use my fingers to push it back into her. Paint her thighs with it. Write my name across her skin. Then I'd have her lick it off my fingers, tasting all that I left inside her.

Because she is mine.

Even if I don't deserve her.

Even if I don't deserve to touch her, let alone live out any of my depraved fantasies.

I've spent too many years being a person she hates. And that's what makes it worse, thinking that my whole trajectory and life might be different if that night at the Ritz had gone differently. If she hadn't overheard one stupid goddamn conversation. If I'd kept my mouth shut or walked away. If she hadn't made assumptions about herself or what I thought of her.

If, if, if…

Maybe she'd be with me right now, smiling up at me with some smart remark, instead of me alone in my bedroom, cleaning up my orgasm from my hand.

In another timeline, in another universe, she would've fallen in love with me that night. It would've been the start of our life together. I'd have found something to keep myself anchored to instead of floating off into space, hoping to fill it up with fame and money.

In another timeline, in another universe, Nadine Rivera thinks I am perfect.

Perfect for her.

CHAPTER 18
NADINE

I SPENT THE FOUNDERS' bye week splitting time between Erik and Molly's house and my sister's apartment in New York City. It's basically a closet that she shares with another woman on the Lower East Side, but Emmaline's good at picking up men for free drinks and food, so it sort of evens out the price. She's tall and tanned like our father, but blond and blue-eyed like our mother. The finance bros love her, but little do they know she plans on working for the SEC.

It was all going well—Emmaline and I were gossiping and sipping dirty martinis—until Tanner sidled up next to me. I swear he saw Leonardo DiCaprio in *The Wolf of Wall Street* and said, yep, I want to do that. I wasn't interested in him, but he wouldn't leave me alone.

He refused to stop yapping at me about this app he had invested in, moving closer and closer to me, so I told him it "sounds like Yelp."

And when he said I wasn't funny, I told him, "You know what's funny? That thing you think is a beard."

Then he called me a stuck-up bitch, and Emmaline barely held me back from throwing my drink in his face.

What's worse was that the first person I thought about was

Camden. I wanted to call him and relay the events, just to prove that I can and do stand up for myself. I don't need him to be my guard dog or to go around bullying every person—or, really, man—in my life.

But when Emmaline caught me staring at my cell phone, at the last text Camden sent me, a message apologizing again for Valerie and hoping I have a nice week off, she read between the lines.

"You like him," she accused with a laugh.

"I do not."

"You do. Of course you do!" She slapped at my shoulder. "I thought it was odd that you always hated him but agreed to help out." She smiled like the Cheshire cat. "I should have known."

"There is nothing to know."

"Except that you've always been in love with him."

"No. That's not—no."

Her amusement melted into true terror. "Does Erik know?"

"There's nothing to know. Camden and I are…"

"In love."

"Friends."

"Who are in love."

I didn't bother to answer since she was going to concoct her own ideas, no matter what I said. But it did make me a little nauseous when she warned, "Erik is going to flip when he finds out."

"Why would he flip out?"

"Because you're his favorite sibling and it's his best friend, and while I love this as a rom-com setup, I don't think he'd appreciate it."

Although it was a moot point. I'm not planning on acting on any of these growing yet confusing emotions for Camden. As far as I know, he's still with Valerie, and I'm still not sure I can trust him. She clearly dislikes me, and it doesn't make me feel any better about him that he's flirting with me, almost kissing me, while still with her.

It doesn't make sense. He's grown so much since this past spring, and I've learned a lot about the person he is, the person my brother promised he is—a good man beneath all the cocky veneer. I'm just not sure I'd *want* to trust him with my heart. Even if it was an option.

Which it's not.

Yet tell that to my reckless, irresponsible heart that loves Y2K rom-coms as much as Paisley when his stupidly handsome face appears on the television screen.

I'm back in his penthouse, staying over while he plays in Los Angeles. The team flew out yesterday morning, and they won't be back until tomorrow, a whole weekend living here. But, really, I've been here more than I've been at Erik and Molly's house, and I've come to think of this place as "home," as opposed to my brother's.

And all those alarm bells are going ringy-dingy-dingy as my sister's words replay in my head.

"There is nothing to know. Camden and I are..."

"In love."

"Friends."

"Who are in love."

Paisley really doesn't care about football, but she often sits with me to watch the games. I've always followed the sport, although I'm not so sure I'd be as interested as I am if my brother didn't play.

My family—my parents and siblings—are all close, but Erik and I have always been like two peas in a pod. I'm sure if he turned out to be a chess player, I would have been into that, but he happened to have a high athletic aptitude, a serious amount of self-control, and a persuasive style of leadership. He was meant to do this, to be out on that field.

I watch him now, in the huddle, giving directions to his team before they all jog to their positions on the twenty, where Erik puts in his mouth guard. He calls the play, takes the snap from Linley, and drops back a few yards, a pump fake and then a sweet pass to Camden, completely open in the end zone.

They make it look easy.

Erik runs over, jumping onto Camden's back as he tosses the ball to the ref, the cameras zooming in on their smiling faces. My brother's and Camden's.

"That's cute," Paisley signs. "They have a handshake."

It is. The adorable little two-step they do, adding a shimmy and explosion after the fist bump. It reminds me of little kids.

Doing what they love to do.

What they dreamed of doing.

I couldn't be happier for my brother. And for Camden.

When he tugs his helmet off, his open mouth is set wide in a smile that makes my heart flop around beneath my ribs. Especially because there are quiet moments I notice him blinking away redness in his eyes. Moments I know he's thinking of his parents, sinking into the ever-present grief that never fully goes away but ebbs for a while. Only to flow back in when he's unoccupied.

When he realizes I'm watching him, that I've found out his secrets, he usually offers me a smile and says he's fine.

He's always *fine*.

But not always happy.

And I think…

I think I'd like to make him happy.

A few minutes later, the half ends, and both teams head to the locker rooms. As they do, the camera moves to show fans in the stands and one particular woman in a box suite, Valerie Blondeau.

She's in a tiny cropped top, jeans that appear painted on, and a flannel button-down in maroon and gray. With her long hair in a high ponytail and the no makeup, makeup look, she is effortless. Fun. Beautiful. The type of woman expected to be with a professional athlete.

I once read a "diet" plan from the 1950s, and it involved a lot of cigarettes, a surprising amount of vodka, and a bunch of hard-boiled eggs. Sometimes I wonder if that's what it would take for me to look like that, like her. Skinny yet curvy, shiny and bright. Cigarettes to make everything taste like ash and suppress an appetite. Vodka for the right amount of carefree. And enough protein from the hard-boiled eggs to stay upright.

I set my bag of chips aside and suck down a gallon of water, knowing it will never flush out the amount of unnecessary salt from my body, while still hoping I'll magically be able to drop the twenty pounds that gave me stretch marks and a perpetual muffin top.

Not that I can compete with Valerie.

Even if I were to suddenly become a size zero, she'd still have five inches and three cup sizes on me.

Plus a boyfriend named Camden Long.

"Hey," Paisley says audibly, pointing to the screen once she has my attention and then signing, "She's got nothing on you." She shrugs and then adds, "Camden is an idiot."

I laugh. "Thanks."

"No, really." Her brows narrowing down in a similar divot like when her brother is annoyed. "You're a better person than she is."

I force a smile, even as it makes me squeamish to put another woman down. I want to be a girl's girl, but envy is a dangerous thing. I swear my fingernails are turning green as I curl my hands into fists, dropping them to my lap.

"She and Camden aren't going to make it," Paisley signs. "They're not endgame."

Am I supposed to believe that means there is an opening for me?

Because that's what my gullible heart assumes.

My stomach twists, and I focus on the talking heads on-screen now that Valerie's face is gone. They pull up video of certain plays, dissecting each one, but I don't care. My brain rewinds every moment with Camden since the first one.

Dissecting them like a talking head. Wondering how they might be different. If I said something different. Or he did.

I've never been much into science, but the butterfly effect makes it seem like Camden and I would be different people right now, if not for one single change in our history.

Would I be sitting here next to his sister?

Or would their parents?

Would I still be teaching?

Or would I be in that box, cheering him on right now?

I will never know.

The second half starts with renewed energy from both teams, and it's a battle. Camden lines up wide, and I find myself leaning forward without realizing it. When Erik snaps the ball, Camden runs a perfect cross route, cutting sharply toward the middle of the field. The pass is on target, and he catches it in stride.

But as he turns upfield, a linebacker comes in low. Camden's legs get tangled up in the tackle, and he goes down hard. I wince, reflexively reaching my hand out to Paisley's arm, squeezing, and she lifts her attention from her phone to the television.

When Camden stays down, Paisley signs, "What happened? Is he okay?"

I don't know, so I don't answer, watching as he remains lifeless on the field.

I hold my breath, and everything seems to move in slow motion as the medical team runs onto the field. Erik is there too, kneeling beside his best friend, his hand on Camden's shoulder pad.

There is movement. They're talking, and I exhale harshly, relieved that he's conscious.

The camera zooms in on his face, and even through the face mask, I can see he's grimacing in pain.

Paisley tugs her arm back, and I realize I'm clenching too hard on her and force myself to release my hold, folding my arms around my bent knees instead. Still, my knuckles are white from my fingernails digging into my palms.

This is what I was afraid of. Not just caring about him, but caring *this* much. The kind of caring that makes my chest tight and the world feel like it's tilting off its axis.

The medics do a couple of tests, ones that I know mean they're checking for a concussion, and from the way Camden shakes his head when they sit him up, I guess he's trying to tell them he doesn't have one, but the league has started to take the protocol seriously.

I'm glad of it.

Especially when they help Camden stand, and he favors his right side. I don't know if it's an ankle sprain, his knee, or even his ribs, but when Paisley signs nervously to me, I attempt to reassure her that they have the best doctors. He'll be fine, whatever it is.

Though he might not be back for this game. Maybe not the next one either.

As they reach the sideline, Camden has his helmet off and looks up toward the stands. For a moment, I imagine he's looking for me.

Of course he's not. He's searching for Valerie, who's probably already making her way down to the field.

The game continues without him, yet I can't focus on anything else. Especially when the talking heads explain how Camden was taken to the locker room for more tests.

My stomach twists, deciding it doesn't really like what we had for dinner anymore.

This is why I can't do this. Can't let myself fall for him completely.

Because I'm already too far gone to pretend that watching him get hurt doesn't feel like I'm hurting too.

CHAPTER 19

CAMDEN

IT WAS one of those hits that takes a minute to recover from. Knocked the wind out of me and tweaked my knee. I came down hard on my side, and it laid me out.

Only until I could catch my breath and stand up, walk out the pain in my leg. The medical staff is extra cautious and made me go for a more thorough examination. Perform an X-ray of my knee and ankle since I've had previous injuries to both, but after I received the okay and got taped up, I went back out onto the field, having missed a few series and a touchdown scored by one of our running backs, Shaun Campbell.

We end up beating Los Angeles by seven points, and adrenaline courses through my veins as I step into the locker room, with the entire team celebrating. It's a tidal wave of laughter, shouting, sweat, and the sweet high of victory.

We're on a winning streak, and Coach gives us a short speech, telling us to enjoy it, which earns a few jeers. "Big Dog" Baynard lets out a couple of rough, low barks, and Shaun jumps on top of a pile of linemen, howling, catching a ball tossed to him.

All around me, my teammates make plans, talking about where they're going and who they're going with. Before, I would have been one of them. I'd have found a bar and ordered bottle service. I would have stayed out until everything closed down and then found someone's house to head to after. I'd have thoroughly *enjoyed* it.

Now? I'd rather relax. Watch a movie. Text Nadine. Ask if she saw the game. Because of course she did. Ask her if that hit I took looked as bad on television as it felt in real life. I know she'd respond with something sassy about the way I played, and maybe I'd have the balls to ask if she'd kiss it better when I returned home.

After some rounds of backslaps and rehashing of plays, I head into one of the shower stalls. I let the steam envelop me and wash away all the sweat and grime of the field, checking over my body, glancing at the new scrapes and bruises. A never-ending count.

But god does it feel good to be winning. To know I'm performing exactly how I'm supposed to be. Turning the tide of public perception.

As much as I'd like to pretend it doesn't bother me, it does. Who doesn't want to be loved?

I finally feel like the media has moved past the shroud of what happened with my parents and are focused back on me as a player. And without any outstanding antics, I can appreciate what it feels like to be loved simply for doing what I do best.

When I finally emerge from the locker room, changed and with my bag in hand, I run right into Valerie, where she's waiting in the friends and family area. There aren't a whole lot because it's an away game, but occasionally, some family members will travel or friends will meet up to get together.

She is the last person I expect to be here. Smiling at me.

"Hey there, big shot." She's dressed in the team colors, a tiny purse over her shoulder, her cell phone in her hand, held up like she might take a picture.

"Hey." I skirt my gaze around, checking to see if anyone has spotted her or us together. Valerie does have the tendency to call attention to herself even when she's not trying. Right now, she's trying.

She steps closer to me, wrapping her arms around my torso. "You played great out there."

I stiffen, attempting to push her away without *pushing* her away. "Thanks."

"What's wrong?" She pulls back to search my face. As if we didn't break up. As if everything has been normal for the last two weeks and she didn't tell me I'd regret it. That I'd come crawling back.

But she's the one here.

She may live in Los Angeles, but there is no reason for her to be at my game.

Unless she wants to come crawling back.

"I don't know why you're here."

She frowns. "I'm here to see you, obviously."

She acts cute, crowding my side, sliding her hand over my chest, though I'm not having it, and I step back, putting some distance between us.

"I don't know what you think is happening here. But it's not. It's over," I say, looking straight in her eyes, and she holds my gaze long enough that I think maybe she's the one who needs a scan for a concussion.

"Seriously?" Her expression darkens. She's not confused. She's simply never been turned down before. "*Her?*"

Valerie can't even say her name. She can't fathom that she's not the center of the world.

But she is certainly not the center of mine. Not even in the same universe. I shrug, stepping back from her. "Yeah."

Her face flushes with anger. "After everything we've been through? You're really going to let it go?"

I'm not sure what she's referring to. We haven't been through much. I've had my life upended in the last six months, but she couldn't seem to care less.

"We've had some fun, but like I said, this isn't working anymore."

She huffs an irritated sound, drawing her hand over her ponytail, swinging it over her shoulder, pulling herself together. Drawing the shades down over her emotions. "You're really going to choose her over me?"

I nod. Without a doubt. "It's always been her."

But she doesn't believe me, so I make sure she understands. "I will *always* choose her."

Valerie points her finger at me. "Fuck you, Camden." Then she turns, shouting it again. "Fuck you!"

All eyes are on her as she stalks away. "You'll never have it as good with her as you did with me!"

She storms off, the furious click of her heels echoing down the hall, and I exhale, shoving my hand through my hair. Feels like exiting a haunted house at a carnival. Coming down after the jump scare.

Months ago, having one of the most well-known models in the world showing up at my games unannounced to basically stake her claim would have made me proud. Now, I'd rather stick my hand in a meat grinder than deal with her. Deal with the stares of everyone around me.

I avoid the questions thrown my way from teammates and random strangers as I head to the team bus, where I find my usual seat next to Erik. He looks up from his phone when I slouch down. He gets right down to it. "So, you broke up with Valerie, I'm assuming."

"What gave it away?"

"The stomping and yelling."

I press my hand to my temple, grunting.

Erik laughs quietly next to me. "Are you expecting a congratulations or commiseration?"

"Neither."

He types out a quick message, probably to Molly, then pockets his phone. "You done for good?" When I nod, he leans over, lowering his voice. "Can't say I'm mad over it." When I hum an agreement, he goes on, "I heard her say something about you being with someone else."

"I'm not with anyone else."

"But is there someone else?"

I cross my arms, staring out to the front of the bus, waiting for the rest of the team to file in so I can get the hell out of here. Back to my hotel room and away from my best friend. Because I can't be honest with him. I can't tell him that I've fallen in love with his sister.

"Yeah," I eventually concede. "There is someone else."

"Really?" The surprise in his voice has me turning to meet his curious gaze.

I don't know why I feel the need to defend myself or my feelings, but the words tumble out before I can stop them. "She's special."

"Damn. You're serious about it." His humor ceases immediately. "You *are* serious about it."

I nod even though it wasn't a question.

He smiles then. "Good for you, man. I'm happy for you. Finally finding what I've been talking about. A good woman settles you down."

That's how I feel with Nadine around, settled.

She reminds me that there is so much good in the world. That *I* can be good.

"I was worried there for a minute," Erik goes on, fiddling with his earbuds. "Thought you might have something going on with my sister since she's been at your place so much."

I stare at him unblinking, but he doesn't notice as he takes his phone back out to find some reality dating show. "Because I love you like a brother," he says, elbowing me as he laughs to himself, putting in his earbuds. "But my sister is way too good for you." Then he presses play, gesturing to his phone. "I gotta catch up so I can talk about it with Moll tomorrow."

I force a laugh. They watch reality shows together, and

maybe if it didn't feel like he punched me in the throat, I'd find the eccentricities of his marriage sweet.

I don't.

Not when I'd like to punch him in the dick.

Make Kai an only child.

I know Nadine is too good for me. I don't need him pointing it out.

But it doesn't stop me from opening my text thread with her. It's well after midnight at home, but I send her a message anyway. One I'm hoping shows her that I can be good.

I can be good for her.

I'll be good *to* her.

> We're headed back to the hotel now. Not sure if you watched the game or not, but I took a pretty rough hit. Gonna ice and watch a movie.

Shockingly, she answers.

> 10 Things I Hate About You?

Probably, but I don't tell her that. I make sure Erik can't see my phone as I respond.

> Why are you still up? You should be in bed.

> I am. Just not asleep yet.

I try desperately not to picture her in bed.

Definitely not in *my* bed.

> I did watch the game. How are you feeling?

> A little sore. Nothing some rest won't fix.

> You're not going to go out?

> Nope

A minute passes before she messages me again.

I saw Valerie at the game.

I didn't know she was coming. I didn't ask her to.

You don't need to explain it to me.

I do.

We broke up.

Before bye week. When she called

I don't want to finish the sentence. When she called and basically talked shit about Nadine. Like she did tonight.

I broke up with her then.

I just didn't know how to tell Nadine. I didn't want to tell her and have it be a *thing* between us. Because what if she doesn't actually care? What if she really does think I'm a piece of shit? She is too good for me, and I'm not sure I'd be able to take it if she ever said it to my face.

It's why I haven't been able to confess how I feel.

Why I haven't been able to face her like a man.

But I can text her. Tell her behind a screen.

She's not in my life anymore.

Honestly, my feelings changed for her a while ago.

Months ago.

You really don't need to explain it to me. You don't owe me anything.

I do.

I owe you everything.

She doesn't reply, and with everyone finally on the bus, the driver pulls out of the stadium, and I let my head sink back against the rest, unable to put my phone away. Hoping she'll text me back, but unable to say what I really want to.

Not with her brother laughing about some new bombshell and one of my teammates reminding me of my past. "Yo, Long. You coming out with us?"

"Nah. I'm in for the night."

JD shouts from the back, "Somebody throw me a sweatshirt. I'm freezing."

Someone else, "Why?"

"Hell has frozen over."

Laughter rings out, and I roll my eyes, though I don't take offense. If some ribbing is what it takes to prove I'm not the man I used to be, I'll happily take it.

I shoot off one last message to Nadine.

I miss you.

CHAPTER 20

NADINE

IT HAUNTS ME. Those three words.

I miss you.

I think of them when Camden arrives home from his road trip, looking a bit worse for wear after that hit and the travel.

I miss you.

I think of them as I play on Erik and Molly's living room floor with Kai, making him giggle with funny faces during my day off.

I miss you.

I think of them as I head back to Camden's penthouse, knots in my stomach at what I can expect to be our conversation, but he has an early appointment with his PT, so he only has enough time for a jut of his chin and quiet, "Morning, Riv" as he scoots out the door.

I miss you.

I think of them as he comes back after his day of practice, sitting down to have dinner with Paisley and me. We made a simple lasagna.

He loves it, helping himself to a second plate, complimenting us. Saying it's better than what his chef makes.

Camden and I haven't been openly hostile in a long while,

but we also haven't been this awkward. We can barely look at each other. Both of us aiming questions at Paisley so we don't have to talk to the other. And she notices, frowning.

"What the hell?" Paisley signs, nose scrunched in disgust at each of us, in turn. "Stop being so weird."

Then she grabs her plate and leaves us to our middle school standoff.

He sits across from me, eyes coasting everywhere but in my direction.

Like at my eighth-grade graduation dance, when I'd been so sure Toby O'Roark was going to ask me to dance. He kept finding me from the other side of the auditorium, and yet he never came over.

I wait and wait and wait for Camden to say something, but he never does.

So, I offer a subdued, "See you tomorrow," and head home.

It's the next morning when he already has my tea steeped and waiting for me when we both finally try.

"I wanted to ask—"

"We should—"

"You first."

"No, you first." I gesture. His cheekbones flush a ruddy red, and I'm right back to that dance with Toby.

"I was hoping you'd come to my game on Sunday," he says, one hand on the counter, the other pushing the mug of my morning Earl Grey toward me.

"You want me to bring Paisley?"

He nods, motioning vaguely, and it's cute. That he's so nervous. None of that overconfident Camden Long I know in sight. But from the way his mouth quirks to the side, I think he likes that he has the ability to quell my attitude now and then.

"I want you to bring Paisley, yes, but I want *you* there," he tells me. "I have seats saved with the other guys' families."

Molly attends every once in a while, but I myself have never sat in the WAGs section. Me being there for Camden would be a declaration of sorts.

Before I can agree, I revisit that text. "You missed me?"

He nods. "I always miss you."

"An uptight bitch?"

"I have never called you a bitch," he says with this finger in the air. "Uptight, yes. Never bitch."

"You told me I needed to get laid."

"It was an invitation, of sorts."

When he shrugs, I lose the fight against my growing smile. "What about the hot tub melting my skin off?"

His eyes rove over me, and my nipples pebble beneath my bra as his gaze practically devours me whole. "There are some things I'd like to melt off, yes, but…" He skates his tongue over his lower lip, his teeth following before his dark eyes lift to meet mine, and they're practically black. "There are much better things I can think of for your skin."

I shiver, incapable of coming up with any words to respond to his outright flirting. His sexual innuendos.

Clearly pleased with himself and his ability to make me stupid with lust, he smiles and combs his fingers into my hair, holding on to the side of my head, leaning down, his intention obvious, and I lift up, ready to meet him. To finally taste his lips. Learn what his smile feels like against my mouth.

But Paisley stomps into the kitchen, huffing and puffing. I suppose it's because of the big test she has today in science. She hates science. Even more than math.

And I fling myself away from Camden, even as his hands are slow to leave me, his fingers grazing my side as I turn away from him to greet his sister. Being a Friday, he would normally take her, but he's been doing some extra deep tissue massages after that hit aggravated some old injuries. So it's on me to drive her in this morning. I motion for her to take her stuff, and I don't bother saying goodbye to Camden. Not able to form even the simplest of words after those confessions.

At least on his part. I was too mesmerized to tell him how I felt.

That I think I might be in love with him.

I spend the day applying to a handful of graduate programs. Because of Camden's generosity, I have the money and time to earn my degree, so it's only a matter of finding the best fit for me and my goals.

After that is done, I get in a workout with Brendan, who's been a bit standoffish since the display with Camden a few weeks ago, which left him with the impression that we're together. Although, with what happened this morning, I can't necessarily promise that *nothing* is going on. And I don't know how to feel about a man being so possessive over me that he'd try to physically intimidate a stranger. I appreciate a healthy amount of jealousy. I am not immune to it, and I have—admittedly—fantasized about poking Valerie Blondeau's eyes out on occasion, but I'd never actually do it. Only I'm not so sure Camden wouldn't follow through on his threats to have Brendan fired, and isn't that ridiculous? Immature and self-centered?

To be so protective of me that he'd been blinded to the reality of the situation.

Except as I shower off my sweat and change into jeans and a Founders hoodie, I wonder if Brendan did have some ulterior motive. Sure, anyone might be terrified of Camden Long, but if he really wasn't doing anything "wrong," why is he so hands-off now? I've never worked with a personal trainer before, and while Brendan is friendly, and I never got a creepy vibe from him, I suspect that if he's suddenly afraid to touch me, maybe he shouldn't have been doing it to begin with. Maybe his goals weren't all about my fitness.

And maybe I should cancel my appointments with him.

When I pick up Paisley from school, she informs me that she doesn't think she did well on the test, but that she was invited to a friend's house tomorrow. I tell her she will have to talk to Camden about it. If it's okay with him, it's okay with me. I've been volunteering once a week at the school, mostly to help with admin work, but I put my name down on the substitute list and made friends with all of the teachers and secretaries, so it doesn't take much for me to find out more information about this girl and her parents, and they seem like good people.

We're only home for a few minutes before Camden shows up with a gift bag hanging from the tips of his fingers, but Paisley reroutes him immediately, asking if she can hang out with her friend. Begging, more accurately. He flicks his gaze to me, and when I shrug, he says he wants to talk to whoever the friend lives with, and I smile to myself. He'd been so afraid he'd fail at being Paisley's guardian, but he's been doing all the right things. Giving her space to grow and try new things, while also being smart about her safety.

Paisley texts him the contact information for the girl's parents once she has it and then flits off to her room, finally leaving Camden alone with me. And whatever is in the bag he holds out to me.

Without a word, I take it from him and whip out tissue paper to find a brand-new jersey. I barely have it lifted in front of me before he has his hand around the back of my head, forcing my eyes up to his. "If you're sitting in my seats, I want you wearing my name and number."

I don't answer with words. Instead, I hop up onto my toes, throwing my arms around his neck to kiss him. There is so much distance between us, he has to bend, stooping his shoulders, his hands cupping my face, his mouth meeting mine without hesitation. His groan is one of relief, but when I part my lips, his tongue finds mine with a growl. He tastes like mint gum and feels like a man deprived of the sun finally being allowed outside. He isn't soft or gentle. No, he is ravenous. He tangles his tongue with mine, pulls at my lips, almost as if he's afraid the sunshine will fade away, and he's wrangling as much as he can now.

If I thought he was possessive before, it's nothing on this kiss that is like he's trying to inhale me. His fingers spear into my hair, arms towing me to him, but when I'm as high as I can go on my toes, he lifts me up, one forearm banded across my back, the other under my butt. I wrap my legs around his waist, and he pins me against the wall, his teeth scratching my jaw, his mouth landing on my throat, sucking and biting, and I let my head fall back with a moan. "God, Camden."

He doesn't stop kissing and licking at me, but he does readjust his hold, curling his giant hands around my thighs, holding me open and up like it's nothing, and I can feel every hard inch of him between my legs, where he rubs himself against me. "I've wanted you for so long," he murmurs, breathing hard, another torturous grind over where all the blood in my body has pooled. "River," he whispers, almost pained, "River…"

His moan anchors me to reality and the question I've wanted answered for the last month. I tunnel my fingers into his hair, gripping the short strands tightly so he can't nibble on my ear anymore. I tug so he shifts, his face in front of mine, eyes wide, pupils blown, cheeks flushed. He moves, obviously wanting to go back to what he'd previously been doing, but I stop him. "Why River?"

He blinks as if coming out of a trance and slowly lowers my feet to the floor, every soft part of me sliding against every hard part of him, and it takes both of us another few moments to recover. He plants his hands on either side of my head, and I hold on to his T-shirt, steadying myself as I ask again, "Why do you call me River?"

His Adam's apple bobs, mouth quirking in embarrassed amusement. "I've been calling you that for years in my head. I didn't even realize I started actually saying it out loud."

He backs up an inch, enough room so that we're not plastered against each other and I don't have to tip my head back so far. Still, I don't give him an out, merely patiently waiting. He shrugs, a bit sheepishly, as he finally confesses, "Your eyes. I saw you that night…"

"The engagement party?"

He nods. "Your dress was that ice-blue color. Reminded me of a frozen river. Like your eyes."

That's why I'd chosen it. I thought it best matched my eyes, blue with a hint of gray.

He gives his head a rueful shake, smiling, like he can't believe he's about to confess it, but... "I swear I've dreamed of your eyes for the last five years. I see them in my mind when I can't sleep."

"I've been haunting you," I say with a laugh, and he dips his head, kissing my temple, cheek, and mouth.

"Little witch." He goes in for another kiss, but I keep it chaste, my hands on his chest, needing time to process what we just did, what is happening. And I'm not sure if we want his sister walking in on us by accident.

When I relay all of this to him, he nods in agreement but hesitates to step away from me. His gaze tracks over me, heated and longing, and it does nothing to cool my own temperature, calm the racing of my heart, or stop the tingling in my core.

"I should try to call this girl's parents, huh?" he says, referring to Paisley's friend. Still, he stays in place.

"I should go home, finish writing my essay."

"Essay?"

"Some of the programs I'm applying to need an essay."

He clasps my face between his bear paws. "I'm so proud of you. More than anything else, I'm so goddamn proud of you for doing what you want. For not giving up."

I cover his hands with my own, nuzzling into him with a smile. "I'm proud of you too. For proving all those motherfuckers wrong."

He chuckles softly. "I lo—ike you."

I swallow the sudden boulder in my throat, voice paper-thin. "I really like you too."

But it's more than that. I know he wanted to say more than that.

I *feel* more than that.

But not yet.

There is still so much to talk about, to think through, and we can't say it yet.

So he walks me to the door, offers me a sweet kiss on my mouth along with a caress of my cheek and waves as I step onto the elevator, both of us holding each other's gaze until the doors close.

CHAPTER 21
NADINE

I INFORMED Molly that Paisley and I would be at the game, so her look of surprise isn't because I'm here. It's because of what I'm wearing.

"It's not a big deal," I tell her, self-consciously tugging on my new jersey. I paired it with my most flattering jeans and simple flats because even if I'm here to be introduced to the wives and girlfriends of the players for all intents and purposes, I'm not very capable in heels. While I'd been sympathetic to Molly before and her anxiety about looking a certain way because of who she's married to, I didn't truly empathize until right now. Until I feel eyes on me, from all over the stadium, like I suddenly have some kind of reputation at stake.

Yet Camden and I aren't even together. All we had was one hot-as-hell make-out session. Though now that I'm here, it's as if I'm on display to be judged by the other women, the fans, anyone who might suspect why I'm here wearing his name and number, when none of the other WAGS are wearing jerseys. I stick out like a sore thumb.

That voice in the back of my head reminds me that I'm not good enough. I'm a quitter. I'm not smart, and I certainly don't look like the type of person the number one tight end in the league should be with. Let alone making out with.

Molly must recognize the terror suddenly tensing all of my muscles, because she takes my hand in hers, hugging me close to her side, Kai strapped to her chest between us. "You're fine, and you look great. I was just shocked to see you in it."

"So is everyone else," I mutter, but she shakes her head.

"No. Literally no one is. No one knows you."

I bark out a nervous laugh. Because, yes, that's true. "Wonderful."

She laughs too. Hers much looser than mine. "It'll be fun! Come meet everyone," she says, tugging me forward. I take hold of Paisley's hand and drag her behind me as Molly introduces us. There are a bunch of wives and fiancées seated here, some with kids, some with other friends or family, all of them welcoming. None of them says anything about my jersey.

But they are quite interested in Paisley. They all want a chance to talk to her, get to know her more, bring her into the little family they've clearly made here. I spend some time translating for Paisley, but eventually, some of them bypass me and simply type notes on their phones. As usual, Paisley has that bored air about her, but she is a good sport as the only teenager in the entire group.

"See?" Molly flicks her hand out. "I told you it would be fine. Here." She passes Kai to me. "I'm going to help myself to a glass of champagne."

We're seated right in front of a suite that is always reserved for the players' families, and she scoots away for a drink while I pretend to eat Kai's cheek so he shrieks in laughter—my favorite. On the field, the team warms up, and I try not to watch Camden, too nervous now that I'm here in person.

But I can't avoid it when he and my brother are shown on the jumbotron, laughing about something before Camden holds his fist out for a pound. Erik knocks his knuckles then slaps the back of his best friend's head. The exact place my hand had been

Friday night, my fingers woven into his hair as he nipped my throat, sending goose bumps racing over my skin when he'd groaned into my mouth.

I'm sunken deep into the memory of the way he curled his hips up so the length of his hard cock stroked me, and simply recalling it makes me overheat. I all but throw Kai at Molly when she returns, so I can get a drink myself. The largest ice water I can find.

One of the wives, Maureen, who's married to the kicker, approaches me with a smile, effectively ending my panic attack of lust, and I fall into easy conversation with her. We chat all through the pregame and into the first quarter, until her husband is called out to the field. He puts the first points on the board, and by the time I go back to my seat, I feel more at ease. Paisley seems to be enjoying herself too. Her cell phone is actually away as she alternates between watching the game and playing with Kai.

By halftime, I'm more than comfortable, and I can actually see myself here in the future. If Camden and I continue down this path we're headed, I wouldn't mind being friends with these women. I wouldn't mind exchanging numbers with them. Molly explains how they all help one another out. The more veteran wives each "adopt" a rookie wife or girlfriend to show them the ropes. There is, of course, some drama, one or two who don't get along with the rest, but for the most part, it's nothing like a reality show. I should have known because if it were, Molly would never be able to stand it. But I guess I had to witness it with my own eyes, to really look past the stereotype.

And I've never felt like more of a bitch.

Had I always been so judgmental?

I guess so.

First, Camden.

And now, these women.

"Am I a terrible person?" I ask Molly when the third quarter starts, and the second glass of champagne must be hitting hard because she giggles uncontrollably.

"I'm serious," I tell her, which only makes her laugh harder.

"I know. That's what's so funny."

I wait with a scowl until she calms down enough to speak. "You're not terrible, but you are hypercritical. Probably because you're so critical of yourself."

"Okay." I take my hand from hers, playfully knocking it away. "I'm not paying you enough to psychoanalyze me."

She claps for a play, a short pass Erik completes then leans into my space. "But that's the whole thing, isn't it? The harshest judges of others are projecting from themselves." When I grimace, she apparently thinks it's a green light and goes on. "If you never feel good enough, of course you'd find it easier to think others around you are assholes or stupid or whatever negative and most likely inaccurate descriptor you want to fill in the blank with. Because you want to believe you're already above them, so you won't be hurt by their rebuff."

I jerk back. "You don't need to read me to filth here. I thought we were having a good time."

"We are." She smiles sickeningly sweetly before lowering her voice to a whisper. "Because you're in love, and now you feel bad for judging him before. It's making you rethink your entire life, and I like watching you squirm."

I cough a laugh and push her away. "Now you're being an asshole."

She grins, taking my hand once again. "No. I'm not."

"No, you're not," I agree, and we watch the next few plays until the Founders finally score a touchdown, both of us jumping up to cheer. But as the clock ticks down to the fourth quarter, I feel a noticeable shift in the atmosphere. It started with Shayna, one of the wives, showing something on her phone to another, and now they're whispering and casting furtive glances in my direction.

When Molly notices, she takes it upon herself to find out

what's going on, and I try to ignore the twisting in my gut. Whatever it is, it has to do with me, and I know it can't be good.

Out of the corner of my eye, my friend slides her phone out of her pocket and studies it for a minute before returning to me. "It's Valerie," she says, holding out her phone to me, so I can view the screen. On it is a social media post. A beautiful black-and-white shot of Valerie, set against what appears to be sand and ocean, a shadow of a palm tree in the corner with a caption about the sun being the best cure for heartbreak and that karma will take care of men who cheat.

Without naming any names, Valerie Blondeau basically told the world that Camden Long cheated on her. I look up from Molly's screen to a mix of curious and accusatory stares from the other women, and it's clear they've put the pieces together. Since I'm sitting here in his jersey, I'm apparently the one he cheated with.

Even though nothing happened between Camden and me while he was with her, the heat of embarrassment and shame creep up my neck. This isn't how I wanted things to come out, and certainly not in such a public way. I'm not even sure what Camden and I are to each other, but now it seems like everyone —the wives and girlfriends of his teammates, who, in this instance, are everyone that may be in *my* future—has come to their own conclusions.

The game continues, but I can barely focus on the action, hyperaware of every whisper, every sideways glance. Not only from the WAGs, but from anyone in the crowd. I debate whether to stay or leave, but it's Paisley who taps my elbow and asks to go. I know she saw the post, and I know she's lying when she says she's not feeling well, offering me an out.

I take it, accepting Molly's hug, and return a few waves of goodbye, some understanding eyes, some disapproving glares. I'm so in my head about it all, I barely notice how long it takes our private car to chauffeur us back home, only that I'm in time to catch some of the postgame interviews on television. The

Founders won by a few points, though I'm so nauseous about everything, I don't care.

Paisley doesn't stick around as I tie myself up in knots, doomscrolling. Valerie's post has taken off and already hit the sports podcasters, throwing in their two cents about Camden's state of play and if his extracurricular activities are getting him in trouble, but that's completely absurd. Camden's been playing better than ever. Besides that, Valerie's social media post has nothing to do with Camden and everything to do with her need for attention.

Yet with the thousands of reposts and comments, it's clear many people agree with this person, and they want to know who he cheated on Valerie with. Helpfully, she's been going around hearting comments that defend her and leaving little nuggets about not trusting nannies and "never believe him when he says he's not in love with the help."

The help.

She could not be more insulting. Not only to me, but to all caretakers.

And even though she never mentions my name, she's all but calling me out publicly. Camden has always been careful to keep Paisley out of the public eye, but it wouldn't be difficult to find out who I am. I mean... I am mentioned on Erik Rivera's Wikipedia page as his sister. I have been known to appear in the background of photos online. It's not like I'm completely new to this, but the frenzy Valerie has whipped up feels mildly threatening.

My stomach churns, and I force myself to put my phone down and really consider what the possible outcomes of this are. A plausible but least likely scenario is some creep on the internet connecting the dots and blasting it out everywhere that I am the apparent "cheater." The more likely scenario is that this will all blow over in a day or two, because some other celebrity will do or say something that sucks up all the oxygen, but that doesn't make me feel any better.

Because even if I know the truth about my relationship with Camden, I don't know anything about his past relationships. I don't know if he was faithful to Valerie or any previous girlfriend. He has a bad-boy reputation for a reason.

And what I can't parse out is exactly how I feel about that.

The front door of the penthouse opens quietly, but I spin around, nonetheless, realizing I've lost so much time to my anxiety-spiraling tonight. The moment Camden's dark gaze find mine, all of it crashes down on me, and tears flood my eyes.

CHAPTER 22
CAMDEN

I'D BEEN FUMING. It was all anybody could talk about as soon as the game ended and I'd been notified of Valerie's dumb fucking social media post. I figured I would ignore it, but I couldn't with my teammates giving me shit about it and Malcolm leaving a terse voicemail to call him back. Even the security guard at the parking deck asked about it.

I wouldn't have cared if I didn't know that Nadine was involved. All I wanted was her in the stands and to be proud of me, but it was Erik who informed me she'd left the game early. Molly had relayed the message to him that Paisley wasn't feeling well, but I had a hunch it wasn't the truth.

Nadine was upset, and she had every right to be. I expected her to be pissed and maybe go a couple of rounds about what a jerk I am—and more than likely that I deserve every bit of scorn from every corner of the world after cheating on Valerie. But what I don't expect is those river eyes to fill with water and her face to fall when I open the door at home.

"Riv." I approach her with my hands up. "What's going on?"

She wipes at her face, but by the time I reach her, her cheeks are wet again, and I use my sleeve to dry them. It doesn't last long, and I hold her head between my hands to kiss her. It's chaste but tastes salty, her mouth soft yet unforgiving.

"You saw?" I guess, and she nods, lips brushing mine. "I'm sorry," I whisper against her mouth. "I—"

"I'm not sure I can do it."

"Do what?"

She sniffles. "I don't know… It's a lot, me and you, and I don't think—"

"Stop. Stop." I step away, releasing her face to take her hands in mine. "Just stop, okay? We have to talk about this. Please?"

She lets me lead her to the living room, but she chooses to sit on the other couch instead of next to me. I blow out a breath and scrub my hands through my hair, attempting to gather my thoughts about everything.

"First of all, is Paisley okay? Erik said you two left early because she wasn't feeling well."

Nadine shakes her head. "She's fine. She's watching a movie."

I swallow past my cottonmouth. I was right, and they left the game because of the post. With my elbows on my knees, I fist my left hand over my right so that I don't close the space between us. I recognize she needs it, but it's a gulf. A chasm I'm worried can't be bridged.

"I don't know where to start," I admit honestly as she still refuses to meet my gaze.

She sniffles again, lifting an apathetic shoulder, eyes focused on where her toe is dug into the rug. "I thought I'd be able to do it, but I'm not sure I can. If this is what it's like to be a part of your life… All this speculation and ridicule, it's a circus."

I can't disagree. My behavior has been clownish at times, and now it's all coming back to bite me in the ass.

She finally lifts her bloodshot eyes to my face, dragging her fingers under her eyes and nose. "You know, while I was at the game, I had this epiphany that'd I'd been wrong all along. About you, about the other wives and girlfriends. I had all these assumptions about what type of people they were." She shakes her head, sawing her teeth over her bottom lip, as if keeping herself from crying again. "I felt so bad for judging them, for spending so long judging you. But then Valerie posted that, and I know…" Her voice wavers. "I know the truth about us, but I don't know the truth about anything else. I only know that you have a whole history I may have been *right* about."

I can't stay away from her anymore, and I fall to the floor, crawling to her, placing my hands on her legs, cupping my palms around the backs of her denim-covered calves. "I can't change my past. I wish I could, but I can't, and I'm so sorry any of it might blow back on you, because you don't deserve it. You are perfect."

She covers her face with her hands and mumbles, "I'm not perfect."

"Riv, please, look at me." She does, and I bring her hands to my lips, kissing her fingertips. "You're perfect for me."

Her breath hiccups, but she doesn't respond, lips pursed, eyes swimming with water.

"Give me a chance. Give *us* a chance. *Please.*"

She squeezes her eyes shut. "I don't know."

"I'll tell you anything. Whatever you want to know, I'm an open book."

A moment passes where I'm not sure she's going to take me up on my offer to answer her questions, but she eventually blinks her eyes open. They're dry and narrowed on me. "Did you cheat on Valerie?"

"Yes. Once, a few months ago while I was in Florida."

"Did you ever cheat on anyone else?"

"No. I swear, and I won't ever cheat on you."

She huffs one single, annoyed laugh. "That's good, I guess."

"Honey, please." I dip my chin, practically prostrating myself. "You know me. You know the real me. I did it because I was pissed at myself and trying to fill up the holes in my life. It sounds shitty, but it didn't mean anything. And this will sound even worse, but—" I lick my lips, preparing for more honesty than I've ever given any other woman "—Valerie and I were never that serious. It's not an excuse, it's just the truth. I didn't feel bad about it at the time because I assumed she was also fooling around behind my back, but I didn't care. I never cared about anyone the way I do about you. And I know my word means nothing right now, but I promise I would never cheat on you. You've been tucked away in my heart for so long, I think I became used to living life with you there. Looking forward to the one day of the year I'd be able to see you. When I'd feel alive again. Because every other day, every other woman was background noise. It's always been you, even if I didn't know it. You have always been mine. Let me be yours."

Nadine's shoulders rise on a deep breath, her lips parting on her exhale. Yet she doesn't answer for a long time. Kicking me in the gut. "I don't know, Camden. I need time to think."

I place my head on her lap, taking a few breaths, letting a tendril of hope weave its way around my ribs like her fingers do when she combs them through my hair. She's not pushing me away. It's not *no*.

We stay like that for a while, me kneeling on the floor with my hands wrapped around her backside and my cheek against her knee as her fingers drag through my hair. Pure bliss.

And if this was ever all she offered me, I might be satisfied.

"I made plans for us for Thanksgiving. Erik is going to host," she tells me eventually, and I bite back a smile. If she's making plans for *us*, that's got to be a good thing. "Since you're playing on Thursday, we'll eat on Friday. Most of my family will be there. I thought it would be nice for you and Paisley to come."

She doesn't need to spell it out. We're orphans now. My sister and I don't have anywhere to go for the holidays, and I appreciate Nadine taking the reins on this since I'd been avoiding it. Figuring I'd order food from somewhere for Paisley, if she wanted.

The shine has all but faded on the idea of holidays. What is the point of celebrating anything if our parents aren't here for them?

I lift my head and slowly reach my hand between us so she has time to stop me if she wants. She doesn't, so I curl it around her neck, guiding her toward me for a kiss that she barely returns. A mere graze of her lips against mine.

"Take all the time you need." I tuck loose strands of her hair behind her ears. "I won't push because I want you to be sure I'm not the guy I used to be. I'm different, and I want to be different for you."

She nods, and I press one last kiss to her forehead before standing and stepping away from her, leaving her with one last warning. "But as soon as you give me the word, I'll be all in. There is no one else for me. You're my endgame."

Then I turn and give her the time she's asked for.

But the Thanksgiving game was a disaster from the start. We were down by two touchdowns at halftime, and I couldn't seem to focus on anything except the fact that Nadine still hadn't given me an answer. It's been almost a week since our talk, and I've been on my best behavior, giving her the space she asked for. But as each day passed without a word from her, my frustration grew.

To make matters worse, I realized halfway through the third quarter that the bracelet Paisley had made me was missing from my wrist. I cursed under my breath, scanning the sidelines for any sign of it. It was a small thing, a simple braided string, but it meant the world to me. A reminder of the bond I shared with my sister and the new life we were building together.

It was gone. Like our chances of winning this game. We fought hard in the fourth quarter, but it wasn't enough. The final score was 24-17, a crushing defeat by Chicago on our home turf.

I stalk off the field, ignoring the reporters clamoring for a quote. All I want is to go home, take a hot shower, and forget this day ever happened. Yet when I arrive at the penthouse, I find a surprise waiting for me on the kitchen counter.

There, next to the Founders cookie jar that had appeared a few weeks ago for Paisley's favorite double stuffed Oreos, is my missing bracelet and an accompanying note in Nadine's handwriting. *Found this. Thought you might want it back.*

But she's nowhere in sight. I've become used to her waiting up for me, and disappointment washes over me even as I tie the bracelet back on my wrist. I snag a sports drink from the fridge and gulp it down, staring at my reflection in the glass doors directly across from me as I contemplate checking in on her. It's after midnight, and while today is just another day for me, other people like to think about what they're grateful for.

I wonder what River's grateful for. If she thanks God every night for me, like I do her. That she was made exactly, perfectly, the way she is. Whip-smart brain, even smarter mouth, and a gentle, loving heart. One that is big enough to care for a former bad-boy athlete and his little sister.

After tossing the empty bottle in the recycling bin, I head over to Rocky and Balboa to offer them their nightly pets then force myself to my room.

I cannot go back on my word.

I told her to take all the time she needs. Even if it kills me.

Even if I only want to go into her room to tuck her in and kiss her head.

I have to prove that she can trust me. She can believe me when I make a promise. When I eventually tell her that I love her.

CHAPTER 23
NADINE

ERIK AND MOLLY'S household is pure chaos. Laughter and music and so many people they put out folding chairs for more seats. The scents of roasted turkey, garlic mashed potatoes, and my father's famous empanadillas and coquito float from the kitchen. Molly isn't much of a cook, nor was anyone interested in standing in front of the stove for hours on end to feed over a dozen people, so she had our meal catered, but Dad couldn't *not* bring the food and drink he'd grown up on to show off to the newbies. He hands out the little turnovers and passes around glasses of what is essentially Puerto Rican eggnog, waiting patiently for their review. Most everyone usually enjoys them, but for those who don't, they tend to pretend to keep him happy.

Between the Riveras—our parents and all five of us kids congregating together, as well as Felix's girlfriend—Molly's family—including her parents and brother—and Camden and Paisley, it's a nice time. We eat and laugh and eat some more.

I watch Paisley have fun, loving that she can easily communicate with everyone because they all know ASL, and my mom takes an immediate liking to her. No one will ever be able to replace her parents, but Paisley stays by my mom's side most of the day.

At some point, my gaze drifts across the room to where Camden stands, cradling Kai with an unexpected tenderness. The sight of this giant man, cooing at my nephew, nearly brings me to my knees, and I think back to last week when he crawled to me, literally on his knees, all but begging me to give him a chance. Give us a chance.

As promised, he has not pushed me about our conversation. He's given me space to process my feelings and think about what I want. We have both gone through enormous changes this year, and I'm not someone who is able to make decisions on a whim.

I have to think and overthink. Make sure I've considered every angle and have processed every possible outcome. It's not the best way to cope with anxiety, but it's simply what I need to do to feel comfortable.

And watching him with Kai cements what I know to be true —he is who I want. He may not be perfect and has done things that I don't agree with, but he's changed. He said he wants to be better for me, and I believe him.

I've witnessed it.

I know his heart.

I know that, deep down, he is a man who wants a family. He wants his sister to be safe and happy, and he's trying so hard to show the world that nothing he's been through has broken him, I'm afraid he will crack.

If he'll allow me, I'd like to be his soft place to land. I'd like to be the person who holds him together when he needs it. Show him he can break and still be loved.

He lifts his gaze as if he knows I'm staring at him. There is a softness to his dark eyes, a vulnerability he doesn't let anyone else but me see. The raw and unguarded part of him.

For a moment, the room falls away. Everything goes silent, and it's only the two of us. Acknowledging the shift that has taken place. It might as well be the tectonic plates moving for how my heart leaps out of my chest.

His lips curve into a small, private smile, and I feel my neck and cheeks heat, a whole silent conversation floating between us.

That I'm ready.

And he's all in.

At his single dip of his chin, I know we'll be leaving soon.

With Erik and Molly hosting everyone, and most of my family and Molly's staying over, I will be sleeping at Camden's tonight so they have an extra bedroom to use for whoever needs it. And it could not have worked out better, according to the way Camden carefully sets Kai on his play mat and makes his way to me, his tongue sweeping over his bottom lip before his top teeth drag along it.

With a scruffy jaw and thick cream sweater pushed up to his elbows, he's killing me. Death by lust suffocation. I barely manage an inhale when he asks, "You almost ready to go?" When I nod, his answering grin is feral. "Me too."

Though it takes another hour to get through all of the good-byes as if we won't see each other tomorrow, and by the time I'm finally seated in the front seat of Camden's car, I'm buzzing with nervous energy. Paisley passes out almost immediately in the back seat, her cell phone held loosely in her hand, head tipped backward, mouth open. I swear the girl could fall asleep anywhere, at any time.

But up front, I'm wide awake. My skin electric when Camden moves his hand from the gear shift to my thigh, squeezing with a rumbled, "I love this."

He tugs at my plaid wool skirt that comes to my knees but is hitched up because of his efforts, rubbing his palm up and down my leg, from mid-thigh to my knee, where the top of my boots hit. "Like a naughty schoolgirl."

I adjust my position, spreading my legs a bit wider, and even though he keeps his attention on the road, his fingers inch up higher, closer to the sensitive place between them. I keep my voice as steady as possible when I tell him, "You have a teacher look about you today. Just add in your glasses."

With his perfectly tailored brown pants and cable-knit sweater, he could pass for old money or an academic. I don't mind either one, but he clearly has a preference.

"You role-play?" he asks, and my pulse accelerates. "I can keep you after class for detention and teach you some things."

I swallow thickly. "Not particularly interested in that fantasy."

"No?" His fingers tighten to a bruising grip. "What are your fantasies?"

I check over my shoulder to make sure Paisley is still asleep before answering. "I'm not sure it's all that exciting."

"Tell me."

I tug at the collar of my shirt, suddenly shy.

"What?" He squeezes my leg even harder.

"I'm asleep, and you…" I clear my throat as he shifts, and I understand his need to move. I feel it too. The need to crawl out of my skin. Only to make a home under his.

"Tell me, honey." Desperation drips from the endearment. Like his life depends on it.

"Lately, I've been fantasizing that you come home and find me asleep. You wake me up by sliding inside me, and by the time I open my eyes, you're already almost there."

"Fuck me." He groans and removes his hand from my leg to readjust himself. "You know how many times I've wanted to go into your room? How many times I've thought about sneaking under your covers? And you've been fantasizing about *that* the whole time?" He grunts. "I'm dying here."

I might laugh if I weren't close to expiring myself.

Merely admitting that has turned my nipples to hard points, and I can feel my heartbeat pulsing between my legs.

"I think about using you however I want," he confesses, driving with his left hand on the wheel, his other over his apparent erection. "You never say no to me. Whenever I want to fuck you, no matter where or when, you never say no."

I inhale sharply, imagining it. Being bent over the kitchen

counter as soon as he walks in. Pushing me to my knees in the shower. Stripping me down on the terrace at night, sinking into me as the city lights twinkle around us.

I find myself nodding, grating out an "Okay," and he blows out an audible breath.

The rest of the ride is silent, save for the quiet music or the hum of the engine. By the time he parks the car in the garage, I'm hot and sweaty. In the elevator, I fidget with my hair, trying to cool off my neck while Paisley leans into her brother's side, yawning. Upstairs, she shuffles off to her room, and as soon as her door closes, Camden takes my hand in his, practically running with me down the hall to his bedroom.

I've seen it before, with the glass wall and neutral tones, but I've never stood here in the middle of the room while he's circled me. His eyes are almost black as he drags his fingertips over me, blazing a trail in their wake. When he finally stops behind me, his mouth is hot on my neck, and I am on fire.

Needy and overheated. My clothes are itchy and heavy, and I help him to undo the buttons of my blouse, peel my skirt down over my hips until I'm left in only my bra and underwear. Then he spins us to the mirror so I can watch in the reflection as he learns the topography of my body. His hands cup my breasts. They're small, and I might be self-conscious about them if not for the way he murmurs words about how he can't wait to kiss them. Then he smooths his palms over my stomach to my hips that are so much wider than the rest of me, down to my dimpled outer thighs. He tells me how much he loves my legs, how he often finds himself staring at my ass. "You are perfect. Exactly the way you are."

So, no, I don't care I'm short and pear-shaped, that my breasts are nothing to write home about, or that I have a PMS breakout on my chin, because Camden can't get enough of me.

"You're so beautiful," he rasps against my ear, a moment before nibbling on it. "And you're mine."

I nod, turning in his hold to work on his belt. "*You* are *mine*."

He curves his hands around my jaw, smiling into a kiss. "I'm yours."

He sweeps his tongue into my mouth, not bothering to help me with his zipper or pants, and I let out a small, frustrated growl, which earns a laugh.

"A little help," I say, and he steps away only long enough to whip off his sweater and step out of his pants. Then he's back on me again, mouth seeking, hands roaming.

Mine are too, fingertips tracing over the hard muscles on either side of his spine and down his sides. When I trail over the ripples of his stomach, he sucks in a breath like it tickles, so I do it again, and he pulls on my lip with his teeth in reprimand. Then he unclasps my bra so it falls off and continues on to my underwear, soft pink with lace on the sides, making a sound of approval.

He drops to the floor, but even on his knees, his head is level with my chest. As his hands work on removing my panties, he sucks on both of my nipples, drawing them to almost painful points. But it's his hum of satisfaction that sends a wave of electrical current to my clit. It throbs, and I rub my thighs together for some relief, but he catches them in his hands, stopping me. "I'll take care of you. Spread wider, honey. I got you."

The first caress of his fingers over me is a promise. The second, though, comes with a threat. "Keep them wide."

"Or what?"

"Or we skip me being nice to this pussy, and I get right to pounding you. Using you how I want."

"Is that how they teach you to talk to girls back in the cornfields?"

He arches his brow. "River."

I arch my own. "Camden."

"You're about to learn how this corn-fed boy can fuck."

"I'm looking for—oh!" I gasp when he invades me with two thick fingers. Given no warning, it's a shock, but not unpleasant. He laves my nipple with his tongue as he slides his digits in and out of me, coating them with my desire, using it to moisten my clit, and then his thumb is there, pressing and circling, as he finds the spot inside me with his index and middle fingers.

"Oh god," I moan, my legs unsteady, and he has to wrap an arm around my waist to keep me upright. Needing something to hold on to, I let my head and shoulders curl, my fingers digging into his hair, cradling him to me, a buoy in the ocean.

Each twist of his fingers and lick of his tongue sends me further out into the depths, waves of pleasure washing over me until my skin pricks with goose bumps and stars fill my vision.

"I'm gonna… I'm gonna…"

"Mm-hmm. Mm-hmm." He murmurs around one of my nipples as if he knows, urging me on. I crash, my orgasm causing my knees to give out, but he's there to catch me.

Although I'm barely allowed more than a few breaths before he bends, weaving his arms between my thighs and around to my back, creating a sort of seat for me. Because then he lowers his mouth to me for one experimental lick. I shudder in his hold, and he chuckles, a puff of his warm breath hitting my already oversensitized flesh. "Yeah, I'm gonna love this the most."

Then he lifts me up, standing with me on his shoulders, his head between my legs, and I shriek, yanking at his hair in terror. He moves like it's nothing. As if I am no more than a feather as he walks to the bed and sets me on the mattress, all the while his mouth never leaving me.

And I've never been so turned on in my life.

"That was really hot," I say to the ceiling, and I feel his grin against the curve of my hip.

"Impressed?'

"Yes, actually." I giggle drunkenly, and he tightens his hold on me, keeping my legs spread wide, his hands clamped on my waist, putting me on full display.

He kisses the very center of me tenderly, as he'd kiss my lips. Then he shocks me. "I don't do this often, so I need all the points I can get."

I lift my head to meet his eyes over the length of my bare torso. "What do you mean, you don't do this often?"

"I can't remember the last time I went down on a woman."

I let my jaw hang open in surprise, and he pulls me down the bed an inch, making himself comfortable on the floor as he explains, "Sex has been transactional for me, and I was almost always on the receiving end. I didn't have to do it. I didn't want to, but…" His gaze drifts down to the most intimate part of me, and he inhales deeply. "If it's okay with you, I'm going to stay right here for a while."

"Yeah." I'm like a bobblehead. "S'okay with me."

"Good," he whispers against my clit, and I reflexively jump a little. He makes a sound of interest and then does it again. And again. Alternating between blowing a stream of air and licking it, learning how to make me moan and tense and dig my fingers into his hair. He does indeed stay there for a long time, simply playing. He finds out what I like, what *he* likes, and how to make me cry out. I laugh when he bites at my inner thigh and then lifts my hips for a better angle. He flicks his tongue, and I hiss. Suctions hard, and I jolt. He hums against me, and I feel it everywhere. Even in my toes.

When he's finally done exploring and learning, I'm practically liquid. Only then does he toss my legs over his shoulders and focus solely on my clit. He sucks on it, humming once again. Telling me without his words that he knows I'm about to orgasm, letting me know that when I fall, he'll be right there, waiting.

"Mm-hmm. Mm-hmm."

I'm not sure why I find the soft yet demanding sound so hot, and I come with nonsense words rolling off my tongue, spine arching off the bed. When I finally settle with a punch-drunk grin on my face, Camden leans up, his mouth shining wet. "Yeah, fucking love that."

"I fucking love you."

CHAPTER 24
CAMDEN

"YOU *WHAT?*" I fly up the bed, holding myself over Nadine, hands on either side of her head on the mattress. A lopsided smile graces her face, her eyes heavy lidded. She's never been more beautiful, even if she's out of it.

She blinks, dazed. "Hm?"

"What did you just say?"

"When?"

"Now." I sigh, dropping my chin toward my chest. "I said I fucking loved doing that, and you said…?"

She strokes her hands over the back of my head, urging me to lift it, and when I do, I find her a little more clear-eyed, but confused, her brows furrowed. "I don't know what you're talking about."

I skate my tongue over my lips in frustration because I *know* what I heard, but her flavor is distracting, and I lower myself, leaving openmouthed kisses along her collarbone. I curve my hand around the outside of her breast, brushing my thumbs over her light brown nipples. "I heard you say something," I tell her, then scrape my teeth over her skin, peppering kisses along the insides of her breasts. She has a red birthmark over one of her top ribs on the left side, and I kiss that too. "I want to hear it again. Make sure I didn't imagine it."

"I have no idea what you're talking about," she repeats, her back bowing, voice airy. "Really, I—ooh, Cam, please."

I shake my head, nuzzling into her thigh, even as I continue to lazily ease my fingers in and out of her. "No, we need to talk."

"I can't. Not when you're—oh fuck, please. *Please.*"

We do need to talk, but when she tunnels her fingers into my hair and nudges my head, positioning it where she wants it, over her clit, who am I to deny her? Especially after she said she loves me.

"One more," I concede, crooking my fingers so she inhales sharply, muscles contracting. "But then I want to hear it."

"Okay, okay, okay." She wraps her right leg around my head, and I chuckle against her pussy. Which only makes her whimper.

I didn't know eating a girl out could be so fun, but I really do love it. I want to hear all her sounds, see how many times I can make her beg and scratch her fingernails over my scalp. I especially enjoy how she coils tight, contorting into funny shapes, like she cannot physically stand the pleasure. Her little body can't take it all.

But she does.

And she will.

She gives me one more orgasm, pushing up on one hand, as if she might fly from the bed as her inner walls flutter and spasm, and I lap it up, tongue licking between her slit as I gently drag my fingers out of her, only to shove them beneath the elastic of my underwear to grip my cock. Give it *something,* so I can hold off a little while longer.

By the time I'm sitting on my knees, she appears to have caught her breath, though her skin is flushed and glistening with a fine sheen of sweat, limbs limp and completely wrung out. I'm inordinately proud of myself for making her that way.

I crawl up the bed to stretch out next to her, leaning on my left elbow to stare down at her. "River." I wait impatiently for her eyes to open. "We have to talk."

"I can't right now."

If I weren't anxious about finally declaring my feelings, I might find her sex-addled mumbling cute. "Nadine."

She slowly turns to look at me, back to her bratty self. "Don't use that tone with me."

"You weren't listening."

"I was listening fine. I just can't talk."

I roll my eyes. "You were talking fine before when you said you loved me."

She snorts dubiously. "What?"

"You said you loved me. Actually, to be accurate, you said 'I fucking love you.'"

She rears back deliberately, taking me in, eyes drifting back and forth between my own. "You're lying."

I huff. "No."

"I didn't… I…" When I nod seriously, she trails off, her throat dipping on a swallow. "I did?"

"You did, and while I understand you were in a state of sex-fogged euphoria from my pussy-eating skills, I need to know if it was real or not."

Her lips part, jaw working, but she stays silent. Seconds turn into a minute. Turns into a whole goddamn year.

And my rapidly beating heart slows to a crawl, until my lungs burn with the effort it takes to breathe. "It's fine. I get it. You—"

"I love you," she says, cutting me off. "I do. I love you, Camden."

Then I'm the silent one, and she smiles at my gaping.

"Are you that surprised? I thought this might have been a ploy for your arrogant ass to make me be the one who says it first."

No. Definitely not a ploy.

"More like reassurance," I finally say, once my organs and

brain are back to working order. I duck down, tucking my face against her throat. "Because I love you. I love you, River." I wrap my arms around her and roll so I can squeeze her tight to me. Never let her go.

She wriggles, and I permit her to sit up. It's better this way. Because I can look into her eyes, watch her lips form the words when she says, "I know your heart, and I'll take care of it."

She places her palms against my chest, and my nose stings with emotion. This woman. With a heart so big, she's promising to take care of *mine*.

I am undeserving.

Yet I want to be.

"I love you." I thread my fingers into her hair, pulling her to me, kissing her mouth. Speaking my vow against her lips. "You won't regret me."

She melts, her mouth pliant, spine soft, muscles loose. I glide my hands over her, from her head, down her shoulders, along her sides, to her ass and back, the emotion I'd spilled all over my bed fading as my baser instincts take over.

The demand to fuck and rut, to claim the woman I love. Mark her as mine in as many ways as possible. "You ready, honey?"

She nods. "Make love to me."

I smile into a kiss. "Yeah, I'll do that. And then I'll fuck you so hard you'll feel it tomorrow."

She moans her agreement, and I nudge her aside so I can reach into the nightstand drawer for a condom and lube. "Are you on birth control?"

"Since I was fourteen. I have really bad period cramps otherwise."

I stand to kick off my boxer briefs, about to rip open the condom, but Nadine swings her legs over the side of the bed, sitting right in front of me. I hold still as her attention purposefully pours over me, slowing at spots, like my pecs, my hands holding the foil packet, and then landing on my cock, straining out toward her. She reaches out as if to touch me and then pauses, tipping her head back, and it does something to me to see her in this position. Almost like she's submitting to me.

Obviously she is not, and I don't want her to, but I like the idea. I can physically overpower her, but she overpowers me in every other way. I may be much bigger than her and don't plan on being especially gentle sometimes, but she can take me down with a mere word or look.

Like the one she wears now. Wide blue eyes, puffy lips, and an innocent question. "Can I put it on?"

"You can do whatever you want." I hand her the condom. "I might want to use you, but you own me. I'm yours, body and soul."

She doesn't reply, though she does offer me a beguiling smile a moment before she leans forward to put her mouth on me, and the half gasp, half squeak that comes out of me is the unmanliest sound I've ever made. But having her twist her hand around the base while she sucks on the tip is what I've been fantasizing about for literal years. I may not have admitted it to even myself, yet when I needed to get off and had to use my own imagination, it was a head of dark hair I saw. A smart mouth finally silenced because it was full of me.

And it is so good.

So fucking good I'm going to come before I've even had the chance to feel the heaven between her legs.

"Riv, stop, stop." I nudge her away, and she laughs at me, rightly understanding why.

"Quick off the trigger, huh?"

I snatch the condom from between her fingers, have it open and on in seconds, stepping between her legs, looming over her until she lies back on the bed. She smirks at me like she really showed me something. "You better watch how you speak to me when I can make you come in minutes. Make you a whimpering, wet mess."

"You don't scare me," she says with that attitude I love, and I grab the small bottle of lube to squeeze out a dollop, smothering it all over her pussy, making even the trimmed curls above wet before pushing three fingers into her, earning a sharp inhale.

"Thought so." I bend to kiss her throat as I immediately find the swollen spot inside her. "Not so tough anymore."

She squeezes her eyes shut, fingers mindlessly roaming over the bed, searching for an anchor, but when she can't find one, she hooks them around my neck. "Fuck me."

I pump faster. "What did you say?"

"Fuck me," she pants.

"What?"

"Fuck me!" She comes with a cry, and before she can come down, I wrap my hands around her waist, moving her up the mattress to make room for me. I thrust inside her in one go, and my vision blurs for a moment with the rush of pleasure.

But once the immediate spark of ecstasy wanes to a more manageable one, I grit my teeth and balance my weight between my left hand by her shoulder and my knees spread wider, her legs open with her right one thrown against my chest and shoulder. And I fuck her.

I fuck her so hard, the slaps echo around us, and she can't do anything except take it. She moans, face pinching, fingernails digging into my triceps. Watching her reaction, feeling her pussy clench around me, hearing her mindless sounds, it all makes my blood rush in my ears. The familiar burn of an orgasm comes on quicker and stronger than ever before in my life, but I knew this was what it would be like. The first time experiencing it would make me come hard and fast.

Yes, Nadine Rivera makes me quick off the trigger.

But I don't think she cares. Especially when I slip my fingers down to where we're connected and press the bud of her clit so that she falls over the edge one last time, and I'm almost too late in pulling out of her, the euphoria too big to find my way through, but I do.

I pull out of her and rip off the condom in time to aim the line of my orgasm onto her. Ropes of my come land on her stomach, pussy, and thighs, but I keep stroking my flagging erection until I'm empty. Until every last drop lands on her pretty, golden tanned skin.

I stare in satisfaction, hoping to burn the image of her stretched out below me and wearing my come into my brain. When she blinks her eyes open a few moments later, she repositions her head to see what I've done then quirks an eyebrow at me in question.

"I'm going to get tested by the team doctor. I want you to get tested too, so next time, we don't need a condom."

She doesn't react. Only focuses her gaze on where I drag my fingertip through the lines on her and draw random shapes with it. Like I'm finger-painting. "I want all of this inside you," I admit, making a heart over her belly button before signing my name just above her pubic bone, and then rubbing it all over the insides of her thighs. "I want all of this dripping out of you. I want to come so deep inside you that—"

I barely stop myself from confessing my most depraved fantasy—that I want to impregnate her. That I want to make her mine in every way, including putting my baby in her.

But I think we've had enough confessions for the night and rein it in. "I want you not only to be sore the next day, but I want to be able to use my come as lube. I want to return home from a game and fuck you while you're wearing my jersey, and then I want to fuck you the next morning while you're still sleeping, but you'll be so wet and warm, I'll slide right in. I want to come inside you. Let me come inside you."

She studies me for a moment, and I'm worried it's too much, but then she curls her dainty fingers around my wrist and lifts my hand, sticky with my orgasm, to bring it to her mouth, where she sucks on my fingers.

"You are filthy, aren't you?" I murmur, feeling my dick stir to life again, and she sends me a sardonic look.

"*Me?*" she says around my ring finger. "You're the one with a breeding kink."

I automatically glance down to her flat stomach, and she laughs, setting my hand over it, my fingers spanning across her middle and up to her ribs. "Yes, I will get tested, so we don't have to use a condom. Yes, I want you to come inside me. Yes, I eventually want children, but that's a long way off."

"But for now, we can pretend?" I hedge, and she nods.

"Practice makes perfect." She tows me down to her, nipping at my bottom lip. "But the first thing we need to decide before you put a baby in me is what we do about us."

"About us?"

"Your life is public, and I'm not saying I want to hide our relationship, but I'd like to stay out of the public eye as much as possible. I'm not going to give up my career for you, no offense."

I chuckle against her throat. "None taken."

"I have things I want to accomplish as Nadine Rivera that have nothing to do with being Camden Long's girlfriend. I know what it's like. I know how Molly struggles with balancing her life with Erik's, and I don't want that for myself."

"I get it," I tell her, cradling her head between my hands, holding myself over her in a plank on my elbows. "But Molly's work is on social media. She's posting every day and working with brands and doing that whole influencer thing. You can do whatever you want, stay in the shadows or be out in the spotlight, I don't care. Only that you're with me."

She considers me seriously, nodding after a minute. "Okay."

"But while we're on the subject, I do think we should keep us on the down-low for now. I'm going to need to talk to Erik, and I don't want to do it while we're in season."

She doesn't seem to like that idea.

"You're his sister, and I think he's going to need to be eased into the idea of us being together."

"Why do people keep saying stuff like that? Emmaline said the same thing. That he'll flip when he finds out."

I tilt my head in question. "Your sister knows about us?"

"No. Well, she had an idea. When I stayed with her in New

York, she figured something was happening between us and basically said Erik would lose it. Why? It's not like he's an unreasonable guy."

"No, but you're his sister, his favorite sibling, and even though I'm his best friend, he's seen me at my worst, and he said he would never want me to date one of his sisters."

"When?"

I shrug my shoulder, settling my lower half in the pocket of her open legs, reflexively pushing her thighs wider with mine. "For some social media thing. They asked us which teammate we wouldn't want dating our sister, and he said me."

"That's for social media, though. He didn't really mean it," she says, though she's lost some of her vigor. Like she can understand Erik's point.

I can understand Erik's point.

I was a dick. I made bad decisions, but I am going to try my best to show everyone, including my best friend, why I deserve a chance with Nadine.

"Either way…" I place kisses along her breastbone. "I want to wait until after the season to tell your brother."

"What about your sister?" she asks, playing with the hair at the nape of my neck. "Because I'm pretty sure she suspects."

"I'll talk to her. Explain the situation because I'm not going to keep my hands to myself in my own home."

"Can I sleep in your bed?"

I lift my head, surprised she'd even ask. "You better."

She shimmies her shoulders, getting more comfortable, almost as if she plans on sleeping in my bed *now*.

But that's not happening.

Not for a long while.

"Up," I tell her, tugging on her hand. "On all fours. I have a few more condoms we can use tonight."

CHAPTER 25
CAMDEN

AFTER THE THANKSGIVING GAME, we had a few days off before we were back to our regularly scheduled program with a Sunday game, and since it's a light day before travel, I scheduled a cupping session to help relieve the tension in my back after our walk-through on the field. I'm pulling my T-shirt over my head as I head down the hall when Malcolm finds me. He claps me on the shoulder. "How are you?"

"Didn't expect to see you today."

He fixes his tie. "I'm making the rounds."

"Checking up on all your babysitting duties."

"Unfortunately, but not for you," he says, then gestures around us. "You've done well the past few months."

I scoff. "Wasn't it you warning me to think with my head and not my dick just a few days ago?"

He shrugs. "Every man needs a reminder every once in a while, but you handled that situation very well."

He means I kept my mouth shut about Valerie's online revenge post and let the scandal-in-the-making fade into nothing.

"I'm proud of you for turning it all around," Malcolm says, and I loop my arm over his shoulders, jostling him.

"Does that mean I'm off your naughty list?"

"As long as you don't mess up again."

"But you'll miss me. I know you will."

He shakes his head. "One of these days, I'll have all of you miscreants off my list, and I'll finally be able to go on vacation without receiving a phone call that one of you has driven off a cliff or impregnated Miss America."

I point my index finger in the air. "I'd like to note, I've done neither of those things."

"Thank the Lord. Just cool it on the racing and keep it in your pants, and it will stay that way."

"I'll try my best." I hold out my hand for Malcolm to shake, feeling like I've been let out of detention early. While I've lost my desire to race, I've put all of my energy into Nadine. So, no, I won't be keeping it in my pants.

Especially when I arrive home to find her leaning over the kitchen counter, peeling a mandarin orange. She must've been at the gym—working out with her female personal trainer—because she's in one of her matching spandex outfits, the fine baby hairs stuck to her temples and neck with sweat.

She smiles my way. "Didn't expect you home so early."

I don't bother even greeting her, simply cross the room in three strides, capturing her in my arms, loving the way she laughs into a moan when I tug on her ponytail, angling her head back so I can kiss and suck on her throat. "You smell so good."

"I smell terrible." She attempts to push me away with her ass, but all she does is grind it against my swiftly growing cock.

"No." I lick at her skin and use my other hand to grip her chin, slanting her mouth to mine. "You smell like sweat and oranges." I kiss her, making sure she knows I love her scent, her flavor, gliding my tongue along hers then across her bottom lip, nibbling on it. "You taste like it too."

Intoxicating.

In the last few days, we've done nothing but have sex any time she's at my place. She went back to her brother's house to spend more time with her family after we got together and has slept there every night since, though she'll be back in my bed this weekend, even if I won't be there. Simply knowing she's there will make me feel better, though.

I've kept myself buried inside her whenever possible, which has not been all that often. Between my practices and Paisley's schedule, it's an hour or so total before Nadine has to go back to Erik's and pretend like we're not together. I had a conversation with my sister, so she knows Nadine and I are in a relationship, but that she is the only one to know and she needs to keep it a secret. She was elated to find out that she was right because she "knew we were in love the whole time."

When I told her, she danced around and clapped, signing so fast, I had to have her repeat it three times. Apologizing for thinking I was Joey Donner, asking to be the maid of honor at our future wedding, and promising to keep our relationship a secret for now.

So while Nadine and I try to keep our hands off each other in front of my fifteen-year-old sister, when she's otherwise occupied, my hands are on my girlfriend.

And she has yet to say no to me. Like I fantasized.

"Bend over," I order. "Farther."

Nadine forgets about her orange and curls her hands around the edge of the marble, angling her hips so far back, her chest almost touches the counter, and I drag her bike shorts down her legs, finding her bare underneath.

"Filthy fucking girl." I roam my hands over the globes of her ass and between them. "You knew I was going to be doing this and wanted to be ready, huh?"

She glances over her shoulder, trying on an attitude. "Maybe I don't like wearing underwear when I work out."

I smack her thigh. "Or maybe you wanted me to know, drive me wild thinking about it later."

I don't let her answer because I bend, swiping my tongue over her slit, stretching her cheeks with my hands, giving me room to tease her all over. She wiggles her hips, groaning softly when I lap at her clit, trying to make her as wet as possible since I don't have any lube close and I'm too impatient to give her the few orgasms she deserves right now. I just need to be inside her.

Keeping one hand on her hip, I put her into position, while I work on shoving my sweats and underwear down enough to free my length. We've both been tested and cleared, so we haven't used a condom since that first night together, and I'm able to thrust inside with nothing between us.

As always, the first grip of her tight heat is painfully good, and I hiss as I find my vision and footing before inching out and in a few times. But my girl's as impatient as I am today, arching her spine and pushing against me. So I give her what we both want and fuck her hard and fast.

"Yes, Camden," she pants out, and I love my name on her lips anytime, but especially when her head is thrown back and her fingers are scrabbling for purchase.

With such a big height difference between us, I'm always hunching over and bending my knees, but I'm so focused on being inside her that I wrap my hands around her hinged hips and lift her up, so her toes no longer touch the floor. She squeals in surprise before it melts into a moan when I grit out, "I got you. I got you."

And I do.

I won't let her go. I won't hurt her.

I only want to love her.

As long and as often as possible.

Whether it's with a hug or earning a playful eye roll or a slow, drawn-out orgasm, I want to give her everything she needs to keep her happy.

In the few short days I've been able to indulge in all of my fantasies—chaste and innocent or completely depraved—I've come to know her well. Like the fact that her love language is quality time and that she doesn't have a favorite holiday and would live somewhere with warm weather year-round. She used to love playing Barbies as a kid because she would set them all up as her students so she could teach them, and she still keeps in touch with her college friends and former colleagues from her school. She eventually wants two or three kids and would like a refrigerator that makes crushed ice because it's her favorite kind. I didn't know people could have favorite kinds of ice, but I do know what Nadine Rivera looks and sounds like when she orgasms, so I know she's close now.

I am too. I'm always close when I'm inside her, continually on the edge, only barely holding out because I go over my stats in my head, trying my best to ignore her whimpers that rocket my adrenaline.

"Get there, Riv," I grunt, on my way to pleading, and set her feet on the floor, so I can loop my arm around her, circling her clit with my fingers, finally sending her soaring.

She takes me with her, inner muscles clamping around me as she chants *yes, yes, yes* quietly. I keep pumping into her, making a mess of us, watching as my come leaks out of her, smearing on her thighs.

"So hot," I rasp, and she eventually lifts her head from the counter to meet my gaze over her shoulder.

"Filthy fucking boy."

I grunt a chuckle. "Damn right. But I'll clean you up." I carefully pull out of her and hike up my sweats. Then I sweep her into my arms, carrying her like a bride to the bathroom. "Take a bath with me."

"Well, if you insist," she says like she's put out.

I set her down on the counter of the sink to run the water, adding some oil. I strip first, turning away from her to check the temperature, and that's when I feel her behind me, hands touching the circular bruises on my back. "Tender?"

When I shake my head, she kisses one before removing her clothing. I watch her pick up her pile of clothes and mine to put in the laundry bin, hidden in the closet, unafraid of being naked in front of me and behaving as if this is her house too.

I want it to be.

Strolling about in nothing but her birthday suit, grabbing new clean towels, and helping herself to stepping inside the tub. When she realizes I've been leering at her like an idiot, she raises her brows. "What?"

"Nothing. I just love you, is all."

Her smile is a direct hit on my heart, and she sits, leaning forward to make room for me behind her in the bath. When I bought this place, I made sure that the tub would be big enough for me to soak in, but I'm eternally grateful Past Me chose the biggest one, large enough for Future Me and Nadine to comfortably relax in. I prop my arms up on the sides, and she lays her head against my pec, the water steaming around us.

"How was your day?" she asks, and I let my head roll on the rounded lip behind me.

"The usual pregame stuff, but I had a visit from Malcolm."

I've told Nadine all about my babysitter, and she snickers. "What did he have to say?"

"That I've been such a good boy, I'm officially off the naughty list."

She breathes an amused sound. "Must mean the higher-ups are proud of you."

I couldn't give a shit about what Debra Rosenstein or anyone else thinks about me. Only that my family is proud of me— Paisley and Nadine. Everyone else can fuck off.

"He told me to make sure I'm not racing and to keep my dick in my pants."

"You already failed that one."

"I know." I slip my hand below the water to cup her pussy. "When I have a live-in sex doll, what else am I supposed to do?"

She rears her elbow back, nailing me in the side. "Hey, ow! Riv, that hurt."

She clucks her tongue. "Did not. You're made of rock."

"Yeah, I know." I rub my dick against her lower back to make sure she can feel exactly how hard I am.

"You are exhausting."

"As if you don't love it." I drag my tongue over the shell of her ear and smile against it when goose bumps appear on her flesh, even under the hot water.

"I can't *only* be your live-in sex doll, you know. I sent in my last application."

I squeeze her waist. "Nice. Which one?"

"St. Joe's." She proceeds to walk me through the pros and cons of each graduate program she's applied to, all of them located in Philadelphia. She explains the difference between what she can do with her master's versus her doctorate, and how she hasn't decided how far she wants to go but is leaning toward her PhD, though she's nervous about it because she fears she won't be accepted to any of them.

Which is ridiculous. She's applied to four schools, and even though she's capable enough to get into all four, she has a hard time staying positive. She struggles with her confidence, so I do my best to hype her up as she talks. Reminding her how smart she is, that she's worked hard, and it will pay off in the end.

When she's finally done word-vomiting all her worries, I gather her up closer, crisscrossing my arms around her middle, and hold her tight. "I love you and I know whatever you decide to do, you'll be amazing at it, but I hope you'll still be my live-in sex doll."

She breaks out in a giggle, and I press my face into her neck as she heaves a sigh. "You are relentless."

"But you love me."

"But I love you." She turns, offering her mouth for a kiss. "Thanks for listening to me yap."

"One of my favorite things to do."

She reaches behind me to brush her hand over the hair at the nape of my neck. "I guess we need to get moving. Have to pick up Paise soon."

I agree with a hum and retrieve the soap. We take turns washing each other, and she laughs when I tell her I want to use her shampoo and conditioner for my hair so I can smell like her. She obliges with a huge goofy grin.

It matches my own.

Then we get out, dress, and hop in my car to pick up Paisley.

Together.

CHAPTER 26
NADINE

THE FIRST TWO weeks of December, Paisley and I went a little nuts on the Christmas decorations, but she missed being at her home in Iowa for the holidays, and I wanted her to feel as "at home" as possible, so Camden's Amex got a good workout with lights and wreaths and the most obnoxious illuminated snowman we could find to set out on the terrace. Camden, the grinch, put the kibosh on a real tree, so I bought a nine-foot faux silver fir that we put in the corner by the guinea pigs, decorating it with a mix of new ornaments and ones Camden had saved from his parents' house.

I did my best not to cry when he stood on the step stool to place the star on the top before folding his big body around his sister, both of them in tears. But it was no use. Camden and Paisley cried because they're grieving, and me because the two people I love most are hurting, and I can't do anything to help.

Now, I pull out all the ingredients for a box cake from the refrigerator, having suggested we do something special to celebrate their mom's birthday. They've been quiet lately, anticipating this day, and I reminded to Erik to make sure he's checking in on Camden more than usual. Keeping his spirits up.

It's one of their parents' first birthdays not on this planet, and I'm desperate to ease the sting.

So I told them that when Camden came home tonight, we'd make a cake together and then watch a Meg Ryan rom-com because she was their mom's favorite. Both Paisley and Camden have inherited Lorraine Long's love of rom-coms, and I thought it might make them feel close to her today to do something she would love.

As soon as Camden shuffles in the door, he drops his bag and kicks off his sneakers before sinking into my open arms. He's bent over, his face in my throat, arms around my waist, as I rub my hands over his back and neck. Instead of going home to Erik's house last night, I stayed over after Camden asked me to, his eyes bloodshot.

"I don't think I'll be able to sleep tonight," he said. "Please stay. In case I can't."

I answered by kissing him, reassuring him that I wasn't going anywhere. He did end up struggling to sleep, and I lay with him in bed as he alternated between crying and telling me memories. Then early in the morning, only two hours after he'd finally fallen asleep, Paisley made her way to our room. She crawled under the covers on the other side of me, and I held her hand as she silently wept.

Now, I kiss his jaw. "How was your day?"

He mumbles something that sounds like "Fine."

"Did you talk to Pearce?" When he nods, and I urge him to lift his head, meet my gaze, I can tell practice was rough solely from the set of his brow.

"I'm just so…tired," he says after a while, and I guide his head back to my shoulder when his eyes go glassy. "I'm tired of feeling like this." He tightens his grip on my sweat shirt, the one I stole from him that fits me like a dress. "Like it'll never go away."

He sniffles twice then clears his throat and stands straight, backing away from me a step, and he looks exhausted. From lack of sleep and from the weight of his grief. I know how much he wishes he could change the last few years and how he constantly replays the final conversation he had with his parents. No matter how often I tell him, Erik tells him, the team psychologist or counselor, he hangs on to it. Thinking that his parents left this earth being ashamed of him.

It's not true. From everything Paisley has said, and from hearing all the wonderful things about the Longs, I know how they really felt about him. It's simply an unfortunate coincidence that a perfectly normal parental conversation has become Camden's nightmare.

And there is nothing I can do about it. Nothing I can do to soothe him besides tell him that I love him, his parents loved him, his sister loves him. Remind him that he's a good man, and if his parents could talk to him now, I'm sure they would say the same thing. They would be proud of how he's taken care of Paisley and showed the world that he is not the disappointment he once was.

"You hungry?" I ask, and he nods, so I direct him to sit at the eat-in counter while I heat up one of the meals his chef has prepackaged for him. This one with salmon, green beans, and pasta, and I try to keep his spirits up as he eats by talking about my day. Mindless stuff about Christmas presents I bought for Paisley and how I grounded Jelly today for chewing through one of the wires for the tree lights, which wins a laugh before Camden corrects me on his name, having yet to win the battle with Paisley and me to call the guinea pigs Rocky and Balboa instead of Jelly and Bean.

By the time he finishes eating, Paisley wanders into the kitchen, so we get to work baking. It's no big feat, but having their hands and minds busy helps, I think.

Paisley laughs when Camden smears a fingertip worth of pink icing on her cheek, and they both carefully decorate the cake with the piping bags I bought, attempting some swirls and flowers, shaking lines that read *Happy Birthday, Mom!*

When it's finally finished, I place a couple of candles on top and light them. We don't bother singing, but we do all take a minute to watch the flames flicker, and I blot my eyes when Camden takes Paisley's hand, a silent communication passing between them before they lean over to blow out the candles. They're both quiet as I cut them pieces, ushering them into the media room, where I've already cued up *When Harry Met Sally*, and we eat their mother's birthday cake while watching one of her favorite movies.

I've never cried more during a rom-com, but I've also never witnessed two people finding a bit of peace from such a profound loss.

And later, after Camden finds me in his bed after lying with Paisley until she fell asleep, he kisses his appreciation of me all over my skin. Whispers his love as he wraps his big body around me and finds his home. One I promise he'll always have with me.

Days later, I hold my cell phone to answer Camden's Face-Time call.

"Shouldn't you be asleep?" I ask, even though it's barely after nine o'clock there. I'm already in bed, the same one I've shared with him for the past few nights. Erik had texted, asking me why I haven't been home to sleep, and I told him the truth—I didn't feel like I could leave Camden and Paisley right now.

"Almost there," Camden tells me now as he sets his phone up on what's probably a dresser to strip out of his clothes. "Just got back from dinner. What did you and Paisley do today?"

"I took her to meet up with her friend at a school basketball game."

He freezes, bent in half, mid-removal of his pants. "Basketball game?"

"Yeah. I'm pretty sure your sister has a crush on one of the boys who plays on the team."

He huffs and tosses his clothes into his bag before taking his Prada toiletry kit and the cell phone into the bathroom with him.

I've made fun of him endlessly for having a designer bag for his toothbrush and paste, but my man likes fine things. Including designer bags for his soaps.

"What's his name?" Camden asks as he sets his phone—me—down on the counter, so I'm staring right at his abs.

"I'm not sure. She hasn't said anything outright, but from how she was acting, I suspect she likes him. A couple of the boys came over to chat with them after, and she went red as a tomato."

"Not sure how I feel about this." Camden proceeds to brush his teeth, his mouth filled with foam when he bends to spit in the sink and finally moves so his face is in frame, meeting my gaze. "I need a full name, address, and report card."

"You're ridiculous."

"You have access to that stuff, right?"

"I'm not going to ask the secretaries for his report card, you weirdo."

He rolls his eyes and rinses out his mouth before asking, "What good are you, then?"

"Nothing besides your live-in sex doll."

His smug smile drips with arrogance. "That's right, baby." Then he washes his face and lotions up. When I first learned of his skincare routine, I was really impressed. He takes care of himself. He'll probably look better than me when we're eighty.

I stay quiet, waiting until he finishes, taking out his contacts and putting on his glasses, and I don't mind. I like being with him, even fifteen hundred miles away. Staying on the phone with him while he gets ready for bed is as close as we can be to doing it together in person.

"I miss you," he says once he flops on the bed, lights off, save for one in the corner. Being a veteran player, and one of the top performers on the team, he's given deference for a single room, as opposed to other players who have to share.

"I miss you too," I reply with a yawn as I stick my hand

under the pillow, and he smiles, moving closer to the screen as if to inspect my surroundings.

"Are you on my side of the bed?"

"Yes. I like sleeping here because it smells like you."

He rolls, positioning the phone like we're in bed together, and hums as if he likes my answer, but he doesn't respond. Neither one of us talks for a while. Merely lying in each other's presence.

"Your brother brought up how you haven't been home all week."

"He asked me about it too."

"I was tempted to tell him," Camden says quietly, a secret.

"That I'm your live-in sex doll," I tease, but he ignores it.

"That I love you. I was so close to telling him that even if you weren't too tenderhearted to leave me and my sister alone this last week, I still want you around. Forever. I love you and want you in my house every day."

I rub at the sudden tightness in my chest, blinking away the stinging in my eyes. "I love you too."

"But I'm afraid that one of these days you're going to wake up and realize what a piece of shit I am, and I'm afraid if I talk to your brother, he'll tell me what I already know—that I don't deserve you."

"Camden, no, I—"

"The thing is, though, I don't care. I don't deserve you, but I don't care. I want you, for myself. You're mine, Nadine."

"I'm yours," I repeat. "And you do deserve me. At least, if what you say is true."

"It is." Then he backtracks with a playful quirk to his lips. "Which part?"

I give in to my own smile. "The part where you want to take care of me. When you said the other night you want to make a life with me and buy a big house with room for a couple of kids and a dog."

"I never agreed to a dog," he mutters grumpily, and I laugh.

"You deserve me if you stand by your promise to support me in my career and give me the space to be me, even when your life is so big."

"I do. I swear. These past few months, you've already given me so much, it would take me decades to repay you, and I plan on spending the rest of my life accruing interest on my debt. I look forward to it. Paying back all the love you've given me tenfold."

"Then you deserve me."

He nods, sinking his teeth into his bottom lip. Not in that sexy way of his, but in thought. After a moment, he says, "Every Christmas, my mom made homemade cinnamon rolls. I think I looked forward to those more than the presents."

I imagine Camden as a child, all long limbs and huge appetite, gorging himself on his mother's cinnamon rolls.

"I was thinking we should do that. Start a tradition…or continue it."

"I could find a recipe. I've only ever made them out of a can, but I'm sure we could do it. All of us, you and Paisley included, because I'm not going to be the only one baking."

"Agreed." He grins. "What traditions do you want?"

"I was a big fan of countdowns. Remember those construction paper chains? My mom made them for everything. Countdown to Halloween, countdown to vacation, countdown to first day of school. Whatever it was, she'd have us write down things we were looking forward to, and I always loved that."

His smile grows even bigger. "Yes. I want to do that. And game nights."

"No Monopoly."

He jerks back. "Are you serious right now? You made me fall in love with you, and *now* you're telling me you don't play Monopoly?"

"It is the absolute worst."

His mouth hangs open. "I…truly don't know who you are." He shakes his head, his outrage pulling a few giggles out of me, which makes him give it up. "I love your laugh. Talking to you. Everything. I love it all."

I burrow down into the covers, nestle against his pillow that does indeed still hold his lingering scent. "And I love you. All of you, even the parts you'd rather forget about."

He lifts his fingers to the screen, moving them as if he's touching my face on it, though I can't be sure. "I think we should hang up now, because if we don't, I'll want to stay on the phone with you, and I need to get to sleep."

"Okay." I yawn. "I'll be watching tomorrow. Play hard."

"I will."

"And then I'll be waiting for you when you come home."

"Like the sound of that." He offers me a half smile. "Gives me a reason to win. Make you proud."

We hang up then, but even if he doesn't win, I'll still be proud of him. No matter what.

Though that touchdown he scores in the third quarter pulls them ahead. And that sign he makes at the camera during his celebration? It means "river."

CHAPTER 27
CAMDEN

AFTER OUR WIN IN CHICAGO, I'm riding high, the entire team celebrating our near-perfect record this season. We're in position to carry this momentum through to clinch the division title. Made all the better knowing I have Nadine in my corner.

And in my bed.

It's almost three in the morning, and she's asleep, on my side of the bed, a small lump under the covers. I don't bother with the lights, tiptoeing to the mattress, and when my eyes adjust to the darkness, I think she's wearing my jersey. The outline of my number has a sheen, and when I reach for it, lightly pinching the fabric between my fingers, my guess is proven correct.

My already-excited cock becomes ramrod straight in my pants, and I quietly strip naked then grab the bottle of lube from the nightstand, hoping I don't wake her.

Not yet.

Because this is what I've been waiting for. What I know she's allowing me to take.

Carefully, I pull back the comforter and climb on the bed, wrapping around her body from behind. I roam my hand over her hip, realizing she's not wearing any underwear.

She really is perfect.

Permitting me to live out my fantasy.

Her fantasy.

Her breathing doesn't change as I gently skate my fingers over her, my pulse hammering in my ears. The bedroom is silent, but my heart is beating so hard, I'm not sure how it's not waking her up. If not with the sound, then how it must be banging around against her back.

She stays asleep, her inhales and exhales steady and even.

I slick the lube over the length of my erection and then rub some on her bare pussy. That makes her move, a brief tensing of her muscles, but when she doesn't wake, I lift her top leg and let my cock sink into her entrance. It's a smooth glide all the way to the hilt, and Nadine finally wakes with a sharp breath.

"Cam?" Her voice is a whisper of a scratch.

"Yeah, honey, I'm home," I say against her pulse.

She moans sleepily, arching her spine while draping her arm back and around my neck, fingers in my hair. Neither of us speaks again as I lazily pull halfway out and push back in while I kiss her ear, temple, jaw, any place I can lay claim.

"You can go back to sleep," I tell her after a minute, and I feel more than see her smile.

"Not like this, I can't."

"Maybe I won't finish. I'll just stay inside you, and then we can both sleep."

Her fingers tighten in my hair at the nape of my neck, as if she likes that idea, and I roll my hips, keeping this slow pace. There is no rush. Not when she's sleepy and warm, barely awake.

Being with her, like this, feels drugging. Being pulled under. I don't have that natural inclination to fuck her hard like usual. Simply stay like this, coiled around her, not even a centimeter of space between us, buried so deep inside her, there is no way to know where she ends and I begin.

I keep my right hand on her thigh, slipping the other under my jersey to hold her breast, doing no more than lightly squeezing it, completely uninterested in bringing this quiet joining to a quick end. I want it to go on forever.

Like a dream.

She is my dream.

But then she rocks her hips, bringing us deeper together, and I groan into her neck. "I want to go slow."

She agrees with a hum but continues to move her hips in maddening circles.

"River," I chide, dragging my teeth over her ear.

"Hm?"

"Don't play innocent."

She turns her head, lips finding mine. "I don't know what you're talking about."

She kisses away my amusement, pulling me closer, dragging me down further into the depths of pleasure with her until I can't control the rhythm anymore. I swallow her sighs, hitch her leg higher, push her toward the mattress until I'm on top of her.

"Cam," she groans, cheek against the bed, hands held out at her sides, bound by mine, our fingers intertwined, so she is completely at my mercy. "I'm so close."

I grind against her, hitting the spot that makes her mindlessly beg. It's a tight fit with me caging her in, but I snake my arm between her torso and the mattress, finding her clit with my fingers, and she hisses. "Yes, Camden. *Please*. Don't stop."

I don't. I keep that steady pace, feeling her climb higher, body tensing. Her breaths become shallow pants, her hips uselessly attempting to move, to meet my movements. But I'm too heavy and have her trapped.

"Just take it," I rasp, and a moment later, I feel her clamp down on my cock, a vise grip that almost sends me over the edge, but I hold on as she gives in to her orgasm, going completely rigid and then lifeless as she relaxes.

But I refuse to stop moving inside her, even though my balls are drawn up tight, the base of my spine tingling. I refuse to chase my climax, even though she whispers for me to come.

I hate how desperate, how needy, she makes me feel.

Because I know I'll never get enough.

Fifteen lifetimes with her wouldn't be enough. Not even fifteen thousand.

"Never want this to end," I growl, settling my weight onto my forearms, on either side of her, a shudder rolling through me. But I can't hold out much longer, her sweet sighs too much to ignore, and I let myself have a few more shallow pumps into her before giving in, against my will to never let this stop.

With her body slack under mine, I'm careful not to crush her as I lie on top of her for a moment, waiting until the last after-shocks of my orgasm dispel.

"I can't sleep like this, if that's what you're planning," she mumbles into the mattress, and I skim my hand along her side.

"So much attitude for the middle of the night."

"That's what you get for waking me up."

I turn us both to our sides, staying inside her. "You didn't seem to mind."

She snuggles into me, wrapping my arm around her waist. "I'm glad you're home."

Me too. Glad to be back with her. My home.

A minute has passed when I think she's fallen back to sleep, but she yawns and says, "You played a good game. Thanks for the shout-out in your touchdown celebration."

"I'm glad you saw it." I make myself comfortable, my thighs tucked behind hers, her ass right up against my groin, my cock still deep inside her. We'll have a mess to clean up tomorrow, but I'm too blissed out to care right now.

"So?" she asks, fixing the pillow under her head. "How was it? Reality live up to the fantasy of doing that?"

I kiss the back of her head. "Better. Because you are my fantasy, and you're real. Here with me."

"I'll always be here with you." She brings our clasped hands up to her mouth so she can lay a quick kiss on the back of mine, and the innocent gesture is so heartbreakingly sweet, my eyes and nose sting with emotion. The reflexive action is a display of how she loves me, of how easily she takes care of me, of how it's so natural, she doesn't think about it.

It's all so simple.

That in the dead of night, she's gone and stolen my heart right out of my chest.

The next morning, I shoot up in bed at the sound of screaming. My alarm blared at seven a.m. so I could wake up to take Paisley to school, but Nadine powered it off and told me to sleep. I didn't put up much of a fight. I couldn't.

Not only because I'd barely had four hours, but because when my woman wants to take care of me, I let her. If she wanted to tuck me in and kiss my forehead, I'd never stop her.

But at the sound of her being tortured, I leap out of bed and run into the living room, where I find her blurry figure standing on the couch. "What's going on?"

Without my glasses or contacts, I have to squint to see her tip her head back to laugh at me. "You're naked."

"And you're screaming."

"Because there's one of those thousand-leggers on the floor, and it scared me."

"Well, kill it," I say, stepping toward her, but she jumps from the couch onto me like a wild cat in a tree, clinging to me.

"I can't kill it. They freak me out. Anything with multiple legs." She makes a gagging sound, wrapping her arms and legs around me, so she's piggyback. "Can you kill it?"

"I can't kill anything with my dick hanging out."

"Put pants on and then kill it."

I try to shake her off, but she refuses to let go, so I heave a sigh and head back to our bedroom, where I pull on a pair of sweats and put my glasses on before brushing my teeth. All with her on my back like a sloth. Smiling cutely. Like it's a totally normal thing to do.

"You're strong," she says when I hike her up a bit higher as I shuffle back to the living room and snatch a few tissues from a box, freezing in place to see where the centipede got to, ready to crush it. I stay in a half squat, eyes on it as it scurries across the floor toward one of the windows. I pounce and squash the thing, which earns me a smacking kiss and another compliment. "Fast too."

"Maybe I'll add it to my bio: strong, fast, killer of centipedes." I tap her thigh, assuming she'll get down, but she doesn't. Instead, she rests her chin on my head.

"How long you think you can do this for? It's been about five minutes. You think ten? Twenty?"

"Pfft. Easy."

"Thirty minutes."

"Honey." I angle my head back. "You know how much I squat? Over four hundred pounds. I could go all day with you like this."

"You think too highly of yourself. I bet you couldn't even last an hour with me on your back."

I deposit the tissues and dead bug in the trash can. "Yeah? How much?"

She thinks on it for a few seconds. "Seeing as how you have all the money in this relationship. If I win, you Venmo me one thousand dollars."

"Chump change," I say, knowing it'll make her roll her eyes. Which it does, and I laugh. "And if I win?"

"You won't, but okay… If you win, you can name your prize."

I rub my hands together in my best impression of an evil villain. "Ooh. It's going to be something with sex."

"You're so predictable."

I smack the side of her ass cheek. "Maybe it'll be to gag you, so you're finally quiet."

She nips my ear. "You'd hate that."

And it's true. I would hate it. One of the things I love most about her is her smart mouth.

Although I do like the idea of stuffing it full. "A blow job."

"That's it?"

I shrug. "Yeah, but you let me come on your face."

She actually harrumphs.

"If you're afraid…"

"Fine, fine," she agrees. "But not by my eyes, you deviant."

"Agreed."

We high-five, and she sets the rules. "One hour. With me on your back. You lose if you sit down or fall down."

I'm offended. "I'm not going to fall down."

"If you say so, tough guy."

I make it exactly fifty-four minutes before I literally cannot take it anymore and fall backward onto the couch in the living room. She laughs in glee, calling me a scrawny weakling. So after I'm able to stretch out my back, I haul her over my shoulder and show her exactly how weak I am by fucking her until she screams my name.

Then I open a bank account under her name and deposit a few thousand dollars in it. Knowing it's just the start. Eventually, she'll own everything I do.

When I inform her of this a few hours later, she gives me that blow job and lets me finish on her face.

Like the deviant I am.

CHAPTER 28
NADINE

THE REST of December flies by, and soon, it's Christmas. The league rotates through teams that play on the holiday, and while the Founders aren't, they still have practice for their regularly scheduled game. I drove to Jersey with Paisley for Christmas Eve dinner with my parents and Benedict. Felix was working, Emmaline jetted off to a beach in the Caribbean with some friends, and Erik stayed home with Molly and Kai, sticking to their normal nightly routine, so it was only the five of us. But I thought it would be nice for Paisley to hang out for a bit in the house I grew up in.

Again, she and Mom were like two peas in a pod, and my parents even bought her a few gifts. The same kinds of things they buy every year for their own children: socks, soaps, and gift cards. My parents are practical gift-givers. Even as a kid, I don't remember opening a whole lot of toys, but I actually started to look forward to the new pack of colorful pens and silly socks with tacos on them.

After dinner, dessert, and some rounds of Cards Against Humanity, Paisley and I returned to the penthouse late, though Camden waited up for us. We'd left before he returned home from practice, but he greets us now in plaid pajamas with a reindeer on his long-sleeved shirt.

"New tradition," he declares as he signs then hands each of us a bag. The silent instructions clear. We are supposed to put on the matching pajamas.

Paisley shoots me a look, and I shrug. My man wants a new tradition? He's going to get a new tradition.

"It'll be fun," I sign to Paisley.

"It's pajamas."

"That match."

Camden butts in. "Yeah, and we're going to take a picture with them. Even Rocky and Balboa. Go on. Get moving."

Paisley groans but pivots on her heel to change, and I glance over to Camden, who's grinning with excitement. After so much loss, they both deserve to have joy in their lives. Whenever and wherever they can find it.

Once we're all dressed in our matching plaid, Paisley and I each take one of the guinea pigs in our arms as Camden sets up his phone. He positions us by the tree, his arms wrapped around both of us, and I decide we're going to blow it up and frame it when he shows it to me.

All of us together and smiling.

Then Paisley says she's going to watch a movie in her room, which I suspect is code for texting the boy she likes, but it gives Camden and me an excuse to bring out all the presents we hid from her. She obviously doesn't believe in Santa anymore, but Camden refused to put any presents under the tree yet, arguing that it took all the fun out of waking up to them.

Once they're all placed, we lounge on the sofa together, my head on his chest, his arm around my shoulders. "We're going to go to your brother's place tomorrow for dinner," he informs me. "We don't have any meetings, just practice, and we don't have to be there until ten. Plenty of time for cinnamon rolls and presents. But I want to give you this now."

Then he pulls a jewelry box from his pocket.

I sit up straight with a gasp.

"It's not a ring," he says immediately, as if to calm my racing heart. "Not that kind of ring, I mean."

I gingerly take the box from him as he explains, "I know you like to wear rose gold, so I had this made, but if you don't like it, I will—"

"Oh, Camden." I open the box to find a delicate bracelet with tiny diamonds along a curved cuff, almost like a river, with a chain on either side to fasten it. A matching ring accompanies it, and he turns it over so I can read the tiny inscription on the inside, *love like a river*.

I'd come across a poem a few weeks ago that I shared with Camden, about wishing for love to be like a river, strong and free, finding a love that twisted and turned but always stayed together. I thought it more than appropriate for us, and he loved it too.

A lot, apparently.

I slip the ring on my finger, admiring the tiny glittering diamonds. "I love it."

"Yeah?"

I kiss him and then ask him to clasp the bracelet on me, so it sits next to the one his sister made. "It's perfect."

I hold my hand up, turning it this way and that, the diamonds catching the light. "I feel so bad. All I got you was—"

He clamps his hand over my mouth. "Don't spoil it."

"But you gave me this now," I mumble behind his palm.

"Because it's the first gift. You can open the rest tomorrow."

"Camden," I scold.

"River."

"I don't need or want multiple gifts."

"Until you see them. You might not *need* them, but you'll *want* them."

Camden is one of the most generous people I've ever known, and if he wants to spoil me, he can. He has the means, so I won't ever say no, but it does make the relationship feel a little lopsided. "Just makes me feel a little silly, knowing what I bought you as a gift."

He shakes his head, hands molding to my face. "Whatever it is, I'm sure I'll love it. Besides…" He kisses my lips. "You are my most treasured gift."

I thump his hard chest, biting back a laugh, wondering what the world would think if they knew Bad Boy Camden Long was a total simp. "You are so cheesy."

"Most definitely. Come here." He pulls me into his lap and then turns on the TV, streaming the original Grinch cartoon, at my request, and after it's over, he scoops me up to carry me to bed, where we fall asleep cuddled together in our matching pajamas, though his don't last long.

He wakes up around midnight to strip down to his underwear, saying he's too hot to sleep, yet he has no problem pulling me on top of him. He swears he sleeps better with my weight next to him, which reinforces that I made the right purchase.

Because he grins when he opens my gift the next morning—a weighted pillow and a pillowcase I had made out of my old Montclair State T-shirt. "It's for when you can't sleep or feel anxious on the road."

He gives the pillow a squeeze, arms around it like it's me. "It's perfect." He even puts the pillowcase on it then tugs me to him for a kiss. "Thank you."

Among the miles of professionally wrapped paper torn to shreds are the piles of gifts he bought for Paisley and me: purses, jackets, gift certificates for spa days, and best of all, an easel and paint supplies for his sister since she's recently become interested in painting through the art class she takes. So now she can do it whenever she wants.

After a breakfast of cinnamon rolls, with a large side of turkey bacon and eggs on Camden's plate, he heads out for practice, while Paisley and I laze around, doing absolutely nothing. My parents text me to ask if I'm going to Mass, knowing full well I'm not planning on it, but I'm guilted enough to say a couple of silent prayers and then find homes for my new gifts. A lot of my belongings have migrated over to Camden's bedroom, closet, and bathroom, so when I stay here, I don't need to pack a bag anymore. Erik might not have noticed, but Molly definitely has since she popped her head into my room at their house last week and raised her eyebrows in silent question at the emptiness of it.

Without saying a word, she understood. Because she merely hugged me and said, "I told you so."

She did. All that *Pride and Prejudice* talk. She Jane Austened me.

But then I asked her not to say anything to Erik because Camden and I would tell him after the season, and she easily agreed before helping me pack up a few more of my things.

Now, I'm back at my brother's house with Camden and Paisley in tow, a few gift bags in hand. Molly greets us with Kai on her hip, and I immediately take him from her, smothering his cheek with kisses. Camden leans over my shoulder to coo at him. "What's up, little one? You're getting bigger every time I see you."

Kai waves his chubby hands, reaching for him, so I pass my nephew off to Camden, who holds him comfortably, his forearm under Kai's little bum covered in a onesie. His other hand spans the baby's back, and I'm tempted to give in to Camden's little breeding kink. Seeing his big form cradling that little body is too adorable for my ovaries to stand.

I know that when the time comes, he'll be a great dad. Giving and patient, though I'm sure he'll be soft when it comes to rules. I can already imagine he'll be the good cop, and I'll have to be the bad one.

"All right?" Erik asks, slinging his arm around my shoulders, rousing me from my daydream of Camden on the floor next to our baby, a toddler running behind him.

"Yep. Mm-hmm."

"You were out of it for a second."

"Yeah." I force a laugh. "Tired, I guess."

"Come on." He tugs me to the dining room. "Dinner's ready."

With so few of us, Erik and Molly asked their chef to "whip something up." The supposedly quick meal is filet mignon, grilled shrimp and vegetables, along with salad and mashed sweet potatoes.

We all dig in, Molly, Paisley, and me on one side with Erik, Camden, and Kai in his high chair on the other, having a grand time mushing the potatoes against his tray. The boys talk shop while we chat about the cat Molly's trying to talk Erik into adopting and how Paisley and I have given in to Camden's whims to call the guinea pigs Rocky and Balboa. But since Molly isn't as fluent in ASL as everyone else, I translate for the both of them.

Out of the corner of his eye, Camden must spot the bracelet and ring he gifted me on my hand while I sign because he offers me a sweet, shy smile, turning to watch me for a moment before going back to his conversation with my brother.

But I should have known Erik would clock it, and after we exchange gifts—mostly presents for Kai to open, ripping at the tissue paper, smacking his hands on the little light-up keyboard —he corners me, hands on his hips.

"What's going on with you and Cam?"

"What?"

He tips his head back toward the living room, where his best friend—my boyfriend—is seated between Paisley and Molly, flying Kai above his head. "Is something going on between you two? Are you sleeping with him?"

I don't like the accusatory tone in his voice, or the fact that he says "sleeping with" like it's "murdering people."

I roll my eyes, pushing his shoulder away, so I can brush by him. "Even if my personal life were any of your business, I wouldn't tell you."

He catches my wrist. The one with my new bracelet. "But you are my sister. And he is my best friend."

"Then act like it," I spit, whipping my head around to him. "Don't come at me, asking if I'm sleeping with him as if it's a mortal sin. You wanted me to work with him in the first place. You told me what a good guy he is deep down. And you know what? You were right. So you can shove this holier-than-thou attitude up your ass." I pull away from him, aiming my finger in his direction. "You are not my keeper."

Then I march back to my boyfriend, my brother's best friend, and the man I'm head over heels for.

CHAPTER 29
CAMDEN

AS HARD AS this month has been without my parents, being with Nadine, Paisley, and Erik has made it a bit easier. My best friend has always been open, inviting me to hang out with his family, even before the accident, and having him and his family around now keeps me from sinking into grief. Though I suppose we'll be spending all of our holidays together, once the truth comes out about Nadine and me.

Kai claps, his giggle infectious, after I've thrown him into the air for the fifth time. Molly laughs. "He's not going to want you to leave since you've become his personal carnival ride."

I blow a raspberry into Kai's neck. "Yeah. Uncle Cam is your favorite, right?"

Kai's giggle ratchets up when I tickle him as Nadine returns to the living room, sitting on the floor by my feet. She props her elbow up on the couch cushion, head in her hand, smile radiant. She looks stunning tonight, even in her simple sweater and dark jeans, her dark hair down and shining, river-blue eyes sparkling.

She hasn't taken off the jewelry I gave her yet, and while I'm not able to tell the world about us, it makes me feel better to know she's wearing something that shows she's mine. Even if only we know.

Kai smacks at my cheeks, and I laugh, forcing my attention away from Nadine to the baby in my hands, tossing him in the air again. "All right, all right, you tiny tyrant."

He kicks his feet, enjoying my roughhousing, but I realize his father has yet to return from when he said he was going to grab a drink. "Where's Erik?"

"I don't know." Nadine flicks her hand. "Cleaning up or something."

From the eye roll, I can only assume they've had an argument and that I might be at the center of it.

I'm proven right an hour later, when we're all about to leave. As I slip on my coat, Erik yanks me around the corner. "I feel like something is going on between you and my sister."

I try to play it off with a laugh. "Nah, man."

"She's never home anymore."

I shrug, shoving my hands in my pockets. "You know how it is with play-offs coming up. By the time I get home at night, I'm not comfortable with her driving back here. It's just easier for her to stay at my place."

He eyes me suspiciously, but looking after his sister's safety earns me some points, and he agrees eventually. "Yeah. She doesn't need to be driving when it's pitch black out."

I nod. *Exactly.*

But also.

I have her tucked safely away in bed.

"You sure you're not, like, developing feelings for her?" Erik asks, and for a moment, I wonder if my memories are playing out on my face. If he can recognize that my favorite way to sleep is with her next to me, her hair tickling my neck, restless feet accidentally kicking me in the middle of the night.

I've developed a preoccupation with his sister.

She is everything: my calm, my inspiration, my future.

But he doesn't have to know that.

"The only feelings I have are about finishing strong. We're

two games away from securing the first seed in the conference. That's where I'm focused."

Which is true. I am focused there. Because I know I have the support at home to do so.

I've never been more focused, more in tune with my body and mind. It's amazing how security in personal matters can change a person's entire outlook.

"We get the ring this year," Erik says, holding his hand out to me, and I clasp it.

"Fuck right."

We hug, patting each other on the back before moving to the door where Nadine and Paisley are saying goodbye to Molly and Kai. I give them both hugs and kisses, ignoring the lingering suspicion at my back when Nadine comes with me. There is no good reason she should.

Besides that she lives with me in all but name.

But he doesn't say anything, and she barely acknowledges him with a wave.

"Everything okay?" I ask once we're in the car.

"My brother asked if something is going on between us, but it was more like an accusation."

I blow out a breath, shifting behind the wheel as I pull out onto the road. "Yeah. He's not stupid. He knows."

"I'm sorry about not believing you before when you said he'd be upset. I…"

Assuming she needs it, I reach for her hand, placing our woven fingers together in my lap as I steer with one hand. The car's hum fills the silence between us as Nadine finally finds her words.

"You have nothing to prove to me or anyone else. Only yourself. Prove to yourself that you deserve me. I already know, and I don't care what anyone else thinks about us, including my brother."

I don't react, her words stunning me. She's close to her

family, especially Erik, and to hear she puts me above them is staggering.

"Camden." She tugs on my hand for my attention, and only when I glance her way does she continue, "I know how bad you feel about everything—your parents, the game, all of it. But you need to give yourself some grace. Be proud of who you are."

"Proud?" My heart twists a little, hitting an uncharted part that seems to beat only in her presence, a sliver of vulnerability that is solely for her. "You want me to be my arrogant self?" I deflect, trying to drape some humor over my discomfort, but it barely hides anything, and she sees everything.

"I want you to be the man I love."

I swallow the tangle of emotion in my throat. She wants me to be proud of myself, of my accomplishments, of how I've overcome indescribable pain and faced unmerciful animosity. And I can be.

I can drop the final shield, the last mask of the facade that I'd put on to keep anyone from finding out how worried I was that I didn't belong. I was so scared they'd discover I wasn't meant to be there, that I built up an aloof image to keep anyone from examining too closely.

But all that is done now. I'm finished playing the arrogant fool.

I skim my thumb over her knuckles. "As soon as the season is over, I'm telling him. Everything."

"Everything?" she repeats with a laugh. "I hope not."

"Everything, meaning my intentions."

She leans into the console. "And what are they?"

As if she doesn't know. But I play her game anyway. "My intentions are that I'm going to marry you. Retire at the end of this contract while I can hopefully still walk without too many joints cracking. By then, you'll be done with your graduate degree and have some big-time job, so I can stay home with the kids. Of course, sometime in there, we'll have found a house in the suburbs. Maybe next door to your brother."

"And get a dog."

"No." I send her a bland look, but even if she can't see it in the dark of the car, she laughs. "No way."

"Don't you want little Camden and Nadine Junior to have a furry playmate?"

"They'll have each other."

"Every kid needs a pet. Your sister has the guinea pigs."

"Because you're a bully and a bulldozer, and I never should have given you my credit card."

"Too late to take it back now."

"That's for sure," I murmur against the back of her hand. "Would never want to take it back."

At home, I don't waste any time. As soon as our bedroom door is closed, I peel Nadine's sweater off, needing to *show* her my intentions.

I kiss my love into her throat, along her shoulders, and over the slope of her breasts after I unclasp her bra. I prove how proud I am by getting on my knees, carefully tugging her jeans down her legs and helping her step out of her underwear then tugging her socks off so that she's completely naked. I show my appreciation by laying her on the bed and licking at the very center of her until she's pulling at my hair, begging me to make her come.

So I do. I rotate my wrist, crook my fingers inside her, stroking over that swollen and sensitive spot inside. The way she sighs my name never fails to send a ripple of goose bumps over my skin, and I give in to a shudder before latching my mouth on to her clit, letting her ride out her orgasm on my tongue and hand until she finally relaxes. I suck my fingers clean and then drop a line of kisses along the arches of her feet and calves. I massage her thighs and nuzzle the soft curve of her stomach.

"Six weeks," I murmur as she combs her fingers through my hair.

"Six weeks until the championship."

I nod. "Planning on going all the way to the end, winning it all, and then we're going public. No more hiding."

"No more hiding," she agrees, and I lean over to kiss her mouth, though I don't let her pull me down on top of her. Instead, I stand and strip out of my clothes. She watches as I stroke my hand over my hard length, and she is the sexiest thing I've ever seen in my life. The way she lies in the middle of the mattress, hair splayed out, one hand by her throat, the other absently gliding back and forth across her thigh, legs spread open and waiting. The picture is both beautiful and lewd. Completely shameless. And I love it.

I love her.

"I still can't believe you're mine," I say. "It's a miracle."

"I think the miracle is you having lube," she says as I retrieve the bottle from the side table.

"Why is that a miracle?"

She welcomes me next to her on the bed, eyes bright with lust as I squeeze a dollop of the translucent gel out to spread over my cock. "You're the only man I've been with who has it, uses it. Isn't afraid to."

"As much as I love hearing things you like about what I'm doing for you, I'd really prefer to avoid hearing about other men."

She snorts an amused sound. "You and your delicate ego."

"You got that fucking right." I pull her up on top of me, positioning her knees on either side of my waist, and smooth my palms around her hips, urging her to grind herself over the length of my erection. "You've shattered my ego."

She releases a pleased sound from the back of her throat and arches away from me. I cover her breasts with my hands, molding them, staring at where she moves over me, her pussy sliding along my cock. She rocks back and forth, and I know whenever she hits her clit from the way her breath hitches.

"You're gonna have to do some work to build it back up," I

tell her, smiling when she shakes her head at me like I'm a nuisance. I nudge her to lift up so I can position the tip of my length at her entrance. "Show me how much you love me."

She places her palms on my chest and angles her hips, slowly sinking back down, sheathing me with her wet heat. We both groan at how good it feels, how easy it is for her to move, rock on top of me with how slick we are. The sight of her finding her pleasure sends my own ecstasy skyrocketing. Adrenaline courses through my veins, igniting my skin. She works herself up and down, using her hands on my pecs to steady herself, and I can't help myself at the delightful sway of her tits right in my face. I lean my head up, sucking one into my mouth, scraping my teeth over the tip, and she cries out, her inner walls clenching down on me.

"Oh fuck." She hangs her head down like she can't take it. Nails digging half-moons into my skin. I hope they're permanent.

"Mm-hmm, that's it." I skate my hands from her waist down to her ass, helping her to move when she seems to lose it. I'm close too. "Come on, Riv. Get there."

She does. A minute later, after I've laved both of her nipples to a shine, and she's found a rhythm that has her breathing hard, eyes closed, low moans escaping her mouth.

As soon as I feel that flutter, I turn us so I'm on top and on my knees, her legs up and against my shoulders. I thrust into her once, twice, three times, and I'm coming inside her, panting.

I settle on top of her, between her legs, feeling the warm evidence of my orgasm leak out between her thighs, but I hold her tight so she can't move quite yet. I place my head on her stomach, ear under her breastbone, her heartbeat a steady rhythm.

"I'm proud of you," she whispers after a minute, and I shift, propping myself up on my elbows, so I can hear her better, her voice unencumbered when she says, "And I'll be proud to tell my brother we're together, to tell anyone—everyone—that we're together. That I'm yours and you're mine."

That shattered ego I joked about before? It's actually unbreakable. As long as I have Nadine Rivera next to me, there is nothing and no one who can bring me down.

CHAPTER 30
NADINE

THE ROAR of the crowd shakes the stadium as the clock ticks down the final seconds. I'm in the stands, heart pounding in my ears as I scream. Next to me, Paisley does too. Molly holds Kai tight to her in a carrier, making sure his earphones stay on while she hops up and down, cheering. As soon as the final whistle blows, the noise amplifies even louder. The Founders won the division on their home turf.

"They did it!" Molly shouts, eyes brimming with tears, and I nod, eyes fixed on the field where the team celebrates. My chest blooms with so much pride and joy, I can taste it.

It's delicious revenge.

Down on the field, Camden throws his head back, arms out at his sides, hands fisted as he screams up at the sky like a feral animal. I feel it in my bones.

I know how bad he wants this. How hard he's worked. How he's climbed each and every step to get back to this place. It's not finished, but he's so close to the top. Nearly there.

When I realize that all the families are headed down to the field, led by a team attendant, I motion to Molly, and we gather our things to follow. Paisley and I hold hands as we traipse down the stadium steps and run out onto the field, chaos among the cameras and reporters descending on the players.

I stay close to Molly as she spots Erik first. After our spat Christmas Day, he texted to apologize about jumping to conclusions, and I accepted. Even though he jumped to the correct conclusion. I just didn't appreciate the way he acted as if Camden were below him or me, when my brother, of all people, knows Camden's real character. I won't stand for him talking shit about his best friend.

I will happily be the last line of defense against any and all who want to come at Camden Long.

Molly hugs Erik, and he kisses her a few times then bends to kiss Kai. When he spots me, he holds his arm out for a hug.

"Good work," I shout into his ear so he can hear me above the commotion. "You deserve it!"

"Thanks, Nan." He releases me and offers a hug to Paisley as well. Then suddenly, Camden is there, hauling his sister into his arms. She shrieks and frowns, obviously hating how he's drenched in sweat, his uniform covered with patches of green and brown.

He sets her down so they can have a short conversation in sign, during which she congratulates him before he turns to me. His dark eyes spark with excitement, his grin wide, and I don't hesitate to hug him, though I am careful of how it looks, so I pat his back once. Completely platonic.

"Congratulations. You did it."

"We did it," he agrees with a smile and leans in as if to kiss me, but I immediately step back, slapping his shoulder pad.

"Way to go!"

He shakes his head with a laugh then holds his hand up for a high five, which I meet with a giggle at the situation.

Dorian Green, a wide receiver, jumps onto Camden's back, yelling something indiscernible, and our small group becomes bigger as more and more players join Erik and Camden. Molly,

Paisley, and I take pictures and videos of them laughing and dancing then clear the field with everyone else twenty minutes later.

The Founders team heads toward the locker room, shouts and whistles echoing in their wake as they celebrate their road to conference play-offs, while some family members hang out in the tunnel, chatting while they wait for the players. They have a bye week coming up while the wild card games take place, and I'm sure they're going to enjoy a few days off to recharge.

I assumed Camden would take forever to shower and change, but I feel a tug on my parka while my attention is on my phone screen, double-checking Paisley's upcoming therapy appointment on my calendar. "Riv. Don't turn around. Just step back."

Following his orders, I act like Homer Simpson in that meme, fading into the bushes, and find myself up against a concrete wall with Camden caging me in. "Just a quick…"

He bends down, capturing my mouth in a kiss. As he said, it's quick, barely more than a brush of his lips against mine.

"You played so well." I skim my hand down his shirt. "That catch in the second?" I blow out a breath like it makes me hot, and his hands find my waist.

"I love knowing you're in the stands for me."

"Coulda shown it with a touchdown."

He cocks his head. "I had my highest average yards this game. That not good enough for you?"

I shrug like it's not, and he huffs, lowering his head, speaking his words against my lips. "Let's see if I can't change your attitude tonight. I—"

"What the hell are you doing?"

Camden is shoved sideways, and I realize the huge body in front of me belongs to my brother. I touch his shoulder. "Erik."

He whips his head to me. "No.

"What do you mean, no?"

"Just shut up!" he shouts, gaining the interest of the small crowd of WAGs and players in the tunnel, and Camden approaches my brother with his hands up, like he wants to push Erik. I step in front of him so he can't.

"Don't yell at her like that," Camden seethes, gently setting me aside, all of his focus on my brother.

"Don't yell? You both fucking lied to me! I have every right to yell after the bullshit you two fed to me."

Erik pivots to face me, but I'm so shocked by the last few seconds that I can't form words, even if I wanted to. "It's not…"

"What?" he circles his hand for me to continue. "It's not what? Not what it looks like? Not my sister and my best friend hooking up behind my back after I specifically asked both of you if anything was going on?"

"Okay, yes, that's what it looks like," Camden says with his usual arrogant amusement, but it's not going to defuse the situation and only makes Erik more irate.

"You've got to be fucking kidding me." Erik grits his teeth, and Molly approaches, a timid but hopeful smile on her face, while another one of the wives holds Kai.

"Babe, I think we should talk about this at home. Everyone's adrenaline is through the roof from the game, and it would—"

Ignoring her, Erik swings around to Camden. "I asked you point-blank if something was going on, and you said no, that you were focused on winning."

"I am." Camden holds his arms out at his sides, as if to encompass their win. "We are."

"You *lied*. To my face."

"Listen—"

"No." Erik knocks Camden's hand down. "You listen. Nadine is my *sister*, and you knew how I'd feel about this."

"Exactly why we didn't want to tell you until after the season."

Erik's nostrils flare as he shakes his head. "You fucking

asshole. It never should have started in the first place." He leans into Camden's space, right in his face. "I never should have trusted you with her."

I slip in between them, pushing against Erik's chest so he'll back up. "Don't talk about me like I'm not here, and especially don't talk about me like I'm a child. I am a grown woman with my own mind. I make my own decisions, and nothing between Camden and me has anything to do with you."

He glares down at me. "It has everything to do with me."

I huff. "Now who's the egotistical one?"

Erik lifts his finger to point at Camden but keeps his eyes on me. "Him. And if I thought you'd fall for his act, I never would have suggested you help him out."

"Don't talk about him like that!" I shove at my brother with all my might, moving him half an inch, garnering the attention of the entire surrounding crowd in the process. But I don't care. He's not going to speak down to or about Camden.

"He's your best friend and teammate, and you're the asshole for acting this way. Camden and I love each other."

Erik lets out a single dubious laugh. "He's incapable of loving anyone but himself."

I assumed my brother would be upset when he found out about Camden and me, but this reaction? It's so over the top I might laugh if I weren't so full of rage. "Seriously? Where is this coming from?"

"You *lied* to me. You are my sister and best friend, and you lied to me. You went behind my back, hid this from me, and you think I'm going to be cool about it? I'm his quarterback, and I already lost one ring because of him. I'm not going to lose another. So don't try to pass this off as some insignificant thing that I shouldn't be upset over. I have every right to be pissed the fuck off, okay?"

"Erik," Molly pleads, pulling on his hand, attempting to move him.

He doesn't, merely curls his lip in disgust at me. "You should be ashamed of yourself."

"Hey! Whoa!" Camden all but leaps over me to get to my brother. "Watch your fucking mouth when you're talking to her."

Finally, Erik looks at Camden. Both of them breathing hard, nose to nose, a silent threat hanging in the air. Molly and I try our best to pry them apart, but it's impossible when they're like this.

"You two are ridiculous," Molly hisses at her husband. "Acting like children."

"Let's go home, Cam."

They both ignore us.

Camden puts his finger in my brother's face. "You can say what you want about me, but you don't say *anything* bad about your sister. *Ever.*"

Erik huffs. "I can say what I want to and about my sister. Because she's *my* sister." He bats at Camden's shoulder. "And this is family business, so stay out of it."

That's when Camden swings.

Molly shrieks as the two fall to the floor, rolling back and forth, both of them grappling for the top to punch the other. I heave a sigh, stomping around them for Paisley's hand. A few people—players and workers—rush to the idiots wrestling on the floor and finally pry them apart.

"What the fuck?" one of the other players says, eyes wide, head on a swivel as he takes it all in.

Some of the wives and girlfriends whisper behind me. I hear my name but can't make out anything else as I comfort Paisley, who is confused and shocked.

I am too, but it hasn't quite hit me yet. Like I'm in an out-of-body experience, watching it all from the sidelines.

But then again, from the video that hits the internet seconds later, I can watch it as many times as I want in my own body.

The snarl on Erik's face. The way Camden's fist meets his

chin. The resounding shout of "We're done!" as they're carted away from each other.

That's what it feels like.

Erik and Camden are done.

The team's done.

And possibly the best thing to ever happen to me is done too.

CHAPTER 31
CAMDEN

THE AFTERMATH WAS WORSE than the actual fight itself. But you wouldn't know it from the way every hissed insult and punch landed, according to the angle of the video that made sure our little wrestling match would be immortalized on the web for all eternity.

Erik and I had been dragged apart by Thad Reise, our kicker, and Josiah Beck, a defensive back, along with two stadium attendants. The O-line coach all but carried us to Coach Roberts's office by the scruff of our necks like we were the misbehaving kittens of an impatient cat, hanging out of her mouth.

Not unsurprisingly, Roberts ripped us a new one. Tore our heads clean off and then shoved them up our asses. Then ordered us to "figure your shit out before you lose this season for everyone."

Erik took it stoically, not saying a word, then left with a single nod.

Me, on the other hand? I felt like I had to say something.

"Coach, it wasn't that big of a deal."

"My quarterback and my tight end fighting in the halls is not that big of a deal?"

"It won't affect our play, I mean."

He plunked down in his chair like he suddenly couldn't stand another second. "That's where you're wrong." He scrubbed his hands over his face before meeting my gaze, disappointment wafting off him in such big waves that it threatened to knock me over. "I've been down this road with you before, and quite frankly, I can't trust you when you say it won't affect your play."

"I—"

Coach shook his head, pointing to the door. "Talk to Pearce, get your shit in order, and don't come back until whatever is going on between you and Rivera is put to bed." Then he reached into one of his desk drawers to retrieve a bottle of Tums and chewed a few pills, mumbling, "Close the door on your way out."

So I left and closed the door on my way out, yet again at the center of a mess. The problem child. The Founders' fuckup.

Now, I open my door to Malcolm, whose shoulders rise and fall on a deep breath like he's tired already.

Same, bro.

I gesture for him to enter, and I lead him to the living room where Nadine's reading on her iPad. She's mostly been ignoring texts and phone calls from her family, all of them attempting to understand what's going on, but at this point, neither one of us knows.

I expected Erik to be pissed when I eventually had the conversation with him about Nadine and me, but I did not at all expect the level of anger. I know he's upset we lied, I know he feels betrayed by me, I get it.

And yet, I wasn't going to let him talk to Nadine the way he did.

You want to call me names? Been there, done that.

But no one, not even a member of her family, will say a word against her.

I acted without thinking.

Although, if I'd given it another minute, I probably would have caught him in the chin, no matter what.

He had it coming.

Maybe it had to come to a head. We never actually talked about last year and the Bowl game. We never had any conversations about how he felt about me, and knowing him, he didn't want to. All of his peace and love chi didn't want to rock the boat, especially after my parents died.

My best friend, the saint.

Well. That's done now, I suppose.

It's what he shouted at me as Beck towed him off me. *We're done.*

"Have a seat," I tell Malcolm, gesturing to the other couch while I move Nadine's feet, positioning them in my lap, holding on to them so she doesn't move. I want both of us to be as comfortable as possible for this conversation, which I know will be very uncomfortable.

"Hello, Nadine. How are you?" Malcolm asks after removing his long winter coat, and she offers him a half smile.

"I'm okay."

He nods then shifts his attention to me. "I know I don't have to ask you, but I will anyway. How are you?"

I reply with the fakest, widest smile I've got. "Grand."

"Your charm will not save you with this one." He wiggles his cell phone in front of him. "This wasn't an accident or a mistake. That punch you threw had purpose behind it, so I'm here to know why."

I glance to Nadine, finding her eyes cast down, fingers toying with the edge of the blanket.

"Riv?"

She lifts one shoulder, shaking her head slightly, mumbling, "Tell him, I guess."

I reach for her hand, brushing my thumb over her ring. "Nadine and I are together, and we didn't tell Erik. He saw us and lost it. I punched him because of the way he was talking to

Nadine. Doesn't matter that he's my best friend, brother, team-mate, or whatever. It's not okay."

Malcolm exhales a noisy breath and nods as if it's what he suspected all along.

"But I don't want that becoming public knowledge," I tell him. "Nadine needs and deserves her privacy."

He sends me a dubious look because if it were possible before, it certainly is not now that I got into a fight with her brother and it's all being replayed on every major news outlet, whether they cover sports or not. "Nadine, you are not required to do anything you don't want to, but we all need to understand the severity of the situation."

She nods but doesn't speak. Not until he says, "Social media is not only tearing through Camden, but you as well."

"What are they saying?" She sits up, knocking my hands away from her. Not that she did it on purpose, but at the moment when we should be a team, it doesn't feel like we are.

Malcolm speaks kindly yet firmly. "All of the usual things to tear women down."

"Bitch, whore, ugly...?" she guesses, and he nods solemnly.

My throat constricts like I'm about to puke, and I reach for my water, downing it. But that only makes me feel more nauseous.

Malcolm goes on. "They're blaming you. Already betting the team will lose because of you and—"

"Okay. Okay." I hold up my hands to stop him. "We get the picture."

"But do you?" He aims his gaze at me, irritation radiating off him. Not the empathy he had for Nadine. "We're in this situation because of you. *She* is in this situation because of you."

I feel terrible about what happened, but not so much as when he lays it all at my feet, and I turn to Nadine, biting into her lip to keep her chin from wobbling, eyes glassy.

"Honey, I'm sorry." I lean over, kissing any part of her I can reach—her hand, her arm, her shoulder. "I'm so, so sorry."

"It's okay," she murmurs.

"It's not. It's not okay. It is my fault. All of this…" I close my eyes, dizzy with guilt. "I promised you I'd take care of you, and I didn't. I caused this."

She sniffs but doesn't disagree. She clears her throat and blinks a few times before lifting her head, focusing her winter eyes on Malcom. "What do we do?"

"We start by being clear-eyed about what is going on. I know it's hard to hear, but you should know exactly what we're dealing with so you can make your own decisions."

I'm not sure he's alluding to her making a decision about our relationship or if that's my own insecurities acting up, but my skin heats. "You don't need to do anything," I tell her, weaving my fingers with hers. "This isn't your problem to fix. It's mine."

"But I'm collateral damage."

And her words makes my heart splinter into a million pieces.

I can't argue with her point. I threw the bomb and took her out as well.

"I'm sorry," I say again, then look to Malcolm, needing to fix this. *Hoping* I can fix this. "What's the plan?"

He sits up straighter, tugging on the lapel of his suit jacket, then digs out an iPad from inside his bag. He spends a few moments finding whatever it is he needs and then explains, "The organization is going to put out a statement." He hands it to me to read, three short sentences about tensions being high in the locker room, but that everyone on the team is focused on winning the conference and then the national championship. Essentially saying, there is nothing to see here. "I've also drafted something for you to post, but it's up to you how personal you want to make it. Now that I know the root cause."

I scroll down to read his—my—statement, a bland explanation of the situation basically echoing the team's lines.

"You want me to post this?"

He nods. "And you'll need to answer a few questions at the press call."

I take off my glasses to rub at my eyes. "Okay. I'll do whatever you need me to."

He makes a curious sound. "That was easy. I came here prepared for a fight."

I readjust my glasses on my nose and face Nadine. She still won't look at me. *She* is my fight. She is the reason I fight. But right now, I'm not sure it's enough.

I'm not sure *I* am enough.

And with that fear comes all of my shields. I smirk at Malcolm. "So that's it? This could have been an email."

He rolls his eyes, over my bullshit.

But before he can continue, Nadine stands, collects her iPad, tucks her loose hair behind her ear, then offers Malcolm a smile. "Thanks for coming, but I'm going to…"

She trails off and leaves the room without another word, my heart chasing after her. I watch her until she's out of sight and then stare at the empty space some more.

She is disappointed.

I am a disappointment.

Malcolm heaves a sigh. "Guess we're back to where we started. Everyone thinking you're making this all about you."

He's not wrong.

CHAPTER 32
CAMDEN

WE'RE minutes away from our first game of the conference play-offs, and I haven't felt so unsure about stepping on the field since my rookie year. Outside of calling plays at practice, Erik hasn't spoken to me directly since our confrontation two weeks ago, and although Nadine has tried to act as if she's fine, she isn't. She's kept her chin up, put on a brave face, but I know all this has gotten to her. She's worried her graduate school applications will be affected by the stories on the internet, and she doesn't have many people to talk to who can understand her position. I overheard her on the phone with Molly, but until Erik and I can work past this, they're both stuck in opposite corners. Same goes for the entire Rivera family, seemingly all at a loss for how to overcome the rift between Nadine and Erik.

In a last-ditch effort not to solve the problem but at least win this fucking game, I approach Erik in the locker room. "Hey, we need to talk."

He keeps his attention forward, on the Founders logo on the wall across from him as he completes his pregame ritual—bending and extending each of his fingers ten times. "No, we don't. We need to focus on this game."

"Yeah, which is why I'm telling you we need to set aside all this personal stuff for—"

"It is set aside."

"Not if you can't even look at me."

He slowly turns, *looking* at me. "We need to win this goddamn game, not have our heads clouded with distractions."

Except the more we ignore this, the more it's going to be a distraction. He should know this. He was the one who pushed so hard for me to talk to Pearce this season. He's the one who practices mindful breathing and journals every morning. Where is all that happy horseshit now?

I'm not used to him being like this. Short-tempered and illogical. I can understand acting out of emotion and not the brain— I've been doing that for longer than I care to remember—but for once in my life, I'm attempting to be the problem-solver and peacekeeper.

He doesn't care.

"Let's just go out there and do our jobs," Erik says, brushing by me before I can argue. He didn't even finish his ritual.

But it's too late now.

Time to play.

New England's defense is a wall, but we fight for every yard. On our last possession before halftime, Reise kicks a field goal, putting us on the board, and we spend twelve minutes talking with coaches, aiming to reevaluate and readjust our game to try to take the win.

But the second half is as much of a slog as the first. New England scores seven in the third quarter, and we trail them until the end of the fourth.

Erik calls the play, a deep pass that's risky, but I'm ready. The ball snaps, and I'm off, sprinting down the field. Erik's perfect spiral for thirty-five yards that lands in Aaron Brown's hands after I take out his defense. A second later, the whistle blows, and we've got six more on the board. With the extra point, we take the lead, 10-7, and with only two minutes left on the clock, our defense is able to hold New England back on their final drive.

We win.

By the skin of our teeth.

But it's a win, nonetheless, and I approach Erik with a tentative smile, an olive branch. I hold out my fist toward him as we make our way to the tunnel, but he leaves me hanging, pointedly ignoring it and me as he walks ahead.

So much for setting it all aside.

I make it through the postgame press bullshit, feeding the reporters all my practiced lines about how there is absolutely no bad blood between the Founders' QB and me. That it has nothing to do with his sister, and that it is definitely not because he caught me doing something illegal. As far as anyone knows, adrenaline got the best of me, and I lashed out. Because I'm the asshole. I'm the one who swung. I'm the arrogant bad boy with a record for breaking things, so why not add one more to the tally?

By the time I arrive home, it's after midnight, and I assume Nadine will be in bed. But instead, I find her in the living room crying. She doesn't notice me, obviously hasn't heard me enter the penthouse, and the sound of her sobs shreds whatever is left of my beat-up heart.

I've been following the rules, not only this week, but this whole season. I've kept my head down. I've played my part, done exactly what the team and the PR company have wanted me to. I've practically been a choirboy, and yet it's still not enough.

Not where she's concerned.

Not when the love of my goddamn life can't catch her breath, her shoulders shaking with every inhale, like it hurts.

Fighting Erik was stupid, but I won't apologize for it. I did it because I promised Nadine to always keep her safe, so I don't feel bad about it. Yet that one minute of my anger—whether it was called for or not—has only made her life harder. In trying to do what was right, I hurt her. I made her life infinitely more complicated.

I've broken the one promise I made to her.

The one thing I said I would do to make sure I deserved her.

If I can't make it right with Erik, maybe I can still make it right for Nadine.

I knew all along she was too good for me. The whole world fucking thinks so. And it might be time to let her go. I could actually be the hero of this story, instead of the selfish prick of a villain.

"River," I say quietly, and she turns, wiping her eyes.

"Hi. I didn't hear you come in."

Her voice is ragged, face red, and the pain in my chest moves up to my throat. Guilt and heartbreak rend me in two, but I can't keep putting her through this. I can't keep breaking *her* heart.

I inhale a breath, though it doesn't make me any steadier, as I approach her, saying, "I thought you'd be asleep."

She shakes her head, rubbing her nose on the sleeve of one of my hoodies. "I watched your game and then that interview you did. I...I feel so horrible about all this."

"No, honey, no." I kneel in front of her on the floor. "You have no reason to feel bad. None of this is your fault." I swipe my thumb across her chin, under her wobbling lip. "You are the best thing to ever happen to me. I hope you know that."

She sniffles and dabs at her bloodshot eyes before meeting my gaze, and I rip off the Band-Aid.

"Which is why I think we should break up. Before all this becomes worse. I don't want you—"

"*What?*"

"I can't stand to see you crying, and—"

"You think the way to make it better is to break up with me?"

Like the flip of a switch, there is no trace of sadness, only pure ire. It's actually a pretty good imitation of her brother. How they can press a button for their temper, just like that.

I back up a few inches, explaining myself. "You know it's

only a matter of time before something else happens. I do something else that may hurt you and—"

"Your brain really is full of fucking straw, isn't it? A corn-fed jock with the emotional intelligence of a scarecrow."

"Riv, I—"

She huffs, cutting off my defense. Though I'm not sure what I was going to say to that kind of funny insult. If I weren't confused, I might laugh. "This whole situation is my fault, and I'm trying to make it better, okay?"

"Oh yeah, okay," she mocks, pushing me away so she can stand. "This whole situation is *your* fault. Like Erik has nothing to do with it?" She points at me, shouting at me like I'm her brother. Clearly needing to yell at someone. "He wasn't the one who verbally attacked me and you? He wasn't the one who didn't bother to listen to us and instigated the fight? It was all you? He had his hands tied behind his back, and you whaled on him the whole time. Is that right?"

I hesitate. "Well, no, I—"

"You defended me, like you should have. You told him the truth. You stood up for yourself and our relationship. Yes, you punched my brother and your teammate, but he deserved it."

"Yeah…" I mumble. That's what I thought too, but it's weird to have someone telling me that I'm right. That I did the right thing, and I'm…grateful? Concerned a little? Like we've fallen into an alternate reality.

"I was crying because your team might lose because of me. Because of the tension our relationship has brought to the team, and I feel bad about that because you deserve to win." She closes the distance between us, the anger in her voice down to a simmer. The icy river in her eyes melting when she loops her arms around my neck. "You've worked so hard to get to this point, and I want you to have your comeback. I was crying because I'm worried you won't have it."

This time, I do laugh. "You're so upset because you think we might lose? Riv, that's nothing compared to me losing you."

She smacks at my shoulder. "So then why'd you say you wanted to break up?"

I bend, smiling into the curve of her neck. "Because I'm a stupid man, and I've seen you cry too many times over this, and I don't know what else to do."

"You can start by telling me you love me."

I kiss her throat. "I love you."

"And that you don't want to break up ever."

"I never want to break up." I nuzzle her temple. "I want to marry you."

"Then promise to go out there and win this whole fucking thing and show the world what kind of person you are."

I kiss her mouth. "I'm going to go out there and win this whole fucking thing." Combing my fingers into her hair, I wrap my hands around the sides of her head, bending my knees to meet her gaze. "For you. I don't care about the world."

She blinks away the glassiness in her eyes. "If you give up, all of this—all of my PMS crying—will be for nothing."

I wince, grunting. "I should've checked the calendar. You always get emotional before your period."

"Yeah, I know." She heaves a sigh, like I'm an idiot.

Which I am.

"I'm sorry," I mumble, embarrassed at my terrible idea. So much for being the hero.

But she merely shakes her head, a tired schoolteacher. "I can't believe you thought you could third-act break up with me."

"A what?"

"You need to read more."

I tug her to me, lifting her up so she wraps her legs around my waist, and I carry her to our bedroom. "I've seen what you read, you little pervert."

That earns me a giggle, and I kiss her, hoping to swallow the happy sound. By the time I reach our bed, her cheeks are no longer red from crying, but I hope to make them red for a whole other reason. "What was that I saw the other day? Something about dinosaurs?"

She helps herself to scooting backward on the mattress, shucking my hoodie to reveal a tank top. "A *Jurassic Park* fan fiction I found."

I work her leggings down and off. "*Jurassic Park* fan fiction?"

She shrugs. "I was into monster romance for a while and then started wondering if there was something with dinosaurs. And I couldn't find anything that rang my bell until someone pointed me in the direction of this Wattpad writer, and…" She blows out a breath. "It's basically erotica about a guy who can shape-shift into a dinosaur…'cause science. He finds his human mate, who, of course, is trying to kill him."

I sink to the floor, wrapping my hands around her ankles to pull her toward me. "You really can find anything on the internet, can't you?"

CHAPTER 33
NADINE

AFTER DROPPING off Paisley at school this morning, I head straight to the main office, where the secretary greets me with a warm smile and marching orders for the day, copying and stapling packets because the printer is constantly broken and can never collate correctly. When I run into the principal, she informs me of a long-term substitute position that will be opening up when Mrs. Baker goes on maternity leave and asks if I'd be interested. Of course I am, and she says she'll talk to human resources about it.

For the first time in two weeks, I'm feeling really great. Confident and empowered. So when Camden arrives home a few hours later, I'm waiting for him with my coat on and keys in my hand. Fired the fuck up.

"Hey, what—"

"Your sister and I ate already. I'm going to Erik's house."

His eyes widen. "What are you going to do?"

"What I should have done a long time ago. I'm going to put my foot up his ass."

He grins and holds up his hand. I smack it aggressively, but he likes it, swatting my ass on my way out. "That's my girl!"

"Pretty sure Paisley's got a boyfriend," I toss over my shoulder, but the door closes on his question.

"She *what*?"

I don't have anything specific in mind to say to my brother when I get there, but I listen to Camden's pregame playlist, letting it pump me up on the drive, and by the time I park, I think I could put on a helmet and do some damage on the field.

Erik answers the door, surprise coloring his face. "Nan? What are you—"

"We need to talk. *Now*."

He glances over his shoulder toward the living room, where I can hear Kai babbling and Molly responding.

"I don't think—"

"I don't care what you think right now." I push past him into the house and wave at Molly. "I need to take my brother out back."

She smiles. "Of course."

So I wrap my hand around the collar of Erik's T-shirt and pull him behind me.

He wriggles out of my grasp. "What the hell are you doing? This is my favorite shirt, and you're stretching it out."

"Oh, poor you."

It's January and cold, but I slam the back door shut after he follows me onto their back patio, the string lights above providing illumination in the pitch-black night around us.

Erik crosses his arms over his chest, a familiar stubborn set to his jaw that runs in our family. He's not often one to deploy it, but that streak is there, nonetheless. Along with the temper. The one that got us into this mess. "If you're here to lecture me about Camden—"

"I'm here to lecture you about being a jackass." His eyebrows shoot up when I poke him in the chest. "You want to be mad at me? Fine. Be mad. But don't you dare take it out on Camden when he was defending me. Don't you dare punish your team because your ego got bruised."

"My ego?" Erik's voice rises. "You lied to me, Nadine. Both of you lied to my face for months."

"Because we were afraid of your reaction, and apparently we were spot-on!" I throw my hands up. "You're being unreasonable and dramatic and—"

"Dramatic?"

"Yes, dramatic. You're acting like Camden committed some unforgivable sin by falling in love with me. Like I'm some helpless little girl who can't make her own decisions."

Erik's jaw works, but he doesn't respond immediately.

"I know that you hold yourself to impossible standards and you think you're above the mere mortals you deign to walk the earth with, but people do dumb shit all the time. I'm not defending us lying to you, but this right here is proving the point of why we did. Granted, it's a little over the top. I understand that QBs need to feel important or whatever, but even this—" I lift my hands, gesturing as if to include this conflict between us "—is too much for you. I mean…this is 2000s rom-com level drama."

"This isn't some childhood drama, Nan," he says, like I'm the ridiculous one. "You know how I feel about honesty. About how hard I work to keep a tight circle of people I can trust around me."

"We didn't lie about killing somebody. We lied to protect your stupid season. Camden needs this championship win, and since he knows how you feel about him—how you think he's not worthy of me—he didn't want to wreck the team's chances. Or our chances of being together." I huff, a white puff of air clouding in front of me. "That tight circle of people you trust is about to get smaller by two if you don't fix this. I know Camden has tried to talk to you, and I also know that you started all this by planting the seed in the first place, by saying he wasn't good enough for me."

Erik opens his mouth to argue, but I stop him. "You were there for him in Iowa, at the funeral. You know how hard this year has been, and I can't believe you'd ever say that. To his face!"

My brother's shoulders droop, as if he's finally understanding exactly what his past actions have done.

"You told me that Camden isn't the man he portrays, and you're right, he's not. He's amazing. He's generous and kind, funny and smart, and he respects me. I've never had a man who supports all of my decisions like he does. So I'm not sure if you said that shit to him as a joke or if you truly believe it, but either way, it was wrong. *You* were wrong."

Erik scrubs his hands over his face, his defensive wall beginning to crack, so I take another swing, intent on ripping the whole thing down. "You want to know why I love him? Because he sees me. Not Erik Rivera's sister, not the family disappointment—"

"You're not the family disappointment."

I ignore his placation and keep on going. "He sees me for exactly who I am and loves me anyway. He believes in me when I don't believe in myself." My voice softens, just a little. "Remember when Dad didn't want you dating Molly in high school? Said she'd distract you from football, take away your focus. But you knew what you felt for Molly was bigger than that, important enough that you could work through all the hard stuff, right? Well, that's how I feel about Camden."

"That's different," Erik says, like he's exhausted by this conversation. So am I, but I'm not done fighting. I will always fight for Camden and our relationship.

"How? How is it different?"

Erik runs a hand through his hair, shaking his head. "Because I've seen him with other women. I've seen how he treats relationships like they're disposable. I've watched him make bad decision after bad decision."

"And you've also watched him change. You've seen him with Paisley, how he stepped up when his world fell apart. You've seen him work harder than anyone to prove he's not the person everyone thinks he is." I take a breath. "You're his best friend, Erik. And you told him point-blank he's not good enough for me. Do you have any idea what that does to someone who's already struggling with their self-worth?"

Guilt flickers across Erik's face. *Good*. He should feel bad.

"He loves you like a brother. Your opinion matters to him, and instead of supporting him, you made him feel like he had to choose between his best friend and the woman he loves."

Erik goes quiet for a long moment, staring at the floor. When he eventually speaks, remorse lines his words. "I just... I don't want you to get hurt."

"Then trust me to know what's good for me. Trust that if Camden ever did hurt me, I'm strong enough to handle it. And trust your best friend to be the man you know he really is."

Erik takes a few deep breaths before finally lifting his gaze. "I fucked up."

"Yep."

A small smile tugs at the corner of his mouth. "You're going to drag this out, aren't you?"

"Deservedly so, yes."

"Rivera guilt trip," he murmurs, and I agree with a nod. All of us five Rivera children needing to be the best isn't a coincidence. We've been guilted and conditioned into thinking there was no other option. If our parents could overcome so much, there was no excuse for us. It was the best or nothing at all.

We all speak guilt fluently.

My brother pulls me into a hug, and the tension I've been carrying slowly drains from my shoulders and back. "I'm sorry," he says. "You're right. I was being an ass."

"You were being protective. I get it. But Camden and I don't need protection from each other. We need your support."

Erik nods against my hair. "I'll talk to him. Fix this before the next game."

"Good. Because I'm not losing my boyfriend or my brother over this stupidity."

He rubs at his jaw. "Boyfriend, huh?"

I show him the ring and bracelet Camden gave me for Christmas, and he makes a curious sound.

"It's serious, then? You really love him?"

"I really love him, and he really loves me too."

Erik exhales noisily, doing his yoga breathing. "Okay. If you're sure about it, then I'm behind you both. Now, can we go inside? I'm freezing."

"All part of the punishment," I say, eyeing the goose bumps on his arms, bare from his T-shirt, before heading inside, where I drop my coat on one of the kitchen chairs and help myself to their pantry, where I know his stash of peanut M&Ms is hidden. My eating them is also part of his punishment.

He takes Kai, pointedly not mentioning my eating his snack, and gives Molly and me some time alone. These last two weeks have been weird between us.

"I tried talking to him," she tells me once he's out of the room. "I'm so sorry about how everything went down."

"I know. It's okay."

"It's not." She frowns. Molly is conflict-averse. She's so afraid to hurt anyone's feelings that she avoids confrontation at any and all costs. "It wasn't right, and I brought it up, but he's so stubborn, and I…"

She starts to tear up, and I reach for her hand. My sweet friend doesn't have to explain. I already know. She wants to support her husband, especially during these high-stakes games, and I am positive she did try to talk to my brother, defend Camden and me. I hug her. "I love you."

She sniffles. "I love you too, and when I grow up, I want to be just like you."

"Full of anxiety and self-doubt?"

She coughs a laugh. "No. You lead with your heart."

"Even when my heart tells me to call your husband a jackass?"

She smiles, leaning into my side. "Especially then."

I dip my head magnanimously. "Saving the world, one jackass at a time."

CHAPTER 34
CAMDEN

I'M WALKING out of the weight room when Erik stops me in the hall. "Can we talk?"

I hold out my fist for some of the other players as they pass, all of us on the offensive team finished our morning workout. When the last one has moved on, I finally turn my attention to him. "Yeah. I was going to grab lunch."

He nods and follows me as we head to the cafeteria. "Nadine came to see me last night."

"I know," I say, because she didn't come home until after I was already asleep. She apparently stayed to hang out with Molly, but we didn't have the chance to talk much this morning because I came in early for a physio session. All she told me was I should expect Erik to talk to me.

But I didn't anticipate his doing it now. In the middle of the day.

He doesn't say anything until after we've picked out our food. A grilled chicken wrap with a side of sweet potatoes and a chocolate-and-peanut-butter protein shake for me. A turkey cheeseburger, fries, salad, and Greek yogurt for him.

"It was an overreaction," he says eventually. "I'm sorry. I never should have said what I said that day or...any other time. I was pissed off because Nan and I, we've always been on the same side, and it suddenly felt like we weren't."

"Yeah," I agree, after wiping my mouth with a napkin. "Because you chose to switch teams."

"Can you honestly tell me you'd be totally cool if you found out one of your teammates was sleeping with your sister?"

"First of all, I love Nadine, so you can stop talking about our relationship like she's some random hookup. And secondly, I hope that once Paisley is old enough…like forty, she'll have enough sense to make a good choice in her partner. So I might not be totally cool with it, but I wouldn't flip out like you did."

He exhales noisily, closing his eyes for a long moment, probably doing his mindful breathing thing. When he meets my gaze again, he says, "I flipped out because you lied to me, she lied to me, I found you kissing her in the tunnel after our game, and to top it off, you're my best friend. You don't think it made me feel shitty that you felt like you couldn't come to me? That's why I asked you, why I asked both of you."

I set my elbows on the table. "Yeah, I get it. That was my decision. I asked her to keep it quiet, but only because I did want to talk to you…eventually. It's not exactly an easy conversation to have after all the shit you've said."

He nods slowly. "I know, and I'm sorry. It's only that I've had to pick up the pieces from things you've broken so many times, I didn't want to have to do it again. With my own sister."

Although I know his words are coming from a place of protection for Nadine, it doesn't make them any easier to hear. That even my best friend believes I'm going to fuck up this relationship.

"But I also know how big your heart is, and when you want to do something, you'll do it. So I'm hoping that you'll follow your heart and not your gut when it tells you to do dumb shit."

I give in to a laugh. "Well, I tried to follow my gut the other night and break up with her when I saw how upset this rift between you and me was making her, and she verbally stuffed me into a locker."

"You tried to break up with her?"

"I thought it was the right thing. She told me I was an idiot."

He hums, squinting, like he does when he's studying a play or film. "You would've given her up because of all this?"

"If it would make her happier, yes, absolutely. But I guess she likes me too much."

A smile slowly unfurls across his face, and I relax. He's right. I should have had this conversation with him from the beginning, but I was too afraid I wouldn't have been able to prove that I deserved Nadine yet. At least now he knows, that she comes before everything. Beyond family or football, she is number one in my life.

"I'm sorry I ever said I wouldn't want you dating my sister. I still don't think you're good enough for her, because no one is—"

"You're right about that."

"But if she is going to be with anyone, it might as well be my best friend."

Erik holds out his hand to me, and I clasp it in mine, both of us standing to hug.

"Love you, brother," he says with a slap to my back.

"Love you too."

He actually chuckles. "Guess Nan's got you in tune with your feelings too, huh?"

"She's got me in tune with *a lot* of things."

He puts his hand up, grimacing. "None of that. Please. I'm eating my lunch."

I grin as I sink back down to my chair. It's good to have him back, and while we finish up, we discuss the game on Sunday.

The conference championship against Arizona.

It'll be a tough one with a wide receiver who currently holds the record for most yards and a fast-as-fuck rookie running back.

But we're tougher.

And we kick the shit out of them with a final score of 31-7.

It feels so damn good to win, even though Nadine stayed home with Paisley because school midterms wait for no one. Including professional football games.

I stalk back to the locker room to find a text message from Nadine that is merely all exclamation points, and I smile the entire way home, knowing she'll be there, waiting for me.

She leaps at me as soon as I open the door. "You did it!"

I press my face to her neck, inhaling her scent, and kick the door shut behind me. "We're going to the Bowl, baby."

"I'm so proud of you." She forces my head up so she can kiss me. "I love you so much."

"You tired?" I ask since I'm so keyed up, I won't be able to sleep until well into the night, and when she shakes her head with a big grin and sparkling eyes, I carry her to bed. "Good."

She doesn't wait for me to take off her clothes, dragging her long-sleeved shirt with Paisley's school's name over her head. She kicks off her joggers while I toss my pants and shirt behind me, all my focus on the woman kneeling on the bed, biting into her lower lip as if she can keep her smile from growing. But it's the brightest thing in this room. Even more than her words when she says, "I can't wait to see you lift the trophy above your head. Tell them you're going to Disney."

I step out of my boxer briefs. "You want to go to Disney?"

She waves away the thought. "You know I hate lines. Plus, I'm going to start that long-term sub position, so I won't have time."

"Right." I close the distance between us, smoothing my hands around her waist, pulling her against me, trapping the length of my hard cock between us. "*Miss Rivera.*"

She laughs into a kiss. "Don't try to start that role-playing."

I slip my hands beneath the elastic of her underwear and squeeze that juicy backside of hers. "Then what game do you want to play?"

"The one where you show me you love me."

"That's not a game, honey. That's my life." I lower her down to the bed, sliding her underwear off. Her bra goes next, so she's completely naked, all lovely and bare for my taking. Gazing up at me with such adoration in her blue eyes that I'm not sure I want to move. I don't want to blink and miss any of the love she's sending my way.

"Make love to me, Camden."

It isn't the first time she's directed me to make love to her, but there is something about it that feels different this time. Now that we're not hiding anymore. Now that our families know and soon the world will too, it's almost like it's more real. The connection and promise of our future.

It's really and truly making *love*.

Creating something new.

As always, I blurt out the first stupid thing that comes to mind. "I can't wait to have a baby with you."

She rolls her eyes, playfully pinching my side as I lower my weight on top of her. "I can't wait to marry you. Have a whole life with you that we build for ourselves."

In all of my appointments with Pearce, I've come to realize that in losing my parents, I've gained a new understanding of life. I have been fundamentally changed in how I view the world and what I want out of it. Or more accurately, how I want to leave it.

When I think of the lives my parents lived, I always thought they were small. But aren't we all? Arguably, my career isn't as important as what my mom and dad did. In fact, their work was probably of greater importance than mine will ever be. My job just so happens to be watched by a lot more people with a lot more sponsors. But my parents kept the world spinning.

If I were to suddenly die tomorrow, the only thing anyone would have to say about me would be my athletic stats and records. Other than that, I've done nothing of real substance. But I want to.

I want to spread joy and do good. I want to leave the world

better than I entered it, and being with Nadine inspires me every day in ways I never thought possible. To ask how I can help instead of waiting for someone else to do it. To speak up when something is wrong instead of assuming someone else will.

I am a better man because of the unfortunate journey I have had to undertake after burying my parents. But that ultimately led me to Nadine, so it isn't *all* bad.

Their absence is still a huge hole in my life, but I am learning that I can fill those empty spaces by taking care of those around me, whether I know them or not. I'm not the selfish bastard I once was, and I don't plan on ever going back.

I kiss my adoration into Nadine's skin. Lick my gratitude against her pulse. Embrace the future we'll have together with whispered words about how proud I am of her and that I look forward to the day I can call her Dr. Rivera and then Mrs. Long.

By the time I wipe my mouth with the back of my hand and lift my head from between her legs, she's agreed to everything I want, including four children and a vacation home in Iowa. Because as small as I thought my parents lived, I need my kids to know the impact one person or place can have on someone. I want them to know my mistakes and learn from them, to understand that it's better to keep close to those corn-fed roots than act out some fake fantasy born of fear.

"Tell me you love me," I say as I push inside Nadine. "Tell me, River."

"I love you," she whispers, lids heavy, fingers in my hair.

I roll my hips, hitting the spot that makes her whimper. "Again."

"I love you, Camden."

I reward her with a kiss and another stroke, filling her to the hilt. With her right leg up and wrapped around my elbow, she's wide open and mewling with every slow thrust. I make sure she can feel every single inch.

"*Yes*, I love you," she moans. "I love you. I love you."

I like hearing it because of my ego, but more than that, I need to be reminded that she chose me. Despite my past and my reputation, she is here with me. She loves *me*.

"God, yes, there. *There*, Camden, please."

I don't stop, merely watch as ecstasy passes over Nadine's face, her eyes closed, forehead wrinkled like she's in pain, when I know it's the purest kind of pleasure. The same that I'm struggling desperately to hold on to, but it's too difficult. When she writhes like that, soft sighs escaping the back of her throat, I am completely unable to hold off the impending orgasm.

We both reach the peak together, my panting breaths against her throat, her fingers fisted in my hair, and when we both finally return into our bodies, I lean over to see her eyelids flutter open, a sluggish curl to her lips.

"I think I saw it. What the future looks like," she murmurs, and I carefully pull out of her so I can lie by her side, though I cup my hand over the soft flesh between her legs, gently pushing the warm trickle of my come back into her.

She doesn't mind. I've done it so often that she spreads her legs a few inches, providing me with more room. For as much as she teases me about it, I think she likes it. Likes that I want to *breed* her. Put a baby in her.

It's going to happen after all.

"What does our future look like?"

She smiles up at me. "Beautiful."

CHAPTER 35
NADINE

I'M SWEATING. My custom Founders jacket is long gone, leaving me in only a tank top and jeans. The curls I put in my hair are forgotten about since I pulled most of it up into a quick knot on the top of my head, trying to keep cool. But none of it's worked.

My nerves have not let me sit down once since the teams took the field, but I don't think any of the fans here in New Orleans have either. The constant roar of the crowd has become background noise, and I grew accustomed to the tumbling avalanche in my stomach around the third down of the first quarter.

The halftime show was cool, though.

Not enough to keep me from feeling like wanting to puke, but a nice reprieve, nonetheless.

San Francisco has put in the work, and we've been trailing them the entire game. After a completed lateral pass from Erik to one of the receivers who was taken out at the fifty-three-yard line, I cheer at the first down, and while the refs move the chains, I glance around at the faces in our box. All of us are here: Mom, Dad, Felix, Emmaline, Benedict, and a few friends, as well as

Paisley, Ava, and her family, whom Camden flew in from Iowa for this.

I shake out my hands as the Founders set up for another play. A loud chant of "De-Fense" picks up from San Francisco fans, while I can hear random shouts from Philly fans about "Shove it down their throats!" and "Punch 'em in the nuts, Ship!"

Kenyon Shipley is an outstanding and formidable offensive lineman, and since he often blocks for my brother's rushing yards, I agree with the sentiment, screaming out, "Take them out, Shipley!"

On the jumbo screen, I watch Erik give the signal, then take two steps for a pump fake, only to streak down the field, gaining twenty yards. Another first down and that much closer to the goal.

"I'm so nervous," Paisley signs to me, hopping up and down on her toes. She and Ava spent all day yesterday making bracelets, and every single one of us in this suite is wearing one of their woven good luck charms. Erik has one too, on his right wrist, his throwing arm.

"They're in shotgun," Benedict says from behind me. "They're going for a pass." He makes his way down to my side. My youngest brother and another NFL hopeful, though he unfortunately doesn't have the height of his peers, but he works hard to make up for it with his speed as a receiver. "Look, look." He points to the field. "Bet they're gonna go to Long."

"Really?"

Erik threw to Camden in the first quarter, and it was picked off. That's what set the stage for this battle, and I worry about what's going on in my boyfriend's head. Hoping that he's staying focused and in the moment and not letting anything else cloud his concentration. Including a chant of "Flounders! Flounders!" from the San Francisco fans.

"You've got nothing, Rivera!" someone shouts, followed up with, "You're nothing, Long."

Benedict physically restrains me from crawling out of the box to go confront that motherfucker, and Molly holds my hands to keep me in place as Erik does indeed drop back for a pass.

That hits number 88 in stride.

Camden doesn't stop.

He runs the last few yards to the goal and then keeps going. All the way to the padded wall underneath the stands.

I scream so loud and long that I almost choke. On the field, the Founders jump and dance, celebrating the touchdown. Camden spends a few seconds doing his usual thing before he looks right at the camera and signs his nickname for me. Then he spins around until he finds the suite we're in and holds up thumb, index, and pinkie fingers to sign "I love you."

All of us in the box repeat the gesture, but it's Paisley's grinning face on the jumbotron that receives the biggest cheer.

The referees bring everyone back, and the Founders go for the conversion. For the first time in the game, they finally pull ahead.

I spend the rest of the half holding my breath, praying for the kick to go wide when San Francisco lines up for a field goal, but it sails between the posts, and I groan audibly with all the other Philly fans.

So with the Founders only one point away from winning the whole damn thing, my father starts praying the rosary, and I squeeze Molly's hand tight as we watch our men line up for one final drive down the field.

Erik is sacked on the first play, and I can imagine how all the players' adrenaline is sky-high. From here, I can see one of the coaches on the sidelines repeatedly batting at the air, palms down, as if ordering the team to settle down. Philadelphia needs to score here and run out the clock to win.

I'm dying inside.

My legs are barely able to hold me up.

Behind me, my father starts praying in Spanish.

Emmaline's stopped drinking, and Felix is holding Mom up against the railing, like she might fall at any given moment.

And I get it.

"Here we go!" Benedict shouts through cupped hands. "You got it!"

The ball is snapped, and as the seconds tick down, Erik scrambles, evading a tackle, only to pitch it over to Camden, who is tackled out of bounds. Enough for a first down.

Molly closes her eyes, bouncing Kai in the carrier on her chest, muttering, "Please, oh please, oh please..."

For the next minute and a half, the Founders slowly but surely move the ball up the field, a few yards at a time, not risking any long passes that could be intercepted. Until they're within field goal range, and Thad Reise jogs out onto the field.

His percentages have been amazing this season, but my muscles are clenched so tight as he lines up that my toe begins to cramp.

For how raucous this stadium was the whole game, it's quiet now, tension rippling around the stands. Every single person is either hoping he'll miss or make it.

The ball is snapped, put in place, and then lifted into the air. End over end over end and through the uprights.

That's it.

Game over.

And I just about burst open with joy. The Founders have won the whole damn thing!

I scream and cry until my voice is hoarse, hugging and kissing every single person in the box before we are escorted down to the field, where it is utter pandemonium. Confetti covers every last inch. Hats, shirts, and towels with the Founders logo and championship title are distributed. It's chaos.

But Camden finds us. He lifts Paisley and me up at once, each of us under an arm, and I think he might be able to move a mountain right now for how he's feeling. He gives each of us a kiss on the cheek then sets us down, placing a hat on Paisley's head. Tears spill down my cheeks as Paisley signs to her big brother that she knew he could do it, and he, in turn, tells her that he did it for her.

Then he pivots to me, a grin splitting his face, and bends to wrap his arms around my thighs, lifting me up in the air, so I can reach him better with his pads on. I brush his sweaty hair back from his brow, drag my thumbs across his flushed and damp cheekbones, wipe a smear of dirt off his jaw.

"How do you feel?" I ask, and he shakes his head as if he can't even find the words.

"Like I'm floating."

I wrap my hands around his head, kissing his mouth, knowing that for the rest of my life, I will remember the smell of sweat and the taste of tears that accompanied this euphoria.

As soon as he sets me down, a reporter approaches him with a camera and microphone, and I step away, but he holds tight to me, keeping me next to him as the reporter interviews him about the game and the touchdown that was basically a redo of last year's game.

"Do you have any statement you want to make to your naysayers?"

"Yeah." He smirks, and I know that *look*. "I'm still here, and I told you, you can't bring me down. And Lionel Barry? You can—"

I slap my hand over his mouth, keeping him from finishing that sentence, which I'm sure was "go fuck yourself." The reporter laughs good-naturedly, flicking his gaze between Camden and me, clearly wanting to ask about us, yet not. Instead, he says, "What about the people who've helped you this season? How have they brought you to this moment?"

Camden licks his lips, taking his time as he formulates his answer, his fingers wrapped around mine the whole time. "The coaches, the staff, my teammates, they've all not only stood behind me when I needed them, but next to me. I owe this entire season to their support. Rivera is not only my quarterback, but he's my best friend, my brother. He walked every step with me on this journey, and while I wouldn't wish my experience on anyone else, I hope everyone has a sibling by choice in their life, because their love is not born but given. It's really special."

He pauses to smile at Paisley and to clear his throat of the rawness in it before he continues. "My sister made me this bracelet," he says, showing it off, "and it's my good luck charm. Her faith in me has changed my life. This win is for my family, my sister and my parents. I hope they're watching over me now and that they're proud."

I swipe the back of my hand over my cheeks, blinking away my blurry vision in time to see Camden staring down at me. "And, of course, I would never have made it here without the love of my life. She has held me up and continues to every day. I'd never have this comeback without her convincing me that there was one to be made. That I could be redeemed."

Then in front of the reporter, camera, and all of the world, he yanks me to him and kisses me.

Someone—I think Emmaline—shouts, "Hell fucking yeah!"

Someone else—I don't know who—adds, "Now that's what I call a kiss!"

And I laugh against his mouth because everything they say about Camden Long is true. He's one of the best tight ends to ever play professional football, an arrogant asshole, and the sexiest man walking God's green earth.

Then again, I'm biased, and maybe it's just me.

The only one who can bring the King of Football to his knees.

Literally.

EPILOGUE

CAMDEN

It's the middle of April, and I'm enjoying my off-season diet of a pastrami on rye from the deli down the street when Nadine tears into the room. "I got in! I got in!"

"What?" Confused, I set down my sandwich and wipe off my fingers to catch her. "What are you saying?"

"I got into Penn."

"You got into Penn?" I parrot, matching her level of excitement and volume.

"Yes! I got into Penn!"

I lift her up, swinging her around a few times as she squeals before holding her up, so she can wrap her arms and legs around me. "I'm so, so proud of you."

The University of Pennsylvania is an Ivy League school with one of the top-ranked education programs in the country. Because of its prestige, they routinely receive thousands of applicants but only accept about a quarter of them.

"I didn't think they'd take me." She leans back to meet my gaze, and I blink a few times to view her clearly through my tears. She had an online interview with them, and she'd sworn they didn't like her. I told her she was making it all up in her head.

Of course, I was right.

"We have to celebrate." I set her down and take off my glasses to wipe at my eyes before grabbing my cell phone to call the building's concierge to tell them I need a bottle of champagne stat. The best one they can find. Personal shopping isn't really in their job description, but seeing as how they want to keep me happy and in the building, they are more than willing to provide it for me. And twenty minutes later, a bottle of Dom Perignon arrives at my door.

Once we each have glasses filled, I tip mine to Nadine's. "To *Doctor* Rivera."

After some more conversations with me and with her parents, Nadine decided that she did eventually want to earn her PhD, and this acceptance is her first step in that direction.

"It'll be a lot of work."

I shrug of her warning. We've figured out our schedule thus far; it won't be a problem in the future. Plus, the program doesn't start until the fall, so we have months to line up help if we need it with Paisley. The little social butterfly has some activity almost every day now. With more friends than she had back in Iowa, she's gained a ton of confidence, and that boyfriend of hers isn't so bad. He's a good kid, but I did warn him that he'll have the entire Founders football team at his doorstep if he breaks her heart.

"I love you," I murmur against Nadine's lips, pulling her against me, and I'm so glad the weather has begun to warm up. She doesn't have as many layers for me to peel off when I strip her naked before guiding her over my lap. She takes over for my hand, stroking the length of my quickly hardening cock, leaving me free to reach for the box I plucked out of the back of my closet. The one I have been hiding from her for weeks.

I open it now, and she gasps in shock, though her face almost immediately melts to a frown. "I cannot believe you're doing this to me *now*. With your dick in my hand."

I grin. "Is there a better way?"

"Literally any other way."

I lift the custom ring between us, this one rose gold to match the other I gave her last Christmas, but with diamonds inlaid around it and a five-carat cushion cut in the middle. She could wear it alone or stacked with the other one, although I plan to keep her dripping in diamonds. Glittering like a winter river.

My River.

"So, what do you say?" I place it at the tip of her outstretched finger. "Will you take this corn-fed boy and make him a man?"

She reluctantly lets her smile loose and eventually laughs. "Might as well. No one else in the world would know what to do with you."

"You got that right." I slide the ring onto her fourth finger then kiss her palm. "No matter what we do, no matter where life takes us, I am yours, forever. I promise to always take care of you, support you, and put your wants and needs before my own. I love you, Nadine."

She bites into her lower lip to keep it from quivering, but she loses out on the battle, and I wipe away the single tear on her cheek. "I think you just wrote your vows." She sniffs a laugh. "Who needs a wedding when we can exchange them right now?"

"In that case, Mrs. Long, I now pronounce us husband and wife."

She giggles, falling against my chest, and I kiss her ear, her temple, her wet cheek. I feel her lips brush over my throat, and her torso expand on an inhale a moment before she sits up, clear-eyed and serious. "I love you, Camden Long, and I promise to always defend you, stand by your side in good times and in bad. I am grateful for your generosity and humor but, most of all, for giving me your heart. I will protect it until my last breath. I am yours, forever."

I curve my hands around her jaw and cover her mouth with mine, sealing our vows with a kiss. One that tastes like champagne and feels brand-new.

It may not be legally binding, but our promises are all I need.

She is mine, and I am hers.

Forever.

That starts now.

With lazy kisses and roaming hands. She sinks down onto my length, and I thumb the bud of her sex, enjoying the sight of her growing blush, the bite of her fingernails into my biceps when she throws her head back, moaning her pleasure.

The spasm of her inner walls triggers my own orgasm, and I hold her tight to me as I release all of it into her, reflexively lifting my hips, pumping into her until we're both spent. Then I carefully reach for the box of tissues, because these couches are leather, and as much as I'm willing to pay for the cleaning service, I think *that* stain would be a step too far for them to remove.

After, we cuddle on the couch, drinking champagne and admiring her new jewelry, idly chatting about taking a vacation this summer before training camp starts or when exactly we'd like to make our marriage official.

The television plays in the background, highlights of a hockey game, and I play with Nadine's hair as we listen to the talking heads argue about whether the Philadelphia Iron will make it to the play-offs. Our city's hockey team hasn't qualified in years, but they're supposedly looking pretty good.

"If only Tremblay could keep his personal matters personal, I think he has the potential to be a star on the team."

I don't follow much about hockey, but I've met Nico Tremblay a few times, and he's never had fewer than two girls at his side at all times. A real playboy. In fact, there's been a story floating around recently about his supposedly giving a woman a sexually transmitted infection. I cringe just thinking about it, how that would affect my play on the field.

Although I can't ponder it too long because Nadine finishes the last of her champagne, and with her ass pressed right up against my groin and my ring newly placed on her finger, I'm ready to go again.

I slide my fingers underneath the panties she'd put back on, and she laughs. "You're kidding. It hasn't even been, like, half an hour."

"Yeah, too long." I suck on her throat. "Let me get you pregnant. Buy two, get one free."

"What?"

"You were accepted into your number one school program, we're engaged, might as well throw a baby in there."

She glares at me. "You think now is the time for me to have your baby when I'm about to start grad school?"

I tip my head side to side. "Might as well really strap you down, you know? Make sure you're not going anywhere."

She snorts a laugh. "Your breeding kink is off the charts. What would Malcolm say about that if he found out?"

"Nothing because I'm firing him."

"He doesn't work for you."

I groan into her neck. "Don't remind me."

———

WHAT'S NEXT?

If you want more Camden and Nadine content, use the QR code to have it delivered straight to your inbox!

To stay up to date with all things Sophie Andrews, use the QR code on the next page to stay in touch!

ACKNOWLEDGMENTS

Publishing is no easy task, and there a lot of people who've helped me put Going Deep into the world.

Thank you to Christina at Concepts by Canea for the amazing covers and artwork. As always, Libby and Lisa have magically made me daydreams into a full story. A special thanks to Linda Hill for being a sensitivity reader and answering all of my questions about the Deaf community. Thanks to my author friends for making me smarter every day and to my non-author friends for cheering me on even when they don't know what it means when I say Amazon rank.

Biggest thank you to all of my readers. Thank you for your DMs and for your early reviews and for making all of this worth it. Without you, I'd literally just be writing these books and reading them out loud to myself like I used to do when I was a kid. And while that's fun, it's so much more fun to know people love these silly little books. I am forever grateful for you.

And if you'd like more information about me, you can find it at https://sophieandrewsauthor.com/

ABOUT THE AUTHOR

Sophie Andrews is a contemporary romance author who writes steamy books that will leave you smiling. As a millennial, she's obsessed with boybands, late 90s rom-coms, and will always be team Pacey. When she's not writing, she's most likely trying to wrangle her children or drinking red wine. Or both at the same time.

ALSO BY SOPHIE ANDREWS

Stone Family

Under One Roof

Just This Once

Right Next Door

For The Weekend

Single Dads' Club

The Rehearsal Fling

The Nanny Tenure

The Dating Pact

The Bartender's Baby

Tangled Series

Tangled Up

Tangled Want

Tangled Hearts

Tangled Beginning

Tangled Expectations

Tangled Chances

Tangled Ambition

Stand-Alones

How to Ruin a Wedding

Love at a Funeral and Other Awkward Conversations

Hart Brothers Novellas

Made Over by Meredith

Wrapped Up in Holly

Collections

Tangled Series books 1-4

The Single Dads' Club

www.ingramcontent.com/pod-product-compliance
Lightning Source LLC
Chambersburg PA
CBHW061608190726
48288CB00007B/2234